Michal's Destiny

by USA Today Best-Selling Author

Roberta Kagan

Book One in the Michal's Destiny Series

Copyright © 2018 by Roberta Kagan

All rights reserved. No part of this publication may be reproduced, distributed, or transmitted in any form or by any means, including photocopying, recording, or other electronic or mechanical methods, without the prior written permission of the publisher, except in the case of brief quotations embodied in critical reviews and certain other noncommercial uses permitted by copyright law.

CONTACT ME

I love hearing from readers, so feel free to drop me an email telling me your thoughts about the book or series.

Email: roberta@robertakagan.com

Please sign up for my mailing list, and you will receive Free short stories including an USA Today award-winning novella as my gift to you!!!!! To sign up…

Check out my website http://www.robertakagan.com.

Come and like my Facebook page!

https://www.facebook.com/roberta.kagan.9

Join my book club

https://www.facebook.com/groups/1494285400798292/?ref=br_rs

Follow me on BookBub to receive automatic emails whenever I am offering a special price, a freebie, a giveaway, or a new release. Just click the link below, then click follow button to the right of my name. Thank you so much for your interest in my work.

https://www.bookbub.com/authors/roberta-kagan.

DISCLAIMER

This is a work of fiction. Names, characters, businesses, places, events, and incidents are either the products of the author's imagination or used in a fictitious manner. Any resemblance to actual persons, living or dead, or actual events is purely coincidental.

Table of Contents

CHAPTER 1

A Jewish settlement in Eastern Siberia, June 12th, 1919

Fifteen-year-old Michal Habelowsky sat on the bed in the room she shared with her sister, Rachel, and studied the beading on her wedding dress. The dress had been handed down through four generations of women in her mother's family. Michal knew that the tiny beads had been painstakingly sewn on by hand. It was a beautiful dress, modest enough to wear standing under a chuppah (wedding canopy) in front of a rabbi. She had only three hours of freedom as a single woman remaining before she would see the man her father had chosen for her to marry. Avram Lippman was his name. He was seventeen years old and apprenticing as a shoemaker. That was all her father had told her about him, nothing more, not the color of his hair, or if he had a gentle temperament. She took a deep breath and wished that she could shake the feeling that she was about to be trapped, caged, forever. But she dared not refuse the marriage, dared not ask any questions. Her father's violent disposition was a secret in the village where they lived. No one suspected that he ruled his wife, son, and two daughters with an iron fist. If Michal had protested his choice of husbands, he would have beaten her until she agreed. Even though her father was a religious man and he knew that the religious text firmly stated that his daughter should have the final say in whether she would marry the man he chose or not, in his own house, Soloman Habelowsky made the final decisions, and no one dared to ever question his choice. For Michal, the only good thing about being married was getting away from her father. After all, from the time she was a child, she had been told that Jews did not marry for love. That was not something she was groomed to expect. Jews married for practical reasons. Most of the girls that she had grown up with spent their time dreaming of their future husbands. When they had a few moments to talk amongst themselves, the girls would giggle and talk about the characteristics they hoped for in a future groom. It was an honor to marry a Talmud scholar or a rabbi. Of course, for most of the girls in this small village it was a dream that would never be fulfilled. In order to marry a learned man, one would be required to support him so that he could continue his studies. The only girls able to provide such a life were girls with rich fathers who were willing to support their sons-in-law or send their daughters to school to become teachers, thereby enabling them to provide for their families. Since they were very young, the girls knew that the most important expectation of them would be to bear many children. Michal was different from the others. Sometimes her mother would worry and say, "Michal, stop being such a dreamer. You sit staring out the window and I wonder what it is that you're thinking about."

"I'm wondering what God has in store for me. I want so much more than what the other girls seem to want. I would love to go to exotic places. Maybe someday even Kiev or Saint Petersburg."

"Michal, listen to me. You will live here in our village, have children and raise them, just like my mother before me and her mother before her. It's a good life."

Michal nodded. She didn't care that her father didn't have enough money for her to marry a rabbi; she had no desire to spend her life serving a pale scholar who sat studying the Torah all day. And after he'd sat in shul (synagogue) for hours, he would come home and she had better have his dinner ready, serve it to him, have all of his clothes washed, and the children fed. It was a high price to pay for bragging that she was married to a scholar. Michal also held secrets in her heart. No one knew that she had done things that were forbidden, things that filled her with guilt and shame. Like an impious woman, she had allowed strange feelings towards a boy, Taavi, to crawl into her mind. If only her father were a different type of man, she could have told him that she would have liked him to make a match for her with Taavi. Taavi was only the son of a carpenter and his father's apprentice. He was no better or worse than a shoemaker. The match would have been acceptable, within her grasp, in fact. Except for her father. The father she'd dared not ever question. The first time Michal saw Taavi she was at the market buying produce. As she was choosing tomatoes from a street vendor, she glanced into the open door of Taavi's father's shop. There he was, deeply immersed in carving the legs of a chair, his forehead lined with seriousness as he carefully whittled the wood. A horse whinnied, distracting him, and he looked up; she turned her head just at the same moment and their eyes met. A strange feeling came over her. It was so coincidental, the way they'd both looked in the same direction at the very same moment. Michal was drawn to him, but she forced herself to look away quickly. After all, it was not proper for a modest Jewish woman to meet the eyes of a strange man so boldly, the way she had done with Taavi. But before she looked away she saw admiration in his eyes and, although she knew it was a sin, she enjoyed the way it made her feel.

Tonight she would lay beside her husband and fulfill her wifely obligations as her mother had explained them to her earlier that day. The very thought of what she must do terrified her. To allow a man to penetrate her body frightened her. Would it be terribly painful? What if Avram Lippman was just as rough a man as her father? What then? Her father was not only harsh, but his fits of anger were unpredictable. An accident such as spilling a glass of milk could send him into a frenzy. However, when she'd lost her grandmother's mezuzah (a piece or parchment with specified Jewish verses from the Torah in a decorative case hung by an exterior door as a sign of faith), she was terrified that her father might be so livid he would kill her, but he wasn't. In fact, he'd been kind and sympathetic. His inconsistency only made him more fearsome. She hated that her father made her feel weak and inconsequential, but she hated to see her brother mistreated even more. Her father had reduced her brother to a sniveling nervous boy who bit his nails and could not concentrate on his lessons at the yeshiva (Jewish institution focused on religious texts)." When the rabbi came to talk to their father concerning the fact that her brother was having trouble in school, her father had promised the rabbi to talk with her brother and help him to find out what he needed or what was bothering him. Instead, once the rabbi was out of sight, her father had beaten her brother until he promised to study harder and never to bring such shame upon the family again. If only she could postpone this marriage for another six months, or maybe a year … But there was no postponing; tonight she would be married. She had already been to the Mikva, where she had spent an hour going through the prenuptial rituals. The Mikva lady had greeted her then escorted her to another room where the woman cut Michal's nails of both her fingers and toes. Next Michal was instructed to try to relax in a tub of warm water before being inspected by the Mikva lady. Inspection was required before entering the holy Mikva bath. Michal was embarrassed, as she had never been naked in front of anyone before. The Mikva lady seemed used

12

to this behavior from young brides. So, she just smiled and quickly finished the inspection. Once Michal was deemed ready, she was led to the bath. Three times, Michal had been fully immersed in the water all the way to the very top of her head. Three times because the word Mikva is mentioned three times in the Torah. She'd repeated the blessings after the Mikva lady, as she was instructed, and then she was allowed to dress and leave. The experience left her unnerved as she walked home on wobbly legs. It had been uncomfortable exposing her body to an old woman. If that had been difficult, tonight, when she would lie with a man, would be horrific. Her heart pounded with anxiety when she thought about what the next several hours would hold for her. Tonight she was expected to perform an unspeakable act with the stranger who was to become her husband.

Again she thought of Taavi, of his bright laughing eyes, which were the color of amber, of his smile. Would she feel differently if it were Taavi she was meeting under the chuppah tonight? Michal couldn't help but wonder if Taavi was betrothed already and, if so, which of the girls in the village would be his wife? The idea of him marrying someone else struck a nerve, and Michal felt tears sting the back of her eyelids. Right now, she hated her father for not even considering her feelings in his choice. But no matter what her new husband, this man whose name she knew was Avram Lippman, was like, she would belong to him. And he would be free to do with her as he pleased for the rest of her life.

CHAPTER 2

Avram Lippman sat outside on the back stairs of the yeshiva with his friend Eleazar. They were taking their lunch break before they would return to their studies. A cool breeze embraced the leaves of an old oak tree. The boys were enjoying the summer weather. It was sixty-five degrees Fahrenheit, and beautiful days like this were rare in the frigid lands of Siberia.

"Are you nervous?" Eleazar asked.

"Yes, of course. How can I not be nervous? Nu*? Tomorrow my life will change forever."

"What will you do if she is ugly?"

"Eleazar? What's the matter with you? If the rebbe (rabbi) heard you he would be very disappointed. You can't judge the heart of a person by their physical appearance."

"Oy, Avram, you forget who you're talking to. I'm your best friend. For years, we tell each other everything. Today, you can't be honest with me?" Eleazar said.

"All right then. Of course it is important to me. If she is ugly, I will have to look at her for the rest of my life. Getting married is a monumental event. It's even a little bit scary. Next it will be you."

"I know. My father has been hinting that he might have a possible match for me."

"My heart pounds when I think that tomorrow, for the first time, I will see the face of the woman who will be my wife and bear my children. For months, I have thought about her before I would fall asleep at night. Will she be kind? Will she be easy to talk with? Maybe … will I even be able to love her?"

"A woman is a wife, for bearing children, not for love. You sound like a goy."

"I know. But you are my best friend. You are the only one who will ever know the secrets in my heart, Eli. So I am telling you. I want that maybe I should have love in my life the way that the goyim do. It is nice to think that a wife is not just a wife, but a companion, even a lover."

"So, I was right, the goisha (non-Jewish) books that you have been reading have been putting crazy ideas in your head. You want a romance. Oy, Avram a romance can be nothing but trouble. Just look at all the problems the goyim have with their marriages. Infidelity. Oy vey."

"Since I know you will never tell anyone my secrets, I will share something with you … Yes, it's true; I do want a romance, a love story."

"You should stop these crazy thoughts before you get yourself into trouble." Eleazar shook his head.

"Yes, maybe you're right. But how should I do that, Eli? It's my heart that wants this, not my head."

"You're expecting too much. When you see her, if she doesn't meet your expectations, you are going to be very disappointed. There is a possibility that you won't like the way she looks at first. But, Avram, it doesn't matter. You have to do what is expected and, in time, you will get used her. That's what everyone says. You know this as well as I do."

Avram nodded his head. "I know. I know you're right."

But all through the afternoon, Avram's thoughts drifted to the following day when he would be married. As he walked home from the yeshiva, he whispered her name softly, "Michal Habelowsky, Michal." She bore the name of the first wife of King David. Would she be as lovely? Eh … he should stop this right now; Eli was right, what if she was not attractive at all? Well, no matter what happened, he would have to get used to her anyway. There would be no going back after the wedding. Suddenly, he felt his stomach turn. He'd created such a fantasy in his mind that he'd been sure that he was going to be happy in his marriage. But, while creating this illusion, Avram had forgotten the possibility that he might not like his new wife. Today, Eli had brought that to his attention, and now Avram was quite terrified. After all, he was not a scholar and was certainly far from rich. In fact, he had been training in his father's shoemaking shop for the past two years. He was to be a humble shoemaker in a small village. So, what kind of a shidduch (arranged marriage) could he expect? If he was to be truthful with himself, he could assume she would not be pretty or smart. But he could hope that at least she would be kind. Even that was not guaranteed. What he could be pretty sure of was that she would be from a lower class family and all of the attributes he had given her in his dreams over the last several months would prove to be nothing but daydreams. Now Avram began to allow his imagination to run away with him. He saw Michal in his mind's eye, a large woman with a complexion of festering pimples or skin tags, a demanding woman with angry piercing eyes. A shiver ran down his spine. It was, after all, very possible that this was what he would see when he lifted the veil from her face tomorrow night.

Still, he was ashamed to admit it even to himself but, more and more as he grew older, and then especially when he turned seventeen, something had happened inside of him that made him like an animal. He had become hungry to do the things that a man and woman did in private together. When he thought about that desire that had taken hold of him, he felt ashamed. And because of that shame, he had never spoken of these growing needs to anyone, not even his best friend Eleazar. In fact, something had come over him and he had sinned against himself. After it was over, he felt sick and swore to God he would never do it again. But then, almost against his will, he repeated the sin. When the need of this sin came over him, he felt that he lost control of right and wrong. He knew better; he knew it was wrong to spill his precious seed without the possibility of a child being created. But then that driving desire would come over him and, although he knew he would regret his actions, he still repeated the sin.

Late in the night before the day of his wedding, Avram tried not to think about the upcoming marriage. Since his conversation with Eli, the thought of the permanence of being married had become repugnant to him. There were too many possibilities of a lifetime of misery.

In the morning, Avram and his father went to the synagogue to say their prayers. Then, as was expected of him, Avram began to prepare for his wedding.

CHAPTER 3

Evening was upon them. Tonight was the wedding.

Once Michal was dressed and ready, her mother came into her room. She was a timid waif of a woman, with darting eyes that were always filled with trepidation. She was like a prey animal, gentle, frightened, and ready to run if the predator appeared.

"You remember what we talked about, Michal?" her mother said, softly caressing her daughter's cheek.

"You mean my wifely duties?"

"Yes. That's what I'm talking about. I know that sometimes these duties are unpleasant, but with God's help, your husband will be kind to you and be quick about doing what must be done in order for you to have children. I realize that sometimes you will dread this, but you must not refuse this to your husband. While he is doing what must be done, you pray as hard as you can that a child will be conceived. Children are God's greatest blessing."

"I am afraid, Mama. I'm afraid that it will hurt. I'm afraid I won't like this man who I am to be with for the rest of my life. I wish I could run away." Michal felt tears begin to form in the corners of her eyes.

"I know." Her mother swallowed hard, "But it is a sin, Michal; you must not feel this way. You must accept your responsibilities. I understand what you're going though. Once, I too was a young girl meeting the man I would spend my life with. Believe me, I know how you feel."

Michal looked into her mother's eyes and felt sorry for her mother. She'd been married off to a tyrant of a man and then had been bound to him forever. Please, God, Michal said a silent prayer, please make Avram be nothing like my father.

"Every woman is afraid on her wedding night. But you will be all right. You'll see. Soon it will be over and you'll say to yourself … there was nothing to fear," her mother said with a smile on her face, but the trace of a tear forming in the corner of her eye.

"But, Mama. I don't want to get married."

"It's time, my child. I am so sorry, my Michal, but your papa has decided and so we do as he says. You will marry tonight; it's time."

CHAPTER 4

Michal stood at the end of the aisle inside the small synagogue and looked out through the veil that covered her face to see all of the people she'd known since she was born. They sat assembled in rows of wooden chairs. All heads were turned towards the door; they were waiting for her to walk towards the chuppah and her new life. At the front of the room, beneath the chuppah, a canopy made of wood and adorned with flowers, stood the rabbi with a table in front of him. On the table was a glass of wine. A strange thought drifted through Michal's mind. Had Taavi the carpenter fashioned that canopy of wood with his own strong hands? Had Taavi sat at his table and carved that very canopy under which a man stood, a man who waited for Michal to come to him? A stranger named Avram Lippman. Even from where she stood, his face was clear enough to be completely foreign to her. How could they have both lived in this small village for their entire lives without her ever having seen him before? As was expected, he wore a black coat that hung below his knees and a tall fur hat. Michal thought that he had a pleasant face. Pale, not sun browned and handsome like Taavi the carpenter. But pleasant enough. Avram was tall and very slender, with dark curly hair that floated around his head and a strong Grecian nose. Michal sucked in a deep breath as the music began. Her father nodded to her and she walked obediently beside him towards her destiny. As they got closer, her body trembled. She wanted to run, but she glanced up at her father, who looked back and gave her a menacing stare. When she saw her father's eyes, she knew that she must face her destiny; there would be no turning back. Seven times she walked, circling the canopy, her heart pounding with fear until she stood beside her future husband. Then the rabbi began the marriage ceremony. The words the rabbi spoke were a blur because her mind was screaming in protest. But she did as was expected of her and said, "I do."

Michal was going through the motions, but nothing was registering with her; it all seemed like a very bad dream.

They spoke their vows. Avram's voice was shaking as he promised himself to Michal.

When Michal whispered "I do," her own voice sounded foreign to her.

Then Avram gently slid the gold band on the trembling first finger of her left hand.

They both drank from the glass of wine. Next the glass was wrapped in a cloth and placed on the floor. Avram's leg was wobbly as he raised his foot over the glass. Then as hard as he could he stomped the wine glass. The sound of glass shattering started everyone cheering. "Mazel Tov!"

Michal felt a sick sensation in the pit of her stomach as Avram removed her veil.

CHAPTER 5

Avram felt his knees shaking as he saw the girl, Michal, walking towards him. He could not see her face. It was covered. He watched her circle the chuppah then stop beside him. He heard the rabbi and repeated as he was told. His heart was a bass drum in his ears. The wine glass was laid at his feet; he broke it with one stomp of his foot. The crowd of people began yelling, "Mazel Tov!" Then, with shaky hands, he pulled the veil back from her face. This was the woman who would be his wife. The woman he'd thought about every day since the shidduch had been made. This was Michal.

Avram drew in a breath and looked directly into the eyes of the girl who stood before him.

She was not only pleasant looking. She was beautiful. She was more than he could have ever hoped for, even in his dreams. Her dark hair was long and fell into spiral curls. Tomorrow, of course, that hair would be shaved. Her mother would come in the morning and shave her head, as was customary. Then she would wear a head cover or a sheitel. From this day forward, once her hair grew back, he would be the only man who would ever see it. As a modest married woman, she would keep her head covered. But right now, the beauty of her thick locks took his breath away. He'd never seen eyes the color of Michal's. They were gray, but not just gray; they were dark charcoal with specks of silver like tiny stars. When he looked at her, she did not return his gaze; she cast her eyes down to the floor. This was to be expected of a good woman. He wanted to lift her chin and give her a reassuring smile. It had not occurred to him until this moment that she too might be frightened of the future. Uncustomary at a proper Jewish wedding, he whispered so only she could hear him. "You are beautiful."

She looked up and met his eyes. Then he noticed that her eyelashes were long and lovely.

Michal smiled and, at that very moment, Avram thanked the stars in the heavens for his good fortune. But, more importantly, at that moment, Avram fell in love.

CHAPTER 6

The wedding celebration passed in a whirlwind of music, food, and dancing. The couple were separated, she with the women, he with the men. But when the party ended, Michal and Avram were alone.

"I hope you enjoyed the food," he said, feeling awkward.

She nodded. "Yes, and you?"

"Yes, very much."

"My mother made the lokshen kugel."

"It was very good."

"Everyone loves her kugel; she uses thick noodles, raisins, and apples, so it is sweet."

He nodded.

Neither of them had tasted the food; both were too nervous about the coming night.

Then he found the courage to ask her the question that haunted the back of his mind. Avram feared what her answer might be, but something inside him made him need to know.

"Were you disappointed?" he asked in a very soft voice.

"Disappointed?"

"Yes, I mean, when you saw me?"

"Oh, oh ... no. I mean, I don't know what I was expecting. But, no."

"I was not disappointed when I saw you," he said boldly.

She cocked her head to the side. He was more outspoken than she'd thought he would be.

"This is difficult for both of us. But I don't want it to be that way, Michal. I know that you must be anxious about tonight. But I want to reassure you that I will be gentle. I promise I will try my best not to hurt you."

She felt her face flush hot with embarrassment. Then she nodded.

Michal prepared for the night by going into the bedroom and changing into her white long-sleeved nightgown that covered her from her neck to her feet. Then she got into the bed under the covers and waited. The weather was warm, but she felt chilled.

Avram gave her ample time to get ready. He was on edge, nervous and unsure of himself. It was essential that he didn't cause her any pain, but he had no idea of what he was doing. He had been told, and he had fantasized about this night, but the reality was much more frightening. What if he failed? He was not supposed to lie down on the bed beside her. He was just supposed to lift her night dress and enter her, then, as he did what was required, he was to keep his thoughts on conceiving a child. Some of the other men told him that they had intercourse through a hole in a sheet. They told him that it was holier, cleaner. But Avram had no plans of keeping himself so separated from his new wife. He hoped that she would not expect this of him. Avram entered the room as quietly as he could, where Michal waited. He carefully removed the light

25

blanket that covered her. It was dark and he could barely see her white nightgown in the sliver of moonlight that streamed through the window. Gently, he lifted the dress. He felt her shiver. But the worst part of all of it was that his penis was not erect. He had no trouble when he was alone and had thought of his wedding night, but now that he was here and it was time for him to do what was expected, he could not. She lay there quietly waiting. He could feel her legs cold and trembling against him. Suddenly, Avram had an idea.

"Michal?" he whispered in the darkness.

"Yes?" her voice was barely a whisper.

"I know that what I am going to ask of you is out of the ordinary. And, of course, you can refuse as a frum (devout, pious) woman, but I hope you will not be offended or upset."

"What is it?"

"Can we just lie here together? Just maybe hold each other? I know that this is a lot to ask of you. But I am afraid I cannot do what is expected like this. Do you understand?"

Strangely, she did. She did understand. "Yes. Yes, Avram. Lie down here beside me and let's just talk. Let's talk about everything."

He felt a tear well up behind his eyes. Could this woman be real or was she a dream? She felt the same way that he did. She too wanted to feel close to him. Perhaps maybe she even had thought about the unthinkable; she might have thought about love.

At first, Avram stayed on the far side of the bed and the two began talking. For a while, the conversation was stilted and awkward. Then Avram told Michal a funny story about one of his friends in the yeshiva and the two of them laughed together.

26

They laughed until their bellies ached. Boldly, Michal moved closer to Avram. He felt the warmth of her body and it comforted him. She seemed to know what he needed and he was relieved. They continued talking long into the night. At some point, their hands brushed. Avram moved closer to Michal and gently kissed her lips. She touched his face. He caressed her body and then, as naturally as God had intended, the two became one. As the sun rose, they fell asleep, and by the time they awakened to her mother's incessant knocking on the door, they found themselves in each other's arms.

Michal opened the door for her mother, who brought food for the newlyweds. Michal knew that her mother had come to shave her hair.

Avram wished that the shaving of Michal's beautiful hair was not necessary. He loved the long dark curls. But this was the custom of his religious sect, and so he sat quietly.

As the first thick dark curl dropped quietly to the floor, Michal was unnerved. It wasn't as if she hadn't known all of her life that this would take place on the day following her wedding, but even with the knowledge, as the hair tumbled to the ground she felt her heart breaking. Michal longed to scream in protest, but she could not admit, not even to her own mother, that she was vain. Vanity was a sin and she had spent many hours alone in her room brushing her long locks. But now, because she was a married woman, every time she menstruated, the Mikva lady would try to shave her hair again. Exposing of one's hair was immodest; it attracted unhealthy attention from men other than one's husband. Michal told herself this over and over again, but she still felt dizzy and horrified knowing what her bald head must look like. Once the shaving was done, Michal reached up and touched her scalp.

"Come, Michal, come and eat now," her mother said, wrapping a colorful scarf around Michal's newly shaven head.

Michal nodded. She had always done as she was told, but right now she wanted to pick up the razor and cut her mother's throat. What was she thinking? It was not her mother's fault. She only did what a good mother was expected to do. The way Michal was feeling, the last thing that she wanted was to eat. She felt sick to her stomach as she reached up and touched the scarf. Her mother was already picking up the hair from the floor. "Go, Michal, go and let me clean up."

Michal just remained in her chair, looking glassy-eyed into the mirror." Her mother leaned down and kissed Michal's cheek.

"You'll get used to it. It's only hair. Was last night all right?" her mother asked.

Michal nodded, not wanting to talk, just wanting to close herself up in a room alone and cry.

CHAPTER 7

That night, Michal and Avram lay side by side in her bed. They had both been raised in Orthodox homes and they both knew that, according to Jewish law, they were not to touch again after the first time they had intercourse for seven days. The initial sexual encounter was a mitzvah, a blessing, but now the couple was required to practice restraint, as they would be expected to for the rest of their marriage. Michal knew that every time she menstruated she would have to wait until she'd gone to the Mikva in order to be declared clean before she could once again lie with her husband. A few days before the wedding, her mother had given her a special scarf to wear when she was unclean, as a reminder to her husband. She was to explain to Avram that when he saw her wearing the special scarf, he was to know that he was not to touch her until she was declared clean again. Not only were they forbidden sexual contact, but their hands must not touch; there must be no contact at all. However, since they had already shared a more tender wedding night than was allowed, they had both made an unspoken agreement to break this rule. And, somehow, each of them, regardless of their upbringing, even though they knew it was wrong, felt comfortable sharing this secret between them. The secret of holding each other close, of joining together before seven days had passed, even though it was considered a sin.

"Do you want me to go to my own bed?" he asked. "I know I should not be lying in bed beside you...."

"Go back only if you want to."

"I'd like to stay here."

"Stay then."

"You feel badly about your hair?"

"Yes. I don't know why. I expected it, but I feel so lost without it."

"Would you believe me if I told you that you are even more beautiful now?"

"No." She laughed.

"You are; now I can see your lovely face even more clearly."

"You are trying to make me feel better."

"Of course I want you to feel better, but that's not why I said that. I said it because it's true."

"You are a very kind person, Avram. I am fortunate to have such a good husband."

.

"Will you try something for me?" Avram asked.

"What?"

"Will you take your nightgown off and lay here with me?"

"AVRAM!" she said, feeling the blush come over her cheeks.

"I'm sorry. I'm sorry...."

There was silence for several minutes, then Michal stood up. Avram felt his heart pound in his chest. He was sure he had offended her. She was going to sleep in the other bed. He was sure of it. Avram swallowed hard. He felt his throat close; there was nothing he could say. He'd made a terrible mistake.

Then, like a miracle, so unexpectedly, Michal pulled the nightdress over her head and quickly got back under the covers beside Avram. He stood and took off his clothes. Then, he too got back into bed.

Neither said a word. Then Avram cleared his throat.

"Thank you," he whispered into the darkness. Putting his hand out, he touched Michal's cheek. Then took her hand and kissed the palm with his warm lips. She scooted closer to him and he took her into his arms. The warmth of his body next to her own felt safe and comforting. He softly kissed the top of her head. She nuzzled into him, no longer wanting any separation between them. He held her tightly, her flesh against his. This was the first time either of them had ever been this close to another human being. Avram felt the side of her breast brush against his chest and his body responded. They would never again make love while still wearing clothing. From this day on, they would lie together naked, as Adam and Eve in the Garden of Eden, lost in love and bliss.

CHAPTER 8

In the morning, Michal smiled at Avram and he returned the knowing smile. Only days before, they were two strangers and now they were not only husband and wife, but best friends. As Avram walked to work at his father's shop, he wanted to call out to the world, "I am the happiest man alive. I am blessed with the most beautiful and kind wife in the entire world. And she bears the name of the wife of King David." While Avram worked, Michal went about making a home for the two of them. She had learned to cook and sew from her mother. When Avram came home that night, Michal had baked a bread and put some bones and vegetables in a pot to prepare a soup for him. It was not the best soup he'd ever eaten, but because she had labored over it, he raved about how wonderful it tasted. He told her about his day, about all he was learning from his father.

Over the next several days, Avram felt comfortable enough to confide in Michal and tell her his private thoughts about some of the customers who came into the shoe shop. Most of the stories were funny because he loved to see her smile. Occasionally, however, he would confide in her and explain how a customer had tried to steal something or take advantage of his father. He would tell her who the culprit was and how angry it made him. She never judged him. It seemed to Avram that Michal was always on his side and that warmed his heart. How could he have been so blessed, what good deed had brought about such a perfect union? God was good to him.

The preparation of their first Shabbat dinner weighed heavily on Michal. She had always had a soft heart and found it difficult to kill a chicken. She didn't want to admit her weakness to Avram. But that Friday morning, he saw the stress in her face and asked what was bothering her. She told him nothing. He touched her cheek and asked again. She dropped her eyes and admitted her problem. Another husband would have been livid. But, gentle Avram just smiled and told her to go to the kosher butcher and purchase a chicken already cleaned instead. It would cost a little more, but her feelings were worth it. She could not help but be relieved. Michal thanked him and kissed his hand.

Avram was happy to oblige. He wanted more than anything for Michal to be happy in her life with him.

July was hot and sticky. When Michal's period began, she insisted that Avram follow the rules and sleep in his own bed. The truth was that she was afraid that if they broke this very important rule, something terrible might happen. After all, she was unclean. It was torture for him, but he knew that he must not so much as touch her hand until she was purified again at the Mikva. But as he lay in his own bed at night, he missed her. He didn't care if she was clean or not, he longed to hold her close to him. It was a sweet pleasure he had quickly grown accustomed to spending his days anticipating.

If she didn't feel so awful, with stomach cramps and bloating, Michal would have missed Avram too. But because of the pain, she tossed and turned all night trying to find a comfortable position. Her periods had been miserable since she had started menstruating at ten. Her mother told her that once she married the periods would get easier on her, but so far they hadn't. Now, her mother changed her initial promise; now her mother said that once she bore a child the pain would cease.

Michal could only imagine the suffering that must accompany childbirth. This was a woman's lot in life, pain and suffering, her mother had told her.

But her mother had said that her marriage bed was to be a part of life that must be endured, and she'd found that her mother was wrong. She cherished the nights she spent in Avram's arms. However, she could understand her mother's viewpoint because of the kind of man her father was. And she thanked God that Avram was nothing like him.

CHAPTER 9

Michal hardly ever thought of Taavi anymore. The only time she was reminded of how attractive he was to her was when she saw him at the market. Their eyes would meet for a mere second. He would look at her in a way that was far too bold to be considered respectful. And, of course, she would immediately look away. Then Michal would walk away as quickly as possible, putting as much space between her and Taavi as she could. Still, every time she saw him, she would return home and not be able to get him out of her mind. She was happy with Avram. The marriage was more than most women could dare to hope for. Michal considered herself to be very lucky. Avram was tender and gentle. He was not rough and was always careful not to hurt her. After all, she knew that there were many men who were like her papa, who resorted to physical abuse against their own families when they felt that the world outside had treated them unfairly. It didn't matter that Michal, her brother and sister, and her mother never stood up to her papa. He was the ruler of the house and, in his mind, he had the right to strike out at the others. Of course, Michal was raised to know that she must always obey her husband and treat him with respect, regardless of his behavior. She must never argue with his decisions. After all, a good Jewish woman was taught as a child that she was inferior to her husband. Michal accepted this as a part of life. And, from the day she met Avram, she decided that she would not give him any reason to beat her. But it had all been for naught because she was pleased to discover that she cared for her husband and they enjoyed each other's company. He was always ready with a compliment on her cooking or a sweet remark at how pretty her new headscarf looked against her skin tone. Michal had no doubt that her husband had deep feelings for her, and what woman would not be happy with that? He did thoughtful things like bringing home a few of her favorite pastries or a small bunch of wildflowers that he'd picked and tied with a ribbon. Yes, Michal knew her life was good, very good. So, what evil thing inside of her still brought about that spark, that desire to sin, when she saw Taavi? She tried to avoid seeing him when she went to the market. But somehow he had a way of finding her. Then he would look at her so brazenly that she feared the other women who were shopping would notice. She would be waiting in line to buy flour and Taavi would walk by; as he did he would stop and gaze at her, his eyes sleepy and soft, then his entire face would break into a smile. It was a captivating smile that he gave her; a smile no married woman would ever return. And Michal did not return the smile. She turned away quickly … although secretly she longed to look back even for just a moment.

Fall brought plenty of grain and butter from the farms on the outskirts of the village. It was a good year and the crops were plentiful, but the government was confiscating most of the food from the farmers, giving them little compensation. This stealing of food by the government was done not only to Jews, but to all of the farmers. Then everyone was given ration cards, which allowed them insufficient allotments to feed a family. Avram had friends who were able to get food through the black market, but it was very expensive. Avram bought what he could. In order to hide some food for the winter, Avram and Michal buried some potatoes in the ground. They would dig them up when they needed extra food, but if the ground was

36

too frozen, as quite often it was in Russia, they would have to wait until the weather broke. Avram purchased as much wood as he was able to get his hands on. It was sure to be a cold winter and they had to find a way to keep the fires going. Some of the men, like Taavi, were strong and able to go the forest and cut their own firewood. But Avram was not so strong. He couldn't cut down a tree.

Winter in Siberia was brutal, but since the revolution had begun it seemed even harder. Michal's father, in his pessimistic way, had assured the family that no matter what happened, whether the czar ruled or the communists ruled Russia, life would never get better for Jews. And, sadly, he was right.

Just before the first of the year fell, several travelers came through the village on their way south. They were furriers and goldsmiths; they came to trade, but with them they brought news of the outside world. They'd told the villagers bits and pieces of stories they had heard. The visitors said that they'd heard that, as the Ukrainian army was leaving Kiev, and before the White Army took over, there were terrible pogroms in several towns throughout Russia and the Ukraine. This was petrifying news because the Jews had nowhere to go, no place to hide. The czar had made no secret of his hatred of the Jews. It had been going on for decades. Soldiers would come into small Jewish villages and destroy them. There would be no consequences for their actions because the czar had convinced the Russian population that the Jews were responsible for all of the country's problems. And this was a way of convincing the people of Russia that, once the Jews were subdued, all of their problems would disappear. This was what the visitors who came through the Jewish settlement in Siberia said. So the people of the town lived in constant fear of what danger might be lurking.

"The Red Army will protect us," Avram told Michal, but she had overheard the men in the village saying that the Red Army had perpetrated plenty of attacks on Jewish villages.

In fact, she still remembered her father talking about the Beilis affair. It happened eight years earlier in 1911 in a suburb outside of Kiev. Traveling merchants who came through the village shared news of the incident. Michal was only seven at the time, but she could clearly recall the fear that the Beilis trial struck in the Jewish community. A Jewish manager of a brick factory had been arrested. His name was Menahem Mendel Beilis. It seemed to Michal that for over a year she did not overhear a conversation amongst adults that did not somehow center on that name. Beilis was accused of killing a thirteen-year-old Christian boy in a ritual murder. The child was found mutilated in a cave. The prosecutor claimed that since Beilis was a Jew he had taken the child and murdered him in order to use the child's blood to make matzo. A tremor of fear spread through Russia as the prosecutor claimed that it was part of the Jewish religion to commit ritual murders. This was the only way, he claimed, that Jews were able to make matzo. It was a ridiculous accusation. Every Jewish person, even Michal at seven years old knew that matzo was made with flour and water. In fact, the color of matzo is white. How could anyone ever believe that it could be made with blood? Finally, in 1913, Beilis was acquitted for the crime, but the damage had already been done. A seed had been planted in the minds of the people of Russia, and the czar used that fear to incite the Russian people to attack the Jewish communities. It had been a terrible time, one she'd never forget. Her parents said that her family was lucky; their village had somehow been spared. They gave thanks to God. But she had nightmares of the horrors that people described in other towns, and she knew that her parents spent every day frightened and worried.

38

Michal wished she could believe her husband that they would be safe. And, because he was her husband and the man of the house, she would never think of arguing with him, but buried deep in her heart were fears and unspoken doubts. In fact, she didn't trust the Red or White Army. Instinctively, she knew that they were both dangerous to Jews.

She'd often thought that the problem lay in the fact that there was no Jewish homeland. Her people were hated everywhere in the world, so no matter where they went they were never safe. She'd heard the rabbi speak many times about the idea of a Jewish homeland. That was because there were always people who expressed the need for a Jewish state. But the rabbi said that they must not even consider trying to build a Jewish homeland. It was against the words of the Torah. He explained the reasons and, for the most part, the congregation agreed with him. But not Michal, she could not understand why. If there was a Jewish homeland, wouldn't the Jews have a safer existence? Michal had heard talk of such a thing, but she was afraid to ask for explanations. Her father had taught her that she dared not question the teachings of those who knew better. Once, before she was married, she'd been serving dinner with her mother to her father and several of his male friends. One of them had made a comment that she didn't agree with. So she'd spoken her mind. In front of the entire group, her father had stood up and said, "You are a woman. And not as smart as you think you are. In fact, you are stupid. So keep your mouth shut and listen. Never speak when men are talking."

His eyes were red, and she saw his hands in fists. Michal looked down at the floor. She was humiliated, but she said nothing. When she and her mother were in the kitchen later that night, cleaning up the mess the men had left, her mother said, "Be glad he didn't hit you."

In spite of the food rations and the coming winter, Michal knew that Avram was hoping that she would soon become pregnant. But each month she shook her head and told him that she was not. She would have loved to be a mother, but at what cost? If she became pregnant, they would have to find a way to feed and care for another person, and right now there was so little they were hardly able to care for themselves. Of course, she would feed the child the milk from her own body, but she had grown so thin that she was afraid her milk would not sustain a healthy child. Michal and Avram were careful to observe every rule of Jewish law except the one about lying together. That had become not only a passionate sexual part of their lives, but a time when they shared all of their inner feelings and the events of their day. Secretly, Avram was afraid that the way he and Michal had given in to passion had angered God. And he feared that might be the reason that they had not been blessed with a child.

Avram walked to shul every Saturday. Every Friday night the couple observed the Sabbath. When she was unclean, the two of them were very careful to have no contact until Michal had been to the Mikva. But still … no baby.

When her parents came to Michal and Avram's house for Rosh Hashanah, Michal's father gave her a menacing look. She knew that her father was angry. After all, she should be pregnant already. Avram did not notice her father's threatening stares. Avram and Michal spent Yom Kippur in temple with Michal's brother, sister, and her parents. Avram's parents were there too. The women, Michal, her sister, her mother, and her mother-in-law sat in the back, which was where all of the women sat. While the men sat in the front. The sexes were always separated.

Michal's mother-in-law watched everything Michal did with a critical eye. And she was demanding in a demeaning way. It was a good thing that Michal's mother had taught her that, as a wife, it was her job to please. She'd been warned from the time she was a small child that she must never oppose her husband or his family. There were many times that Michal had to control her desire to speak out. She would have liked nothing more than to tell her mother-in-law what she thought of her. Her mother-in-law would demand something of Michal, and in her mind Michal would say, "You are lazy and fat, and should try to do things for yourself instead of always ordering me around."

But, of course, she never spoke those words aloud and she asked God for forgiveness for the sin of disrespect that always seemed to creep up in her mind. Still, she had to give thanks. Her husband was a good man, nothing like her father. So, putting up with a terrible mother-in-law was not the worst thing that could happen.

The winter descended upon the people of Eastern Siberia with a blanket of frozen snow and an icy wind that swept down from the frozen lands in the North.

Michal had been babysitting, secretly, so that she could earn extra money. She wanted to purchase yarn to knit a scarf for Avram for Hanukkah. She was almost finished. And, although she doubted that there would be enough money to spare in order to purchase oil or candles to light the menorah, she wanted to give him a gift to show her appreciation for his kindness.

Two days before the first night of Hanukkah, Avram gave Michal a small package wrapped in brown paper and tied with a thin red ribbon. She opened the gift to find nine small white

41

candles. One for each night of Hanukkah and one for the shamos (candle to light the other candles).

She looked up into Avram's kind brown eyes "Thank you," she whispered, her fingers gently caressing the package.

He took her hand in his and held the palm to his lips. "You are a good wife, Michal. You make me very happy."

She saw in his eyes that he spoke the truth. He did care for her. And, because he did, she wished that she could bless him with a child. But no matter how hard she tried, how many prayers she said as he expelled his seed into her womb, she still did not conceive.

CHAPTER 10

By the beginning of February, the temperature dropped to negative thirteen degrees Fahrenheit. It was just before dawn on a bitter morning. Michal went outside and gathered a bunch of chopped wood. Her breath hung in white clouds as she carried the bundle into the house. Then she placed each piece carefully into the fireplace and lit the fire. Next she dropped several icicles into a cauldron she'd place over the flame to melt for coffee; she rubbed her hands above the burning wood. It was not much, but it gave her some warmth. The thick shawl she'd wrapped around her shoulders did little to shield her from the chill that seemed to seep through her skin and settle right inside of her. The water began to boil slowly. Avram was still asleep. The sun was just rising as she gazed out the window. It was going to be another crisp ice-blue day, bright and frigid. As she sat back in the rocking chair that Avram had purchased from Taavi's shop, her mind began to drift. She held the wooden armrest and thought of Taavi's strong hands as he carved the wood. When she'd caught him working intently, she'd found his face even more attractive. The serious expression he wore when he was creating a masterpiece was incredibly alluring. For a moment, she allowed herself to wonder what it might be like to lie beside him, the way that she and her husband had come to know each other. In spite of the cold, her face flushed. How could she ever consider such a thing? She shook her head. "It's a sin to think of another man in that way," she whispered softly to the fire. "And, besides, I am happy with Avram. I don't know why I am even thinking of Taavi. Avram is a wonderful husband."

Then she felt the earth tremble. In the distance came the sound of thunder. She rushed outside to see what was happening. Could it be an earthquake? She'd heard of such things, but had never experienced one. Once she was outside the door, the roar became deafening. Fear struck her heart like a lightning bolt. She ran back into the house and shook her husband awake.

"Avram … get up … come in here now. Something is happening."

Avram sat up in bed. Then he heard the sound. It was upon them now. The air smelled of smoke. Avram ran outside the door of the house. He felt the earth rumbling. For a moment he stood, unable to move. Then he ran back inside and faced Michal. "That is the sound of horses.…"

They heard a man's voice come from down the street. The man cried out in panic, "COSSACKS!"

"Cossacks? Oh, dear God, help us, they are coming. Quick, Avram. Quick, hurry we must find a place to hide," Michal said. It felt as if the horse's hoofs were pounding inside her heart.

A shroud of white fell over Avram's face. "Do you think it's a pogrom?"

She shook her head. "I don't know." She couldn't move for a moment; she was paralyzed with fear.

Then, outside her living room window, Michal saw her friends and neighbors running in all directions. Some of them had not even stopped to put on their coats. They were still in their night clothes. She heard a crash of glass shattering as the odor of smoke grew thicker. Her eyes burned and she began coughing. As soon as she could speak, she said: "Where should we go? What should we do?"

Avram shrugged. He had no answer.

She looked around the house. They had not prepared for this in any way. Why not, she thought? But Michal knew the answer. It was because the people of the small village where she lived believed that they would be overlooked by the pogroms, that God would protect them. They were good people, religious people who stayed away from trouble. And, yes, the people knew that the czar was battling against the communists, but they had little affiliation with either side. Still, it was no matter; the czar blamed the Jews for the communist takeover, and even as the Red Army was descending upon Russia, the White Army still took the time to hire their terrible mercenaries, the Cossacks, to take revenge upon the Jews. The White Russians would offer the Cossacks the opportunity to steal anything and everything that they could find in a Jewish village during a pogrom, with the guarantee that there would be no penalty from the police or the government. The Bolsheviks had promised to protect the Jews once they took over. However, they were not yet firmly in place and there was no government to speak of; the country was in chaos, and anything could happen. Michal scanned the little house she shared with Avram. Her eyes darted to every corner, but she knew that they had no place to hide. Before they could even discuss escape routes, a massive band of sword-wielding Cossacks on horseback was right outside of the house. The horses' breath was thick and white in the icy air. One of the stallions reared up and rose on his back feet to a terrifying height. The invaders, with their long black coats and felt hats, could not be confused with any other group. These were the feared Cossacks. Cruel and barbaric.

Even the word had sent tremors through Jewish communities for as long as Michal could remember. The Cossacks' coats hung open to reveal loose tunics, loose pants, and colorful waistcoats. At their sides, some of them carried sabers, others long spears. Some had long hair that peeked from beneath their hats; others wore no hat but had shaved heads with a single ponytail rising from the center. Thick fur pelts hung about some of their necks, while others wore black felt capes over their coats. One of the Cossacks cried out into the crowds, red-faced with a loud fierce voice, "Christ killers, come and face your destiny. You are the reason that the communists have taken our beloved country!" Then the rest of the Cossacks joined him, "Christ killers...." they screamed. "Come and get what you deserve."

Bearded men with black hats, boys with long pe'ot (sidelocks), women with sheitels (wigs) that had been thrown on their heads without care all ran for their lives as the Cossacks on horseback chopped them down with giant sabers that glittered in the sun and dripped with vivid red blood. Michal covered her ears to the piercing screams. She heard a young child calling, "Mama … Mama...." Michal could not catch her breath. Her heart beat in her throat so loud that she thought the sound must be audible to Avram.

From somewhere down the road, she could hear a woman crying, begging, "No, please, no." Then she heard a group of men who had begun chanting prayers in Hebrew.

From where Michal stood, she could see that across the street, two Cossacks, both with single ponytails rising from their shaved heads, were nailing the door to her neighbor's house shut. Then another Cossack, wearing a gray fur hat and carrying a stick that had been wrapped with hay and set on fire, came riding by and touched the burning torch to the wooden house. It sprung into flames immediately and became a hungry orange beast that began to swallow the structure. The family who lived in the house was trapped inside. Clouds of black smoke rose into the air. The people who lived in that house were the Glickmans; they were friends of Michal and Avram; they had a small child, a girl. In fact, they had been guests at Michal and Avram's wedding. Now, they were being burned alive. OH, DEAR GOD … PLEASE HELP US. Michal said out loud, but her prayers were drowned out by the roar that came from the chaos all around her. What to do? What to do?

"Avram, we have to get out of here. We can't stay in the house. We are safer outside," Michal said, feeling bile rise in her throat. "They are burning the neighbors alive in their home next door."

Forgetting to put on her coat, she and Avram rushed outside. "Let's try to run as fast as we can and get into the forests." She grabbed his hand, attempting to pull him away. But he was stunned with grief, unable to move. The bodies of his friends and neighbors lay bleeding out in the snow. "AVRAM!!!!"

She tried to wake him out of the fog that had taken over his mind, but he refused to be moved. He began to pray. The prayers for the dead….

"Yit'gadal v'yit'kadash sh'mei raba Amein

May His great Name grow exalted and sanctified," Avram said.

"Avram." Michal shook his arm, but he stood, mesmerized, as if he had left the world and was speaking directly to God.

"b'al'ma di v'ra khir'utei

In the world that He created as He willed," Avram continued.

Michal felt tears fall from her eyes as she shook Avram harder. "AVRAM! AVRAM!"

Her grip on his arm did not move him at all. Instead, Avram continued to speak the words of the Mourner's Kaddish.

"v'yam'likh mal'khutei b'chayeikhon uv'yomeikhon

May He give reign to His kingship in your lifetimes and in your days,

uv'chayei d'khol beit yis'ra'eil

and in the lifetimes of the entire Family of Israel."

"Avram, have you gone mad?" Michal shook him hard, but he continued even though he was alone, without the other nine men that were required by religious law to make a minyan (quorum).

People were running all around her. People she'd known all of her life, still in their bedclothes, their bare feet leaving blood stains on the snow and ice. Michal had a vision of her parents and her brother and sister. Where were they? Were they alive? In a split second, without her realizing what was happening, a monster of a man was upon her. He stood at least six feet five and carried over three hundred pounds on his large frame. Throwing her to the ground, he tore the shawl from her shoulders. Michal scrambled to escape, but he kicked her in the stomach and the pain doubled her over. She began to pray. There was nothing else she could do; her husband was lost in another world. "Avram?" she called to him, but she knew he did not hear her. He continued his prayers. With a single slice of his sword, the Cossack beheaded Avram. Michal let out a piercing scream as she saw her young husband's head roll down the hill, blood still spurting from his empty neck. A mahogany bay horse that had been tied to a fence post let out a loud snort. Michal wanted to run, but she was unable to move. Her stomach ached and the ice beneath her prevented her from rising quickly. This had to be a nightmare. How could something so terrible be actually happening? It was no feat for the Cossack to rip the nightdress from Michal's body. She was too horrified to feel any modesty or to be affected by the Arctic winds. She forced herself, in spite of the pain, to rise to her knees. Her feet slipped on the ice, but she finally stood. The massive man grabbed her and threw her down on a patch of ice. Michal hit her head as she fell, but she was numb to the pain. Her entire body trembled with terror. The blood of her husband soaked the snow on the ground beside her. Her own blood trickled from her head wound to blend with Avram's. The Cossack pulled his heavy fur coat away from his body and unbuttoned his pants. Michal felt like she might vomit. She would beg, but she knew it would do no good. He took his penis out of his pants and entered her body. Michal wished she could die; even death could not be as horrible as this moment. He began heaving and grunting like a wild boar. She shivered from the cold and tried to move away from him, but he slapped her face so hard that her lip spurted a stream of blood.

The Cossack closed his eyes in ecstasy and, as he did, Taavi came from behind with the ax that he used to cut wood. The Cossack never heard him. Taavi lifted the ax and planted it square into the massive man's skull. Blood flew into Michal's face. She gagged. Taavi pushed the man off of Michal and lifted her.

"We have to get away from here right now," Taavi said.

"But Avram?"

"Avram is dead. Come on. Before the Cossacks notice us."

Taavi grabbed Michal's hand and she reached down and picked up her shawl, then wrapped it around her. For a moment, she remembered that it is unsuitable for a man to hold the hand of a woman who was married to someone else. But that thought passed quickly as Taavi pulled her by the hand and led her out of the village. He tugged her along faster as they ran through the farms. Behind them, houses and barns blazed. Michal heard the tortured cries of the families and the horrific neighing of the horses that were being stolen from their stalls. She stopped to look for a moment; she was mesmerized, staring at the scene in front of her, unable to move. Taavi tugged her hand harder.

"Don't look back," he said.

"But...."

"Come on … If you don't come now, we will both be dead." He pulled her hand harder and she almost fell forward, but she caught herself and the two of them ran at full speed until they reached the dense forest that lay just beyond.

The trees were close together. The icicles that hung from the branches and leaves of the trees were thick and heavy enough to cut into a man's flesh. Michal glanced up and saw that there were rainbows that the sun was causing to reflect in the ice. A little way across from where they stood, a long frozen dagger of ice fell into the snow, leaving a gap where it had landed. Michal looked up at Taavi with concern in her eyes. But he refused to stop; instead, he continued pulling her deeper into the thick foliage where they would be hidden from the invaders.

Her body trembled with the cold. He took off his coat and put it around her.

"Wear this or you'll freeze. I'll be all right as long as we don't stop moving. It's too dangerous to try to break into one of these farm houses," he said.

"So, where will we go? What will we do?"

"I have an idea."

He pulled her harder, moving her faster.

"I'm still stunned by what's happened," she said.

"We have no time for sentiment. If we are to survive, we cannot think of what we have lost, only of what we must do."

She nodded, but tears filled her eyes. They froze as they dripped down her cheeks. He turned to look at her.

"Please, don't cry. I'm not very good when someone cries," he said. "Now, I know you are scared and that you lost your husband today. I don't mean to seem uncaring. But, Michal, this is a pogrom. They mean to kill all the Jews in this village. We are fighting against terrible odds. The Cossacks are strong. They're cruel and fierce mercenaries. We're lucky we got away. If you dwell on the past, you will not have your wits about you. Until this is all over, we have to be very careful."

"How long do you think it will be before they leave?"

"Tomorrow morning probably. I think they'll stay in town at the tavern drinking until they fall asleep. Then they'll steal what they can and leave. You wait here. There's a farm in the distance; I'm going to break in and take some clothes."

"But we can't be sure that there won't be anyone in the farmhouse. They might shoot you."

"I know, but it's a risk we have to take. If we can't find warm clothes, food or shelter, we will die."

She bit her lower lip. "I'm scared."

"Yes, well, that won't do us much good right now. I'll be back; wait here."

Michal had not realized how cold she was until she stood still waiting for Taavi. He returned with men's pants, a shirt, boots, and another coat for himself. His face and shirt were splattered with blood. She dressed quickly and didn't ask questions.

"Now, let's keep moving until we can find a safe place to stop." She felt as if she could not go any further, but he kept pulling her forward. The cold bit through her skin and she felt like her blood was freezing solid.

Taavi put his arm around her. Michal looked up at him; he was taller by over a foot. She was stunned. It was not acceptable for such an intimate gesture to take place between a man and a woman. "I don't mean to behave disrespectfully, but we are both freezing. We can use the warmth from each other's bodies," he said, reading her mind.

Michal blushed. He was right, of course. But even in the middle of this terrible situation, she was reminded of the inappropriate thoughts that she'd had about him in the past, and she felt ashamed.

"You're shivering and your lips are blue. We cannot wait until nightfall to find shelter. We must find some place warm as soon as possible or we will both freeze to death."

"What can we do? There are Cossacks all around us!"

From where they stood, hidden behind the thick brush, they could still see the pillagers on horseback.

"We must turn and go to the non-Jewish farmers until we can find someone to take pity on us."

"I've never been out of the Jewish section. It is forbidden to have communication with the non-Jews."

"Yes, I know about all of your rules. In my opinion, they are ridiculous."

"That's your opinion," she said, wrapping her arms around herself. Her teeth had begun chattering.

"Never mind. I don't want to have an argument with you. It's a waste of precious energy right now. Just follow me and do as I say."

She felt her back stiffen. He was a man. After all, men had all the power. But he was different from Avram, who was gentle and never made her feel like she was being dominated. He reminded her a little of her father and, for that, she was starting to dislike him. Still, right now, she needed him and so she would do as he commanded.

Taavi pulled Michal's arm, leading her deeper into the forest. Her toes were numb. She felt the wind slice right through her skin. The cold had frozen the tears she'd shed for her dead husband less than an hour ago, and her eyelashes felt heavy and began sticking together. The terror of the pogrom, the screams of the victims, the wild conquering cries of the Cossacks mingled with the unbearable cold of the Siberian winter left Michal exhausted and ready to collapse. It would be easier to just give up, to lie down in the bed of white frozen flakes and allow her body to sleep, a sleep that she knew she would never awaken from. But, Taavi pulled on her arm, the heavier she felt and the slower she moved, the harder he pushed her, the more insistent he became.

"Where are we going, Taavi? We have nowhere to go. I'm tired, I'm weary. I can't go on anymore...."

"Don't even talk like that. I'm taking you to a place that very few people know about. We'll be safe there."

Her shoulders dropped. She had to believe him. He would not let her go, would not let her fall into her final rest. Instead of slowing down, Taavi pulled her harder. The icicles on the tree branches scratched her face. One dropped right in front of her, missing her by inches. She wanted to cry, to cry and cry and cry. But Taavi would not let go of her arm.

Finally, there was a break in the trees. A small cottage stood alone, surrounded on all sides by forest. The house was made of wood painted brown, so as not to stand out to a passerby. In order to find this minuscule shelter, one would have to know exactly where to look.

"Who lives here?" Michal asked. She'd heard tales of the old wise woman who lived in the forest, but she thought it was only a myth. The woman was said to be a witch, to work with herbs and cast spells. People had warned of the danger of the witch in the woods. "Is this the home of the witch?"

"Come on," Taavi said, giving her a tug.

"I'm not going in there."

"You are. You have no other choice. Besides, she isn't a witch at all; she's a woman who makes medicine and delivers babies. I know her. She is kind. She'll help us."

"For sure she is not one of us."

"You mean a Jew?"

"Exactly, she is not a Jew."

"No, of course not. But she is a good person. You are about a minute from freezing to death. Stop asking me so many questions." He was curt, but to the point. He knocked on the door of the modest dwelling. A woman wearing a thick flannel dress and a heavy woolen shawl opened the creaky door. Her hair, as white as the snow, was long and thin, but her eyes were bright, blue as the morning sky on a crisp winter day.

"We need help," Taavi said. "There has been a raid by Cossacks on our village. We are Jews."

The old woman stared at them both skeptically. Her piercing eyes scanned the couple, digesting every detail. She shook her head. "I've been expecting something like this in the village. It's been happening more frequently at all of the towns surrounding us. It was just a matter of time." She shook her head. "Well, come on in. What are you waiting for? Standing outside half naked, you'll both freeze to death. I have a fire going; you're welcome to sit down and warm yourselves."

The orange and red flames burned low, deep inside the belly of a black cast iron stove that stood in the corner of the small room. There was a single bed on one side and a table filled with bowls containing strange mixtures. Michal looked around suspiciously.

"Don't be afraid. You're safe here. The Cossacks are scared of me. They're afraid that demons will descend upon them if they come anywhere near this house." She laughed. "My name is Bepa. Go on, sit down."

Michal settled cross-legged on the dirt floor with Taavi beside her. The room was very warm and it felt good to have that warmth seep into her body. As she began to defrost, she felt the will to live begin to rise within her and travel through her bloodstream all the way to her heart. She was afraid of the old woman. She'd been raised with fears and superstitions that haunted her now as she accepted Bepa's charity.

"Are you hungry?" Bepa asked, already doling out a ladle of soup and tearing off a thick hunk of grainy bread.

Taavi nodded. "Yes, very hungry. Thank you."

Michal thought about all of the rules that she'd grown up with. There was no doubt in her mind that this food could not be kosher. Yet, Taavi did not seem to care at all.

"No, thank you. I'm not hungry," Michal said. "Thank you for taking us in. You didn't have to."

"You both would have died. How could I not take you in?" Bepa said, smiling. "Anyway, you're welcome."

Bepa pulled her shawl tighter around her reed-like body and gazed into the fire. "I'm glad for the company. It gets lonely here sometimes."

Taavi smiled and nodded at her. "I can imagine how you must feel."

"Mostly it's worst in the winter. In the summer I can go outside and walk through the forest. In the winter it's just me and these four walls. And my friend." She pointed to an old docile wolf that lay asleep in the corner.

"Is that a wolf?"

"Yes, Sheba is a wolf. I found her as a cub. She was dying. I took care of her. We've been best friends ever since. Anyway, for the most part, the townspeople stay away from me. Unless, of course, there is a woman having a difficult birth or someone is dying and the doctor cannot be reached in time. Then, they come here. They think I am a witch, but they also think that if they pay me I will bring the child safely into the world or save a loved one. They think my hands are magic." She looked down at the loose skin on her slender hands and laughed.

"Magic?"

"Does it always work? Do you always save them?" Taavi asked, scooping up the last of his soup with a mouthful of bread.

"God, no. I wish I did. Sometimes the medicine works, sometimes not. But I try my best."

Michal cleared her throat. "Are you?" she asked in a small voice.

"Am I what? A witch?"

Michal nodded.

Bepa let out a belly laugh. "I'm no witch, although I've often wished that I was. My mother knew how to work with herbs, with plants and with all the things that grow here in the forest. She showed me how to crush and blend them together in order to make medicines. I grew up learning what to use to cure a fever or settle a cough. It began when I was very small, when my mother took me with her when she went to deliver babies. So, I learned to do that too. But ... no, unfortunately I do not have any magical powers."

Michal knew that she should not be fascinated by this woman. She should be afraid and run away from this house. Yet, she was captivated and she could not run. And, even if she wanted to leave, there was nowhere to run; danger lurked just outside the thick forest.

"You can stay as long as you like. I don't mind if you choose to remain with me until the weather breaks. I have plenty of food. People pay me for my services with food. And, as I said before ... I wouldn't mind having the company. The two of you could sleep over there by the fire and I will sleep here on my bed."

"Oh … we are not husband and wife. We cannot do that," Michal said. "It wouldn't be proper."

Bepa smiled "Of course. Then, I'll move my bed into the middle of the room and one of you can sleep on each side of my bed. That way we can be sure that nothing inappropriate will occur."

Michal eyed the old woman. She's laughing at me, she thought. (Well, let her laugh. I know right from wrong. I will not lose my dignity, my modesty, just because I have been put into this dreadful situation.

CHAPTER 11

From walking barefoot when she and Taavi had first left the village, Michal had lost all feeling in two of her toes. They had turned red and blistered. The boots Taavi had stolen for her were men's boots and they were far too big. Bepa gave her a pair of shoes that were slightly bigger than Michal's feet, but she stuffed them with cotton. However, it was too late to save the toes. They turned black. Michal didn't want to bother anyone with her problems, but when she removed her shoes by the fire one afternoon, Bepa saw what had happened.

"I'm afraid that your two toes that have turned black are going to fall off," Bepa told Michal.

Michal touched her foot and gently caressed the damaged appendages. "I can't feel anything."

"I know. You will lose the toes, but it shouldn't have any effect on your ability to walk. At least from what I can see."

Bepa was right. Michal lost her toes, but she was still able to walk without any problem. Looking at her deformed foot made her feel ill. Alone in her bed at night, Michal wept softly as she prayed, asking God why her life had taken such a frightening turn. She prayed that her brother and sister had survived, but she doubted she would ever see them again. Although she tried to be quiet, muffling the sound with her pillow, Taavi heard her and he longed to comfort her. But he knew she would misinterpret his actions if he dared to enter her side of the room. She would be offended and feel that he had broken some silly forbidden law that had been set in place to keep her pure and above reproach by the Jewish Rebbes. It was all nonsense to him. He didn't want to take her in his arms and make love to her. He only wanted to offer the calm reassurance of a good friend. Well, that wasn't entirely true. But he would never have attempted to carry out his true desires. He respected her.

As time went by, Michal found that she liked Bepa's straightforward ways. The old woman did not flatter or lie, and she never once made Michal or Taavi feel as if they were intruding or that they owed her in any way for her kindness. Michal watched Bepa take a basket down off of a high shelf and fill it quickly with medicinal supplies when a boy from the village came to ask for help for his mother who was having difficulties in childbirth.

"You are welcome to come with me if you would like," Bepa said to Michal.

Michal felt her face grow hot. How could she refuse to help? After all, both she and Taavi were living under this woman's roof, eating her food. The idea of assisting in delivering a baby petrified her. There would be blood, and perhaps even death. Michal looked into Bepa's eyes, which were fixed upon her.

"It's a good thing to have the knowledge of a midwife. You may need to know these things someday."

"I'll come with you," Michal said, drawing a sharp breath.

The peasants whose home they went to were not Jews. They were farmers that lived on the other side of the forest. When Bepa and Michal arrived, the room was cold. The husband sat on a chair beside his wife's bed, wringing his hands.

"Don't just sit there." Bepa looked at the husband sternly. "Start a fire and warm this place up right away. Then bring me a kettle filled with hot water and also bring several clean towels." Bepa spoke with authority.

The woman with an extended belly lay sweating and trembling on a slender cot. Her hair knotted and stuck to her face and neck with perspiration.

"You are going to be just fine," Bepa said, as she smiled at the woman and touched her shoulder.

The man had started a fire in the cast iron stove; it was burning low and beginning to warm the room. After the husband laid the towels and the pot of hot water beside the bed, Bepa told the man and his son to leave them.

Next, she raised the sheet and examined the woman.

"The baby will need to be turned," Bepa said. "This may hurt a little. I'm sorry. I'll do my best to make it as painless as possible." Then Bepa gave the woman a thick rope that she took out of her basket. "Hold on to this. It will help you. Squeeze it when you are in pain. Now, don't push until I tell you to do so. Do you understand me?" Bepa turned the woman's head so that they were eye to eye. Again, she asked, "Do you understand me?"

"Yes...." the woman said in a tortured voice.

Michal watched as Bepa massaged the woman's belly. Then Michal held her breath as Bepa reached inside of the woman's body and gently manipulated the fetus. The woman cried out in pain and Michal trembled with horror. She had never seen a child born, and it was a frightening thing to watch. First there was a rush of water.

"Push...." Bepa said. The woman did as she was told. "Now wait ... wait ... Now push again...." The woman let out a loud groan and pushed. "Again ... push again ... as hard as you can."

Blood covered the bed as the woman's body tore open to allow the child's head and shoulders to come through. And then with the force of a final push, the rest of the small body entered the world.

Bepa held the baby up by his feet and slapped his bottom. A hearty cry came from the infant's lips.

"You have a healthy son," Bepa said. Then she took the knife from her basket, tied and cut the cord. As if it were a doll, Bepa handed the baby to Michal. "Wash him," she said, as she finished helping the woman to expel the afterbirth.

As Michal gently washed the child with warm water, her hands shook. What she had just witnessed was frightening, but it was also miraculous. She felt tears form in the corners of her eyes. Hashem, the Jew's name for God, was here today. He used Bepa's hands to bring a new life into the world. At that moment, Michal knew that she wanted to learn the things that Bepa knew. She too wanted to work as a servant to Hashem, healing the sick and helping to bring new lives into the world.

From that day on, Michal accompanied Bepa whenever the old woman was called upon to doctor a person in need. Michal witnessed three more births and, by the fourth, Bepa insisted that Michal act as the midwife. Michal was nervous, but she had learned enough to carry out the mission.

Not all of the births were successful. Once they lost the baby. It was born dark blue, with the umbilical cord tied tightly around its neck. Another time they lost the mother and the baby. The baby was stillborn and Bepa could not stop the mother's bleeding. These were two terrible occasions. But the bad times occurred much less often than the good. And Michal could not help but love being a midwife. She did not enjoy tending to the sick as much. The vile smells of feces and vomit turned her stomach. But even though sometimes blood, feces, and vomit were present at a birth, at least at the end the reward was a beautiful child.

After they had assisted a young girl in a very difficult birth, the grandmother of the newborn baby offered Bepa and Michal a cup of tea. They gladly accepted. Both the mother and baby had survived. The grandmother claimed that the child's father had been killed by a bear when he was hunting. Michal thought that perhaps the new mother had never been married. Michal decided that it was not for her to judge the woman's moral convictions. She gazed out the window and waited for the tea to be ready. It was a late winter night; outside, the ground was covered with a soft dusting of new fallen snow. The moon lit upon the white blanket and it shone like diamonds.

"Come, sit down at the table with me," the grandmother said, pouring three cups of tea, while her daughter and new grandson lay sleeping in the other room. "I want to thank you both for everything that you did for my daughter and her child."

Bepa smiled and sipped the hot liquid.

"I have no money to pay you. And ... very little food. But ... I can do something for you that I do not often offer to anyone."

Bepa tilted her head. Michal sat quietly.

"I can read your tea leaves...."

"Oh, no," Michal said. "That scares me."

"Are you sure? Are you sure you're not the least bit curious?"

Bepa laughed. "I am not curious about my future at all. I know my future. I will live for a few more years and then I will go to my final resting place. And for me ... that's all right."

"But, you? You are young ... You must be a just a little curious?"

"Yes, perhaps a little."

"Then finish your tea and hand me your cup."

Michal looked at Bepa, who shrugged her shoulders "Do it if you want to," she said. "I don't set much store in these things."

Michal longed to hear what the woman would say. She wondered if the woman would say that Taavi was in love with her. She thought that perhaps the tea leaves might tell her if her brother and sister were alive. Curiosity got the better of Michal, so she drained her cup and handed it to the woman.

Michal smiled conspiratorially at Bepa, as if to say that she was not a true believer, only curious.

The woman took a deep breath. Then she sighed.

"Dear child. I am sorry to tell you, but you have a challenging life ahead of you. There will be much love, but there will be many disasters for you to overcome. You will have to be strong to survive. Yes, I am afraid I see a very hard road that you will travel. You said your name was Michal?"

"Yes, my name is Michal."

"I am sorry, Michal, but your destiny is not to be an easy one."

The woman shook her head as if she were feeling pain. Bepa stood up. "That's enough of this. I think it's time for us to leave," she said. "Get your coat on, Michal. We have a long walk home."

They walked for over a half hour in silence. Then Michal asked "Do you think she was right? She scared me a little."

"Right about your future?"

"Yes, do you think I am going to have a hard life?"

"I think we all have a difficult path to walk. You are strong. If I were you, I wouldn't give what she said very much thought. Just live day to day and do the best you can with what God gives you."

Michal nodded. But that night as she tried to fall asleep, she felt uneasy about her tea leaf reading and wished she had never allowed the woman to predict her future. The last words in her mind as she finally drifted into a fitful sleep were, "Michal's destiny will be a difficult one."

CHAPTER 12

Working with Bepa helped Michal to avoid thinking about the past. She was too busy to allow herself to be still and remember the horror and pain she'd experienced that night at the hands of the Cossack who'd raped her and murdered her husband. Every day was a new learning experience. Reluctantly, Michal had abandoned her need to keep kosher with her food. It was impossible to keep that law and survive. She knew her mother would have died before eating the treif (non-kosher) food that Michal now consumed, but Michal did not want to die. She was young, and through Bepa had found a purpose for her life. A way to make a difference in the world that she enjoyed.

One night when Bepa fell asleep by the fire, Michal took a blanket and gently placed it over the old woman. She turned to find Taavi watching her.

"You've come to really like her, haven't you?"

"I have. I was afraid of her at first, but she is a good woman."

"Even though she isn't 'one of us, she isn't Jewish'?"

"Yes, even though." Michal smiled. "You know, all that has happened has taught me so much. When I was growing up, I believed that I would spend my entire life in the Jewish community. After I got married, I thought that Avram and I would stay together forever, have children and raise them according to Jewish law, the way I had been raised. Now, everything has changed."

"And you are sad?"

"Yes and no. It breaks my heart to think about what happened to Avram. He was always kind to me. A good husband. He didn't deserve to die that way. And of course ... well ... what you saw the Cossack do to me ... still brings me shame."

He nodded. "I know. But don't be ashamed; it wasn't your fault."

She looked away, too humiliated to meet his eyes.

"Still, even with everything that has happened ... at least I have met Bepa and learned a wonderful trade."

"And me?" he said, lifting one eyebrow.

"What about you?"

"Nothing."

"I don't understand." She looked at him and saw the light from the fire dancing in his eyes.

"Well ... you probably don't even realize."

"Realize what?" she asked.

"The way I feel about you."

She felt her face burn with embarrassment.

"Did you know that since that first day I saw you in the square I was wildly attracted to you? And ... even after you married Avram, I still watched you. Do you think it was an accident that I was there at your house when the Cossacks attacked? As soon as the pogrom began and I saw them come riding into the village, I ran to find you. I decided I would save you or die trying."

Her breath caught in her throat. "Thank you."

"Don't thank me. Instead, tell me that the look I saw in your eyes every time you looked at me before the pogrom and even now that we are here together is not my imagination. Tell me that it is real. Tell me that you care for me too."

"Oh, Taavi." She could hardly speak. "We should not speak of such things. I am still in mourning."

"You want me to wait the year until you are done mourning before I declare myself? If that is what you want, I will abide by your wishes. But … Michal … there is no one to judge you now."

"Only Hashem."

"And where was God, where was Hashem when our village was attacked? Where was he when that dirty Cossack chopped your husband's head off? Where was God when that savage tore your dress…?"

"Stop. Stop, please, Taavi. You should not talk this way. We do not always understand God's mind or his intentions."

"Is that what you really believe, Michal? Is it? Then why do you eat the food that is treif that the old woman gives us? Are you a hypocrite?"

"I don't want to talk about this anymore, Taavi. Talking about God this way is a sin. I am going to sleep. Goodnight."

She got up and pulled the curtain between herself and Taavi. In her former life, before the pogrom, she would not have ever been alone in a room with a man that was not her husband. But things had changed. She lay down on the cot that Taavi had made for her and tried to sleep, but she couldn't. Where was God when they were suffering? Forgive me, Hashem. She shuddered in fear at the thought. And Taavi … if he had not appeared … what would have happened to her? Would the Cossack have severed her head when he finished with her and would it now be lying in a ditch somewhere, her blood drying into the snow? Michal bit her lower lip. She was so confused…

CHAPTER 13

Meanwhile, Taavi spent his time repairing every piece of furniture in the old woman's house. He wanted to do as much as possible to earn his keep. All of his life, Taavi had been resourceful. He was not rich enough to rely on anyone but himself, so when he needed to shift in order to survive, he was able to do so without much effort. The old woman had a gun and plenty of ammunition. She kept it, she said, for defense purposes. It gave Taavi an idea. He took it out and taught himself to hunt. Taavi had always been a lover of nature, mostly of animals. However, he knew that they needed meat to survive and the furs could be sold for much needed money. He did not want to use up all of the bullets teaching himself, and so he took branches of trees and fashioned a bow and arrows. Sometimes he caught rabbits or squirrels, which Bepa skinned and boiled. It helped the three of them to survive the vicious Siberian winter. But after a couple of months had passed and the weather was not so severe, Taavi began making trips back to the Jewish village that was still reeling from the pogrom. He wanted to see if any of his friends were still alive.

The synagogue was burned to the ground, only ashes and a few walls remained, half standing. A few of his old friends and customers were still in the village. They welcomed him, glad to see that he had escaped. From his friends, Taavi learned that the rabbi had been murdered and the Torah had been destroyed. He walked the old familiar streets, his heart sick and heavy.

When he passed his carpentry shop, he felt his heart sink even lower. All of the windows were busted out and all of the furniture he'd worked so hard to create, furniture he'd carved so carefully for hours, now lay broken into pieces on the floor. He was ready to leave Russia forever. That was when he began to talk to the other villagers, to see if anyone could help him find a way out of the country. It took several visits, but Taavi was patient and finally he got what he wanted.

That night he returned to the little house in the forest with news.

"I've been to the village," Taavi told Bepa and Michal as they sat around the cast iron stove eating soup. "Everyone who was left alive is terrified that there will be another pogrom."

"I am certain that there will be. These things are not new. They have been happening for generations," Bepa said. "Why don't you stay here, out in the forest? You will be safe here."

"I have no job here. I cannot earn any money here. In fact, that is what I wanted to talk to both of you about. When I went to the village, I found an old friend of mine. He has a brother who lives in Berlin. His brother has a carpentry shop. My friend said that he would contact his brother and perhaps find work for me in Berlin."

"Berlin? Germany? That is so far away," Michal said.

"Yes, I know. But I need the work. And besides, from what I'm hearing, the Germans are educated. They're more advanced than the Russians, a more civilized people. I would be living and working in a big city. Berlin is a lively and exciting place. From what everyone is saying, it's the center for art and science. I'm sure that there's still some anti-Semitism, even in Germany, but the people are not ignorant like they are in Russia. We are surrounded here with villagers who are backward and terrified by old superstitions. They think Jews have tails and drink the blood of Christian babies. Jews are hated and feared in Russia. The czars throughout the ages have caused that. But, I believe Jews are tolerated in Berlin. I've heard that the Jewish community is thriving, that there are Jewish artists, writers, and scientists. What I think is that in Berlin, they leave us alone and we leave them alone."

"But things are changing here. Things will be better now that the communists have taken over," Michal said hopefully.

"Do you really believe that? Russia has always been known for blaming the Jews for all of its problems. There will be problems with this regime too … and then what?"

"My father always said that the Jews needed a homeland."

"And we do … desperately, but for now, we need to get out of Russia."

"Well … if you think that's what's best for you…"

"I do. But, Michal, it's not just what's best for me; I want you to go with me."

She looked away and shook her head.

"I want to marry you."

"I'm still in mourning for my husband. I can't even consider such a thing."

"Times and circumstances have changed us. I have feelings for you. I know you have feelings for me. I respect that you are very frum and it is unsuitable for a man and woman who are unmarried to travel together."

"Berlin is very far away. You are welcome to stay here. I am going out to get some water. I'll be back. I think it's best that you two talk about this alone," Bepa said, and she walked out, closing the door softly behind her.

"Bepa is right; Berlin is very far from here. I think it is very different from everything we know..."

"But I would be very respectful of you. Very respectful. I would not do anything inappropriate. I promise you this. And I would not even consider coming near you until our union was blessed in the eyes of God by marriage."

She liked him. She'd always liked him. And he was there when she was in danger; he'd rescued her. He was a strong man, a man who could be trusted.

"You could stay here with Bepa; I realize that. But I would miss you terribly and you would be wasting your life. Avram is gone, Michal. Your grief cannot bring him back. You're still alive. You're still young. Marry me. Come with me to Berlin, to the city. I will make a nice life for us."

"I don't know..."

"Michal," he said, his voice soft and pleading. Then he did the unthinkable ... he took her hands in his. She shuddered for a moment. It was not right for a man to touch a woman who was not his wife, and especially a woman who was married to another man. He'd promised not to do anything inappropriate, and he was doing something wrong already. But ... she liked him. And she measured the situation. Her husband was dead. There was a very good chance that her family was dead as well. She had come to adore Bepa; she enjoyed the work she shared with Bepa. However, if she stayed in the forest, her days would be spent healing the sick and delivering babies. Rewarding, yes.

Fulfilling, no. Michal took a deep breath. She could not hide from her true feelings. From the first time she'd seen Taavi, she had felt desire run through her like a current of lightning and, instead of disappearing, that current had grown stronger over the last several months. She could not bear to think of being without him for the rest of her life. And she knew that if he went to Berlin alone, she could probably assume that he would not return to Siberia. This was her only chance. All of the religious modesty and all of the rules she'd been raised to abide by began to lose their validity. If she stayed, she would spend her life working with Bepa; it was almost certain that she would die a childless widow. If she left … if she left … she would have a husband, a home … even, God willing, children. Was it a sin to want this life so soon after Avram's death? She trembled as she whispered a prayer to God in her mind, "Please forgive me, Hashem, I beg of you forgive me for what I am about to do…."

Then Michal, with trembling hands, reached out and took Taavi's hands in her own. She could see the shock on his face. He was hardly expecting her to touch him.

"Yes," she said.

"Yes?"

"Yes. I will marry you. I will go to live with you in Berlin," she said and took a long breath.

A smile broke across his face. He laughed out loud. She could hear the joy in his laughter and she began to laugh too.

"You've made me very happy this day," Taavi said.

"And you have made me happy too."

"We will marry in Berlin, where we can avoid the questioning and critical eyes of our old neighbors. Until then, I will observe all of the laws and not take any liberties with you," he said, drawing his hands away gently. "Please don't think I don't find you attractive. I find you beautiful. But, out of respect for you, I will wait."

She knew he was right. If they went down to the village where they had grown up and searched to see if anyone knew where to find a rabbi, there would be questions, there would be judgment. People would condemn her for accepting a proposal so soon after her husband's death. Taavi was right. It was best to leave Russia as soon as possible and go to Berlin.

"How will we get there?" Michal asked.

"I have some money that I saved from when I was working before the pogrom, and I sold the furs from the animals I caught these last few months. There is a man in the village who has a horse and cart. I will pay him to take us to the railroad. We will take a train into Germany. Then, once we arrive in Berlin, I am fortunate to have a job waiting for me. The man who recommended me to his cousin is a trustworthy friend. We will be all right. As soon as we arrive in Berlin, we will marry."

Bepa had returned. She stood listening for a few moments at the door before she entered.

"I was listening and I know you want to go. I will miss you both. I don't think Germany is as wonderful a place as you think it is. And I will tell you again you are both welcome to stay here," she said, leaning against the wall. It was as if she needed support to say goodbye to Michal.

"We want to go, Bepa. We both are very grateful for all you have done for us," Taavi said.

"All right then." Bepa was suddenly strong once again "If that is your decision … then, here." She took an earthenware pot with a heavy handled cover down off the top shelf, where she stored her medicinal herbs. She reached in and pulled out a pile of coins.

"Take this money. I have no use for it here. You might need it to start your lives in a new country."

"We have enough. Thank you," Taavi said.

"Michal has been a great help to me. This is not charity. She earned this money as my assistant. I insist that you take this, Michal. I will not take no for an answer."

Bepa looked at Michal with eyes the color of a blue jay, "Take it!" Bepa said, her voice firm.

Michal took the money.

Bepa nodded and turned away, then she walked outside the cabin to be alone. Michal saw the sadness that Bepa tried to hide as she left and thought, *she doesn't want us to go. She will be alone again and lonely*. A seed of sadness took root in Michal's heart. But before she had a chance to let it begin to grow, Taavi began packing the few things he'd brought with him when he came to the old woman's house. The sound of his movement around the cabin distracted Michal from her thoughts.

"Taavi," she said, her voice quivering, "I don't even speak German."

"Yiddish is very similar."

"Is it? You know, it is said that Yiddish is the language of God."

"Yes, I've heard that old wives' tale." He smiled.

"But it's not an old wives' tale. The rebbe says--"

"Yes, and the rebbe was there to protect you and save you when you needed him, wasn't he?"

She looked away.

"I'm sorry. That was uncalled for. Listen, don't worry about speaking German. I speak fluent German and I can read and write in German as well."

"Really?" She cocked her head to the side. Would this man ever cease to amaze her?

"Yes, really. And, I'll teach you."

"To read and write too?"

"Yes, to speak, read, and write in German."

"Oh, Taavi. That would be wonderful."

"Yes, women should have access to books."

"The rebbe says that it is not good for women to learn. It takes us away from our true purpose of being wives and mothers."

"Again the rebbe?"

"I do want to learn to read and write." She looked into his eyes and her heart swelled. Any woman would find him to be very handsome. He had chosen her, and that made her feel very special. She thought that her life had ended the day that Avram died, but she was beginning to feel the joy of living sprouting inside of her. "By the way, how did you ever learn to read and write in German?"

"My mother taught me."

"How did she know? Who taught her?"

"I'd rather not talk about it, but let's just say … she knew and she taught me," he said, crossing his arms over his chest.

Michal watched him as he talked about his mother. Something seemed to trouble him, but she dared not ask. "Well, I'm really happy that you plan to teach me."

He nodded his head. "You'd better get ready. I would like to leave the day after tomorrow," Taavi said.

So soon? So soon? Michal thought, but she just smiled in acceptance.

Taavi was wrong. It took longer than two days for Michal and Taavi to prepare to make the trip. Taavi's friend who lived in town suggested that Taavi wait for a return letter from his cousin, guaranteeing Taavi work before they took off for Germany. Between the weather and the distance, the letter took two months to arrive. It was not as positive as Taavi had hoped. Yes, the cousin would give Taavi a job, but business was slow. Money was tight. Germany was in a depression.

"Are you sure you still want to go?" Michal asked, when Taavi told her about the letter.

"Yes, I want to leave Siberia. I don't want to face another pogrom."

"But the country is changing. The Bolsheviks are taking over. They hate the czar and they hate the Cossacks."

"Do you think they like the Jews? They say they accept us, but I know better," Taavi said with a hint of sarcasm in his voice. "Everyone hates the Jews…"

"So, if everyone hates the Jews, why would things be different in Germany? Won't they hate us just as much?"

"Germany is a civilized country. I've been told that they are making tremendous advances in science, medicine, and the arts. A country like that would never do something as barbaric as a pogrom," Taavi said. "We need to leave Russia. Whether it is governed by the Reds or the Whites, this country will always be an enemy to our people."

"I've heard differently. I've heard that Stalin wants to give us a part of Siberia as a Jewish homeland."

"I don't believe it. As far back as my father's father could remember, Russia has had pogroms against the Jews. I don't want to stay here. I want to try and find a home where there is equality for our people and opportunities for work. I am resourceful. If I can't find enough to do as a carpenter, then I'll find another job. There are factories in Berlin. There is work in the city."

"Then at least agree to wait until the spring. It will be easier to travel once the weather is a little less brutal. Will you do that for me?" she asked.

"I would do anything for you, Michal. And, yes, if that is what you want, then we'll wait and leave at the first sign of the spring."

Meanwhile, Taavi spent every evening teaching Michal to speak, read, and write in German. Although she was curious, she never asked about his mother again.

And so, after three months of planning, packing, and saying goodbye, Michal and Taavi were on their way to the city.

CHAPTER 14

Berlin, Germany, May, 1920

Taavi set both suitcases down in front of him as they waited on the platform for the train that ran through the Jewish sector of town. Michal was nervous and excited. She had never been so far away from home. A loud whistle alarmed her as the train pulled into the station. A conductor with a dark blue cap motioned Michal and Taavi to go to the last cars.

"People with baggage must ride in the back cars," he said to Taavi.

They boarded the correct car. Michal sat down beside a woman with a cute little girl that appeared to be about five years old on her lap. Michal smiled at the child, who shyly nuzzled into her mother's chest. There were not enough seats available, so Taavi remained standing. Then the train began to rattle and move along the rail. Michal turned her body so that she was able to look out the window. Before she began this trip, Michal had never left the small village where she was born. Every sight along the way excited her and filled her with wonder, even though she was exhausted and hungry, she was mesmerized by the enormous world that surrounded her. The train rambled past road construction and automobiles. Then a large billboard hung suspended on an iron post; it was a picture of a suave-looking dark haired man smoking a cigarette. Michal saw a group of three children playing on the sidewalk. Then the train sped by two women wearing head scarves and house dresses. They were talking across a fence as each of them was hanging their laundry out to dry. There were rows and rows of tall overcrowded apartment buildings that stood in line like soldiers beside the tracks. People sat outside on the stoops, they hung out the windows, and leaned on the buildings. Some of the apartment dwellers had forgotten to close the drapes over their windows, and Michal could see inside; some were eating, reading, or talking. Then she saw one couple making love. She looked away quickly, embarrassed, hoping Taavi had not witnessed the display of what should have been a very private moment.

They arrived at their stop. Taavi grabbed the luggage and helped Michal off the train. The walk to the Jewish sector of town was a short distance. But once they arrived, there could be no mistaking where they were. Although more people filled the streets than Michal had ever seen in one place at one time, they all looked ethnically familiar. Yes, their clothes were different, and their accents were different, but she could overhear the familiar sounds of the Yiddish language. From the open doors and windows of the restaurants, she could smell the familiar odors of Jewish cooking. Men and boys with long curly sideburns called pe'ot and long black coats hurried down the walkways. Some wore tall hats, others shorter felt hats, still others wore yarmulkes. They had stiff white shirts and short hair. Old men with long grey beards walked slowly through the streets. Women carrying baskets of food wore long skirts that reached their ankles and blouses that covered them from their necks to their wrists. But then there were others. She saw a rich couple get out of an automobile; the woman was wearing a fashionable dress and the man looked smart in a well-tailored suit. They entered the diamond cutter's shop. Michal admired the woman's beautiful garment; she'd never seen such finery.

Two women with dresses low enough to expose most of their heavy breasts leaned against a building. Their lips and cheeks had been painted scarlet. One of the red-lipped women smiled at Taavi and winked. Then she lifted her dress to expose her thigh. Michal felt her face turn hot. These women must be prostitutes. She'd heard about such things, but had never seen or been so close to such a person. Taavi did not respond; he ignored the vulgar display, and Michal was glad. She wasn't sure what she would have said or done had he smiled back. A young man with bent up legs and an amputated arm sat on the sidewalk wearing his army uniform. He held out a cup. In Yiddish he asked for a few coins. He said he was a veteran from the Great War. Michal wanted to give him a few of the coins that Bepa had given her, but Taavi shook his head, took her elbow, and led her away.

"It's a mitzvah to help the poor," Michal whispered to Taavi.

"We don't have money to be giving to anyone. Right now we need to find a place to stay and ensure our own future."

She knew that Taavi was not a Talmud scholar. He was a survivor, and he knew how to be selfish when he had to be. So what had she expected? She glanced at him. His face was hard, determined. She didn't like this side of him, this lack of caring, lack of kindness, but she should not have been surprised; after all, he was right. They did need to take care of themselves.

"The first thing we must do is find a place to stay," Taavi said to Michal. He turned to a man who was walking in the opposite direction and asked him, "Where is the nearest hotel?"

The man answered him in Yiddish with a Russian accent. "You are from Russia?" The man asked Taavi.

"Yes."

"Me too. You want a hotel? Or you want to go to the homeless shelter? It is free. You can stay there until you find a place to live and a job."

Taavi looked at Michal. "A shelter? Vos iz dos?"

Taavi had asked the man what a hostel was in Yiddish, and the man explained it was a homeless shelter. "They've built it for refugees. You'll find a lot of other people from Russia staying there until they can get settled."

"Only from Russia?"

"No, from all over the east. Jews running away from the pogroms. It's not so bad here in Germany."

"No anti-Semitism?"

"Ech, I wouldn't say that. But at least they don't come in the middle of the night and attack us. It's not perfect, by any means, but it is better."

Taavi nodded. "Better is a good thing. Where is this hostel?"

"I'll give you directions," the man said and he did.

Taavi and Michal walked for another three blocks. She glanced into various store windows, many of the names of the stores were written in Hebrew letters on the front windows. She saw a large sign for shoe polish and another for chimney sweeps. Children with dirty faces and knotted hair chased each other and played on the sidewalks. Women hollered to each other out the windows of their apartments. A door was propped open to what appeared to be a tavern. In the back of a darkened room, a group of men wearing fancy suits without head coverings sat whispering and playing cards. She bit her lower lip as they continued towards their destination on Wiesenstrasse. When they turned the corner, they saw the large stone building that had a sign hanging from a post that said, "Homeless Shelter." Michal was relieved.

A woman with finger-waved brassy blonde hair that looked as if it had been bleached with peroxide sat at a worn wooden desk. Her nasal voice had a slight twinge of annoyance as she greeted Michal and Taavi. While Taavi was registering with the woman, Michal looked around. There were rows of beds, children playing on the floor, and overcrowded rooms that smelled of dirty laundry, perspiration, and cigarette smoke. The lost and destitute faces of the people frightened her. She'd come to Germany for a better life. Perhaps she should have stayed with Bepa. She reminded herself why she'd come to Germany. She wanted a home, a husband, children, and so she'd followed Taavi.

"This is only temporary," he said, as he came up behind her. It was as if he'd read her mind. "I'm going to go out and find someone who can make us papers for the right price. If we have papers, we can go to the hostel. From what I understand, it is much better there. We must keep a good eye on our things here. I don't trust that they won't be stolen. I am also going to see about the carpentry job tomorrow. So, once we have some income that we can count on, we can feel a little more secure about spending our money to find a place to live."

She felt her shoulders drop in despair.

"Don't be afraid. I'll take care of you," he said and rubbed her arm. "Now, listen. I'm going to leave the luggage with you while I go out and buy something for us to eat. Try and get a little rest."

They found two small cots, she in the women's room, he in the men's. She was beyond tired, but she couldn't sleep. Although it was the middle of the afternoon, people were asleep on their cots. For Michal, the circumstances surrounding her were far too frightening to allow her to close her eyes. She felt that if she let her guard down even for a moment, everything that she and Taavi had brought with them would be taken.

She picked up the suitcase and put it in the bed under her. It was uncomfortable, but at least she knew it would be safe.

Michal lay on top of her suitcase with the scratchy gray wool blanket covering her, watching the other women in the room. She could hear a hodgepodge of languages, but most of the women seemed to be speaking in Yiddish. From the conversations around her, she gathered that all of them were displaced persons, Jews without a homeland. What strange twists her life had taken since her marriage to Avram. She'd grown up believing that she would spend her days in the same village of her birth, bearing and raising children of her own. She would be a frum and faithful wife, going to synagogue, sitting in the women's section every Sabbath, preparing meals, sewing clothing, caring for a home. None of it had happened as she had once believed it would. Well, she dared not linger too long on the twists and turns of her past or she would find herself lost in fear of the future. The only option left to her was to go forward, and so she knew she must. Even though she had no skills to speak of, she wanted to try to find work. Perhaps she might find a midwife who needed an assistant. She wasn't confident that she was skilled enough to work on her own, but she knew she was qualified to be a valuable assistant.

It began to rain outside. Michal could hear the crash of thunder and the burst of lightning. It seemed to shake the walls around her and the walls inside of her heart in unison. Somewhere across the hallway, a fight broke out. The voices of two angry women screeched in Yiddish, echoing throughout the shelter. From what Michal could make out, they were arguing about a hair brush, something about lice in a hair brush. The very thought of lice made Michal's skin crawl and she felt a shiver of disgust run up her spine. LICE!

Taavi seemed to take forever to return. The darkness of evening began to settle over Berlin, and Michal wondered if Taavi had abandoned her. If he had, what would she do, where would she go? She must be crazy to be considering this; why would he do such a thing? Perhaps once he saw the conditions in Berlin, he'd changed his mind about taking on the responsibilities of a wife. Her eyelids twitched with the sting of tears that she was trying to hold back. It was best not to show weakness in this terrible place. These women surrounding her appeared desperate, some with children who they needed to feed; others were alone looking like lost souls. How would they respond if they knew how vulnerable she was? Would they take advantage of her? Steal everything she had? Buried deep in her bra, she had the money that Bepa had insisted that she take. When she and Bepa were alone, Bepa had given her extra cash, but she'd warned Michal not to tell anyone that she had the resources, not even Taavi.

"This is emergency money. It is for you in case you should need it. I am not saying Taavi is a bad man, but you will be alone with him in a foreign country. Just in case you find yourself in peril, you will have at least a little something to help you."

The words reverberated over and over in her mind as she sat on the bed watching the sky grow darker outside the window.

It was nearly eight o'clock when Taavi returned. He'd been gone for over five hours. He knocked on the door to the women's rooms. The head mother agreed to bring Michal out to him. When Michal heard that Taavi had returned, she felt her heartbeat slow down with relief. Then she went to the door.

"Come out; I brought some food and lots of news," Taavi said.

"You were gone a long time. I was worried about you."

"I'm sorry. I wanted to see the carpentry shop, so I walked all over town until I discovered that it is right next door to a hotel on the corner of Grenadierstrasse and Hirtenstrasse. I stopped at the boarding house on Grenadierstrasse. It is a lot nicer than this place. I was thinking that maybe we should eat quickly and then go right over there. This shelter is terrible. It's filthy and it smells like a sewer."

"I would like that," she said.

He brought two thick heels of bread, a small container of herring in sour cream, and an orange. Michal took her suitcase and then two of them went into the communal room. The table was sticky, but there were no napkins to lay out the food. She felt herself wanting to gag. Taavi peeled the orange and split it between them. A crowd of hungry faces with wizened eyes watched them eat. If she wasn't so hungry, Michal would have given her food to one of the children, but she had not eaten since the previous morning and she was famished. The simple fare caused her taste buds to explode and she greedily ate the small portion of food that Taavi had brought.

Once they'd finished, Michal cleaned up the mess. Taavi took their belongings and Michal followed him out into the street.

It was a short walk to the boarding house, but now Michal could see that the streets were populated with prostitutes and men who wore suits unlike the suits of the religious men she knew. She heard two men talking as Taavi hurried her along.

They said something about the odds being five to one. She had no idea what that meant. Odds? Five to one? But there was little time to dwell on that. They arrived at the boarding house at almost nine o'clock.

"We're all full," the guard at the desk said.

"I have money to pay," Taavi answered.

"How much?"

"How much is it a night?"

"Two marks for the room and two marks for me being kind enough to let you in at this late hour," the guard said.

Taavi looked at Michal. She could see the distain he felt for the guard in his eyes. But he said nothing. Instead, he pulled the money out of his pocket and paid.

"Go to the back of the building. You have to take a bath and be disinfected and deloused before you can have a bed. But once you've finished bathing, you will both receive a bowl of hot soup."

Taavi and Michal separated and both went to bathe. Michal was happy to feel the water cleanse her body. She'd felt filthy from traveling and from the shelter.

Once they were both clean, they were offered bowls of hot soup. Then they were given one bed, as if they were husband and wife. Michal was appalled, but she dared not question or complain. This boarding house was much cleaner than the shelter and she didn't want to be sent away. She lay beside Taavi, both of them fully clothed and careful not to touch. At first it was uncomfortable, but exhaustion took over and she felt so safe with Taavi beside her that Michal fell into a deep and restful slumber.

When she awakened, Taavi was not beside her. Michal assumed he'd gone to the carpentry shop to announce that he had arrived in Germany. She stretched and sat up. It was strange to awaken in a place with so many people all around her.

"There is bread and a little butter in the kitchen," a young girl who had been sleeping in one of the cots a few beds away from Michal's said. "My name is Yana; I'm from Bryansk." Yana spoke Yiddish. The dialect was slightly different, but Michal had no trouble understanding her. As time went by, Michal would hear many different dialects of Yiddish, but each would be close enough to the others to be understood.

"I'm Michal. I'm from a small village in eastern Siberia."

Taavi came in carrying a slice of bread and a cup of watered down coffee made mostly from turnips. Real coffee was hard to come by and terribly expensive. With the inflation going on in Berlin, one could easily spend a million marks for a pound. This was a mixture of spices, turnips, a little coffee, and lots of water. He handed the food and drink to Michal and sat on the bed beside her. "I've found a rabbi here. He is willing to marry us. Four men who I met in the kitchen are willing to hold the poles for a canopy. We could be married today." He smiled brightly.

She sipped the hot liquid. There was no cream or sugar, neither was readily available, especially in a shelter. Perhaps they could be bought for a price on the black market, but neither Michal nor Taavi were about to spend needlessly until they had a better idea of where the future was going to lead them. Besides, they had no black market connections. On their way to the shelter they saw men who looked as if they would be involved in illegal dealings, but Michal would not have trusted them.

Looking away from Taavi's eyes, Michal felt guilty. All of her teachings had told her that it was wrong to take a husband so soon after Avram's death. It was disrespectful. But she couldn't live in such close quarters, alone in a strange country with Taavi without being wed. She sighed.

"You're feeling bad about Avram?"

She nodded.

"There is nothing you can do for him anymore. Mourning will not do you or anyone else any good. If you would like, I will arrange a minyan every night for a week. But that is all I can do. We don't have a year to mourn. I have to begin working and we have to get settled into our new life. This shelter is only temporary. I don't plan for us to live here. I want to find an apartment where we can raise a family."

She looked down and ran her fingers over the wool blanket. Tears welled up in the corners of her eyes.

"Michal," Taavi began again, his voice softer, more compassionate than before, "I am sorry. I know you grew up with very strong beliefs about things. I understand that, even though I don't agree with most of it. However, things are not the same for us as they would have been if we were still back in Russia. Now we are here in a new country. There is little time to mourn the past. If we stay stuck in the past, we'll fall into poverty and ruin and miss any opportunities that might come up for a better future."

She knew he was right. It was only guilt and all that she'd been taught that were keeping her from moving forward. If they were to survive, and maybe even thrive in this new land, she must be willing to abandon everything she believed.

"Can you make all of the arrangements?" she asked.

He smiled brightly and gently caressed her shoulder. "Of course."

They were married in a simple ceremony in the main room of the boarding house. Instead of celebrating with friends and family members, they said their vows of eternal devotion surrounded by displaced persons with blank staring eyes, who were lost in a country far from their homes.

Once the rabbi and the four men who held the posts that were draped with a tablecloth to create a canopy had been paid, Taavi slipped a thin gold band on the first finger of Michal's right hand.

For a split second, she remembered how she'd felt when Avram had put his ring on the same finger. Then she forced the thought from her mind.

"Where did you get this?" she asked about the ring.

"Never mind where I got it. Let's just say I got it to show you how much I love you."

"Oh, Taavi, thank you," Michal said. She turned away from him, looked down at her hand, and then at the posts and tablecloth that just a few moments before had been a makeshift chuppah, and Michal began to weep.

"What is it?"

"I don't know. I don't know," she said, shaking her head. She was thinking of Avram, of the future, of this strange country, of this man who claimed to love her. Frozen in time at this very instance, everything in her world felt so terrifying and uncertain.

Taavi took both of Michal's hands in his. "We won't spend our wedding night in a homeless shelter. I wouldn't do that to you. Let's get a room at the hotel next door to the carpentry shop. By the way, I saw the hotel when I went by the shop last night. The hotel looks very nice."

"A hotel?" Michal said. She'd never been in a hotel. In fact, before the pogrom, she'd never eaten food that was not kosher. She felt like she'd fallen into a spiral that was rapidly going downward, undoing stitches of her life. Things were happening so fast that she didn't have a chance to adjust to one strange and new situation before another arose.

"Yes, at least it will be private. Here, we have no privacy."

"Then what, after the hotel … the night … I mean, then what?"

"Shaa, don't be so afraid. Trust me, Michal. I will take care of you. I promise. You're going to have to trust me. We will spend our first night of marriage together in the hotel. I will take you to a restaurant and we will enjoy a pleasant dinner and some wine." He smiled at her and lifted her face with his thumb gently on her chin. Gingerly, she returned the smile. He took both of her hands in his. "Your hands are freezing," Taavi said and held them to the warmth of his cheeks. Then he opened the palms and kissed each one. "Don't worry. After our first night together, we will return here to the shelter. But only for a very short time. Then once I begin working and I get settled in at my job, we'll move. As you know, we have some money, but I'd like to hold on to it if we can. I would like to have my first pay from my new job before we find an apartment to rent. It should only be a week or two and then we will have a place to call our home."

She nodded. He was so strong. It was good to lean on him. "Yes, all right," she said. Her heart pounded in her chest. Tonight she would be expected to allow Taavi to act as a husband to her. There was no doubt that she cared for him. And now that she'd been married to Avram, she knew that sex could be pleasant. Poor Avram, her unions with Avram had been sweet, if not passionate. But, even so, the memories of that terrible day of the pogrom, still gave her nightmares, that horrific Cossack standing over her forcing himself inside of her, invading the most sacred place in her body. She felt as if the small opening to her womb had closed after that assault. It was like her womanly parts had been wounded and now the scar was healing them closed forever. But, even so, more than anything, she wanted children, and the only way to have children was ... It was all so confusing, so embarrassing, so conflicted, how could she ever explain all of this to Taavi?

They walked to the hotel and checked in. The desk clerk gave Michal a sly smile, and she turned away, embarrassed. He is thinking about what will happen between Taavi and me when we go to our room, Michal thought, and even though she and Taavi were married, she felt ashamed.

They walked up two flights of stairs and then found the room. Taavi turned the key in the lock and opened the door, allowing Michal to enter first.

Michal glanced around the hotel room. To her, it looked like a place for sleeping, and also for doing shameful things. There was nothing there but a bed, a small dresser, and a nightstand. Down the hall were two bathrooms, one for men the other for women. It was strange and a little awkward to be confronted by the sight of the bed immediately upon their arrival. The room was pleasant enough, with matching quilt and drapes in a colorful floral pattern. Unlike the shelter, the temperature was perfect, not too hot or cold, and the room had a faint smell of bleach. At least it was clean.

Taavi set their luggage on the floor. Then he sat on the edge of the bed.

"We can lock the door to this room. Nobody will be able to get in here. Our things will be safe. We can leave them and go out. Would you like to go and have dinner?"

A restaurant, a hotel, a city, and a new husband were a lot for Michal to digest. She shrugged her shoulders, then nodded her head.

Taavi cocked his head and looked into her eyes. He raised her face to meet his.

"What's wrong?" he said, his voice soft and kind.

"I don't know," she said and felt the tears slide down her cheeks. "I'm just...."

"You've been through a lot. I understand, Michal. We can go slowly."

"But we only have this one night together of privacy. Then we have to go back to the shelter until we can find an apartment. I feel like we are forced to consummate the marriage tonight. I feel so much pressure...." She gestured to the bed with her hand. "And I feel so afraid, and so ... I don't know."

"Shaaa. It's all right. We don't have to do anything now except have a wonderful dinner. Let's go and enjoy some good food. It's been a long time since we have been able to do that." He kissed her forehead and then smiled into her eyes.

She smiled back. He was kind and gentle. What was she so afraid of? "Can I go to the bathroom and get cleaned up a little first?"

"Of course. There's no hurry."

"I want to take a bath," Michal said. It cost extra money to use the bathtub and hot water, but Taavi didn't mind. She told him how much she loved the feeling of being clean. Even though most people were quite satisfied with a weekly bath, Michal had always bathed more often, twice, sometimes three times if she was able.

"Yes, certainly, go ahead and I'll pay the clerk for your bath. In fact, I will do the same for myself. I'll go the men's bath and you go to the ladies. Then we'll meet back here and go out for a nice meal."

"All right," she said. He was trying to make himself as attractive as possible for her and she appreciated his efforts.

CHAPTER 15

It had been a long time since Michal had enjoyed such delicious food. Everything was served on beautiful china plates. They had brisket and latkes with applesauce. Taavi ordered a bottle of sweet red wine. It tasted similar to the wine she'd drunk when she'd celebrated holidays with Avram. The wine warmed her throat and eased her tension. Taavi made her laugh and she began to feel comfortable, warm, and safe.

Taavi put his arm around Michal's neck as they walked back to the hotel room. Such open displays of affection were foreign to her, but the alcohol and the laughter had brought down her guard. She was far away from everyone and everything familiar. This was to be a new life, a new way of living. Timidly, Michal leaned her head on Taavi's shoulder.

When Taavi closed the door to the hotel room and turned to Michal, she began to feel the effects of the wine wearing off. She was shy and frightened again. It wasn't so much the guilt she felt about Avram as it was the Cossack. If only she could get his face out of her mind and the terrible feeling of his intrusion out of her body. Taavi seemed oblivious to her trepidation. He walked over to her and took her into his arms, kissing her tenderly. She liked him, cared for him deeply, but her body refused to cooperate and she froze, unbending, unyielding. Gently, he tried to remove her coat, but her arms stiffened and he was unable to help her. She didn't want to resist. She wanted a home and a husband; she wanted Taavi.

"It's all right, Michal. We're married. You're my wife. I will spend my life trying to make you happy. Let me get close to you. Please." He touched her shoulder. "Please, stop fighting me," he whispered and began kissing her again. Her lips would not respond. She knew she was pushing him away from her, but she couldn't yield. The thought of being naked, of being touched, her damaged body being explored, sent a shiver up her spine.

"What is it, Michal? You don't care for me? I thought you did," he said, backing away and sitting on the bed. She could see that she'd hurt his pride. As her husband, he had the right to force her to comply with her wifely duties, but she could see that he had no such intentions. "If you don't want me, then you don't have to worry, I won't touch you." He turned away and faced the wall, refusing to look at her. The room was silent, but in the silence, Michal could hear her own soul crying out with deafening screams. But she continued to quietly get ready for bed.

There were so many things she wished she could say. Her heart was breaking; she was losing a man she cared for so deeply, but how could she explain what she was feeling? How could she tell him that she could not forget the horror of the day of the pogrom when her body had been violated? How could she make him understand that she felt unclean, that she felt she might never be clean again? It was a filth that no visit to a Mikva could ever wash clean.

They lay on opposite sides of the bed. Michal shivered as she listened to Taavi breathing. There were so many things she yearned to tell him, so much she wished she could find the words to explain. But her voice had left her; she couldn't speak. Instead, she listened to him until his breath grew slow and steady and she knew he'd fallen asleep. Then she buried her face in her pillow and began to cry softly.

Sometime during the night, Michal drifted into the nothingness of sleep.

In the morning, Michal awakened to find Taavi gone. Her heart pounded hard in her chest. Was he gone forever? Had he left her? After all, she did deserve to be abandoned after her behavior last night. But now, what would she do? Where would she go? A woman alone in such a big and dangerous city. If she had to get a job, she had no real skills. Her hand caressed the money she had buried deep in her undergarment, the money Bepa had given her. It might be her saving grace after all. Michal's eyes fell upon the pillow where Taavi's head had left an indentation. She touched the place where he'd slept. He had meant so well, paying for this fancy hotel room, and taking her out for that overpriced dinner. There was no doubt in her mind that Taavi loved her. So why couldn't she accept the fact that her life had changed and Taavi was her husband now? She owed him the same wifely duties that she'd allowed Avram. It was only fair, only right. Now, he'd left her, alone in a hotel room, without a friend or job, or any place to go because she had denied him. Michal bit her lower lip. The only thing she might be able to do was find a job as an assistant to a midwife. Bepa had taught her enough to allow her to be of some help. But where would she find a midwife willing to take her on as an employee? A shiver ran up her spine. She should have stayed with Bepa. Did she have enough money to travel back to Siberia? If she could get back, then she would return to living and working with Bepa. Michal reached into her bra to count the money. She had not counted it before. How foolish of her. Somehow she believed that she would never need that money. Taavi would take care of her. They would marry and have children. That was how a good Jewish woman was raised to live. The idea of depending upon herself had never entered her mind. Just as she was about to pull the cash that was wrapped in a handkerchief out of her bra, the door to the hotel room opened. Taavi stood there fresh from his morning shower. In his hand he held two cups of steaming coffee and a brown bag that was stained with grease.

"I brought us some breakfast," he said.

She was relieved that he had returned, but she felt terrible about her behavior the previous night. She'd denied him his right as a husband. And she knew that her body would not allow her to succumb to him even now.

"Thank you." Her voice was small as she took the coffee. She took a sip. Of course it was turnip coffee, but at least it was hot.

He smiled. "I found a bakery down the street. I brought some strudel. It's vinegar raisin strudel." He pulled a square of cake from the bag and took a bite. "It's pretty good. There's almost no sugar, but the raisins help to make it sweet." He handed her the bag.

"I'm sorry about last night, Taavi."

He shrugged. "I wouldn't want you to do something you didn't want to do. I'm not a desperate man. There are plenty of women who would be more than willing; in fact, they would want to be intimate with me. If I have to force you, I would rather not make love to you at all."

Make love? She'd never heard such a word. Intercourse was expected of a good wife. It was to be endured for the importance of for producing children. Making love?

"I didn't mean to act that way," she said.

"Forget it," he said. "I'd rather not talk about it. I won't try to touch you again."

Taavi sat on the other side of the bed and sipped his coffee. Instead of looking at Michal, he was gazing out the window. There was so much she wished she could say, yet her throat was closed and as dry as sandpaper. All she could do was watch him in silence.

After he'd finished eating, Taavi turned to Michal. "I'm going to the carpentry shop to let them know that I've arrived in Berlin and am ready to start working. Then I will look for an apartment where we can stay. For today, I will drop you back to the shelter. I'm hoping to have a permanent residence for us by tonight. Once I have everything set up, I'll come and get you."

She didn't answer. Instead, she followed him out to the street. He did not walk beside her.

Taavi left Michal at the shelter with all of their possessions. She wondered if he would return. She couldn't help but understand if he didn't. What a foolish woman she was. Women had endured far worse than she. Was she so childish that she couldn't overcome a tragedy that took less than an hour of her life? There was a very good chance that she could lose Taavi over this. Michal sat on a new cot that she had been assigned. She had no place to go and nothing to do. Then, she saw Yana. She remembered her from the boarding house. Yana was sitting on another cot rolling a small silver tube in her fingers.

"Hello," Michal said from across the room. "Yana, right?"

"You remembered my name."

"Yes."

"I'm sorry. I'm ashamed. I've forgotten yours."

"Michal."

"Yes, that's right. The biblical name. I thought it was something like Sarah or Esther. A biblical name. But Michal ... now she was a lofty woman, mother of King Solomon." Yana laughed.

"It is a biblical name, but Batsheva was the mother of King Solomon."

"I don't believe in any of that nonsense. But Michal is a pretty name."

"My husband doesn't believe in the Bible either," Michal said, shrugging her shoulders.

"Would you like to see something beautiful?" Yana asked.

Michal nodded.

"Look at this."

Michal looked at the silver tube with a thick red tip. "What is it?"

"It's lipstick."

"What do you do with it?"

"Wear it on your mouth. Here, watch." Yana put the lipstick on her mouth. Then she ran her fingers over her lips and smeared a little of the red sticky stuff on her cheeks and rubbed hard until it was absorbed into her skin, leaving her face as if she had a natural healthy glow.

"You look beautiful."

"Would you like to try it?"

"Oh, I don't know. In my home town it is vanity for a woman to paint her face."

"Come on. You're in Berlin now. It can't hurt to try."

Michal nodded and Yana laughed. "You're a sheltered one, aren't you?"

"I don't know what you mean," Michal said, straightening her back.

"Please, don't be offended. I didn't mean to hurt your feelings. Let's try this lipstick on you."

"All right," Michal said, shaking her head. It was hard for her to believe that she had agreed to wear cosmetics. Three years ago, Michal could not have imagined that she would be sitting in a shelter in Berlin smearing red paint on her lips.

CHAPTER 16

While Michal waited in the shelter, Taavi rented a small apartment in an old rundown tenement building just a few blocks from the shelter. The apartment had three rooms: a kitchen with a table and two chairs, a bedroom, and a sitting room. The bathroom was down the hall. The hall smelled of garlic sausages and sauerkraut. Children with tangled hair, dirty faces, and running noses played in the streets outside. Women with deep wrinkles and worn clothing waited in lines trying to purchase whatever foodstuffs their husbands' small salaries would afford them. Due to the inflation, prices changed within hours. In the morning, milk or bread might be a million marks, but by nightfall it could be two million. Taavi began working at the small carpentry shop where his friend from Siberia had sent him. The boss, Moise Rivesman, was a demanding employer. Taavi understood how hard it was for Rivesman to afford to keep him on. There were few sales. Far too many people had begun purchasing furniture from factories. It was less expensive and served the same purpose. Taavi would have easily been qualified to work at one of the factories, but they did not employ Jews. Sometimes rich clients would come from other parts of Germany and even Austria to purchase lovely pieces, which Taavi spent hours slaving over. Other times, Taavi made simpler pieces for the Jewish clientele who lived right in town, which he delivered by horse and cart. Nearly two months had passed and he had not attempted to consummate his marriage after the first time. His pride and ego

103

were bruised, and he swore he would never be that vulnerable to a woman again. When they finished work, Taavi and Lev, his friend and coworker, would go out and spend their money at the taverns. Sometimes they would visit the Jewish prostitutes who stood on the docks.

One night when Taavi was quite drunk, Lev suggested that they leave the Jewish ghetto and go out into the real city to drink at one of the cabarets.

"There are things going on there like you have never seen before."

"Like what?"

"Like things that are different. There are famous psychics that can tell you the future, and sex shows … crazy wild stuff like you have never imagined."

Taavi cocked his head "I don't know. We're Jews. You think it's a good idea?" He was quite drunk. "We could get ourselves into trouble."

"Ehh, don't be silly. Why not? Let's go and see what there is to see, huh? We don't have to tell them we're Jews. I'll change my name. I'll say my name is Stefan. Come on, it will be fun."

"Maybe tomorrow," Taavi said, but he began to think about it. He couldn't help being a little fascinated by the idea. Sex shows? What was a sex show? He'd had quick sex with the prostitutes against the walls in the alleyways, but he'd never even really seen a woman's naked body. The idea ticked in his mind as he walked home.

Michal was awake. "You're very late," she said, "I was worried."

He shrugged. He was glad that she was worried.

"You smell like you've been drinking."

"I work hard. I deserve a release at the end of the day," he said.

"Taavi..."

"What?"

"I don't want to see you fall to ruin."

"You actually care? If you actually cared, you'd be a wife to me."

"I know. I wish I could be...." She took a plate out of the stove. "I kept your dinner warm."

"I don't care about your cooking for me," he said, flinging the plate to the floor. He was suddenly furious, fueled by words he'd kept buried inside of him. He pushed her onto the table. She was crying, but he didn't stop. She turned her head to look away from him as he forced himself inside of her.

When it was over, Michal stood up and straightened her dress.

"I'll be leaving here in the morning," she said, having no idea where she would go. Then she went into the bedroom, slammed the door, locked it, and wept.

The following day when Michal arose, Taavi had already left for work. She dressed warmly and walked to the shelter. The only person she knew was Yana. She asked for her when she arrived, but no one knew where Yana had gone. When Michal left her apartment, she'd felt brave. But here, amongst strangers, she began to feel lost and afraid. It was hard not to notice the men gawking at her. The rooms in the shelter were cold, and she knew that she could only stay for a short time. Then where would she go? What would she do? All she could do was take a train back to Siberia all alone. And she wasn't even sure that the money she had from Bepa would be enough to get her all the way back to Russia. Besides, Michal had never been on her own in her entire life. Someone had always been there for her; someone else had always been in charge. The idea was terrifying. When she thought about the previous night, she hated Taavi. But he was right. He was her husband and she had been denying him his rights for far too long. Perhaps she should go back to the apartment and swallow her pride, then they could try to come to some agreement.

A biting wind slapped her face as Michal walked back to the apartment dejected. She despised herself for her weakness. If only she didn't feel so lost and empty, so powerless. The only thing to do was make things right with Taavi. Just thinking about him made her angry, angrier at herself than at him. The thought of sitting alone in the apartment and waiting for Taavi to come home was unbearable. It was a waste of money to stop at a café and have a cup of tea, but she decided that she deserved to splurge. She entered a corner café, where she sat down at a table for two. Across the aisle sat a young mother with a boy who looked to be about three or four years old. The child had wild hair like a flaming torch and a personality to match. His mother seemed exhausted and at her wits end, as she yelled at the boy to return to his seat and be still. However, the child didn't listen and dashed through the walkways between the tables, as if he were running a relay race. Just as the boy rushed by Michal, he tripped and almost fell forward. Michal caught him before he hit the ground. His mother rushed over and grabbed her son.

"Thank you so much. I am so sorry that my son disturbed you. He is just so uncontrollable at times."

"It's perfectly alright. I understand," Michal said.

"May I buy you a cup of coffee or a sandwich?" the woman asked. "By the way, my name is Gerta Fogelman, and this active little fellow is Samuel, but I call him Sammie." She smiled. Her teeth were perfect like tiny white gemstones, almost iridescent like opals. I'm waiting here for my husband; he had to come into town to see his accountant. It seems that my husband is so busy that we never see each other, so when he invited Sammie and me to come along, I was glad to spend some time as a family. Now, I'm wishing I hadn't come; this child is driving me over the brink of insanity today."

"It's not necessary that you buy me anything to eat or drink," Michal said. "But you are more than welcome to join me if you like."

"I'd love to. It would be wonderful to spend some time talking with an adult my own age for a change." Gerta smiled. "Do you live near here?"

"Yes, just a few blocks away. And you?"

"No, we are Jews, but we live outside the Jewish sector. We own a house in town."

"Your own home, that must be wonderful."

"Yes, I suppose it is. My husband owns a large garment factory. You may have heard of Fogelman's Frocks? My husband is Richard Fogelman."

That accounted for Gerta's lovely cashmere coat with the silver fox collar.

"I'm sorry; I'm new here in Germany. I don't know much about the different factories. But your coat is lovely."

"Thank you. It's a product of my husband's company. Are you married?" Gerta asked.

"Yes. My husband is a carpenter here in this sector of town."

"Do you have children?"

"No, not yet."

"So, not to be nosy, but are you an artist? Or are you employed?"

"No, neither. We've only been in Germany for a short time. I'm not sure what I'm going to do, but I'm probably going to look for work."

"Well, the good thing is, life is changing for women here in Berlin. It now seems as if ladies are permitted to follow their dreams. It's a very exciting time. In fact, if I didn't have a youngster, I would go back to school. Perhaps I'd become a professor."

"I'm not sure what kind of job I can get; I'm not really qualified to do anything at all," Michal said.

Gerta gestured for the waiter to come over to the table. She ordered them both sandwiches, potato salad, and coffee. Then she turned to Michal and said, "I insist that you have lunch with me," and smiled.

Michal liked her right away. The boy was tearing through the restaurant again. The owner gave Gerta a nasty look.

"Well," Gerta said, tapping the spoon on the side of her coffee cup. "I hope you won't be offended by my asking, but … how would you like to work as a nanny for me?" Gerta asked. "God knows the boy is a handful and I could use the help. Then perhaps, if you think you can handle him, I might be able to go to university for a few hours a day."

A Job? This was an answer to Michal's prayers. She would earn money, she could leave Taavi, be free, be on her own.

"Where do you live, and how would I get there?"

"You could take the train or you could stay at our home during the week. I have plenty of space. You would have your own room, and I would pay you salary, plus room and board. If this is acceptable to you, you could return home on the weekend. Would you like some time to think about it?"

Michal glanced outside at the snowy sidewalk, then back at Gerta. The boy was a handful, no doubt about it. The job would not be easy. But she felt empowered; she would teach Taavi a lesson. She would show him that she didn't need him, that he dare not treat her the way he had treated her the previous night.

"Nothing to think about. My answer is yes."

"When would you like to start?"

"Today? I could go home and pack a small bag and meet you back here. I wouldn't be long."

"That would work out just fine. My husband has an automobile. He'll drive us back to the house."

CHAPTER 17

Taavi didn't go home after work. He was ashamed of his behavior the previous night and didn't want to face Michal.

So after work, Taavi and Lev left the Jewish sector of town and went into the city of Berlin. Neither of them had been raised to be religious and both wanted to leave the Jewish ghetto. Berlin was an exciting place to live, and both men wanted to infiltrate themselves into German society. Lev worked as a carpenter, but he had a secret desire to be a painter, a real artist, he always said. Often, he'd spend his meager wages to hire prostitutes to pose nude while he intensely sketched and then painted their portraits. Taavi knew that if he were somehow able to find employment outside the ghetto, he could earn more money. They took the S-Bahn and arrived in a city wilder than either could ever have imagined. Paper boys stood on the street corners, hawking papers that advertised predictions for the future by famous psychics and astrologers. Taavi and Lev continued to amble down the strange streets, looking at the bewildering world surrounding them.

Lev was excited by the newness of everything. This was a place unlike anything either of them had seen before. They peeked inside of an elegant club called the Cabaret Montmartre on the west side of Berlin. On the stage, they saw two women completely naked caressing each other. Taavi was dumbstruck and mesmerized by their beauty. The audience seemed immune. They were a sophisticated group. Taavi watched as a couple got out of a long black car and were greeted by a doorman who wore a special uniform. They walked into the club, never looking at Taavi or Lev, as if both men were invisible. Lev pushed Taavi along. They glanced into the window of another nightclub. This one was called "Marquis de Sade in der Holle." There they saw a woman naked on the stage, hogtied with rope, a stick had been placed between her teeth. A man was standing over her, wearing a black suit and cracking a whip across her back. Taavi trembled. He'd never seen such a heinous performance on a stage and he began to feel as if he'd walked into some sort of hell.

"Come on, there's more," Lev said.

Taavi cocked his head and gave Lev a strange look, but he followed him. He couldn't help it; he was intrigued. This was quite an experience for a young man from a remote village in Siberia.

Women dressed as men with their arms around each other passed by him; they whispered into each other's ears with soft voices. Two men dressed as women with lovely wigs, elegant gowns, high heels, and sparkling earrings slipped in to a doorway that had a marquee above it that said "Cabaret of the Spider." Taavi was not a child, he had heard of such things, but he had never seen them displayed so openly before. He was not offended, but he had to admit he was shocked.

A sign said, "Peep Show," at the corner of two busy streets.

"Let's go in," Lev said.

Taavi shrugged his shoulders. "How many marks is this going to cost?"

"I don't know; we'll see."

They sat down in a booth that was closed off from the other booths so that the customers could not see each other. In front of them was a curtain. Once they paid their money, the curtain was raised. On the stage in front of them was a woman. She was one of the most beautiful women Taavi had ever seen. Her long golden wavy hair reached to her waist. She began to remove her clothes. Slowly piece by piece. Just as she was about to take off her bra, the curtain closed.

"If you want to see the rest of the show, you must pay more money," a man at the door said.

Lev was engrossed; he refused to walk away. He gave the man a wad of paper bills and again the curtain rose. This closing and opening of the curtain for additional money continued until the woman was naked.

Watching her, Taavi was breathless. He'd never seen such a beautiful goddess, and he'd never seen a woman entirely naked before.

The curtain went down.

"Are you ready to go?" Lev asked.

Taavi nodded.

"Wait," the man who ran the show said. He was standing in the doorway to their room. "The next act is something that I guarantee you have never seen before. It's a phenomenon. You just can't miss this."

"What is it?" Taavi asked.

"It's a man and woman in the same body. You can see their parts, both parts in the same body."

Taavi felt a chill tingle in his spine. This wasn't something to be gawked at; this was a deformity. He'd always hated it when he was a child and the freak shows came to town. His friends had been fascinated, but he'd always found himself pitying the poor souls who had been born malformed. "I don't know..." he said.

"Come on, I want to see it," Lev said. "I'll pay if you don't want to."

Taavi gave in; he didn't want to spoil the evening for his friend.

Lev paid and the curtain rose. What Taavi saw standing beneath the curtain took away all of the sexual desire that had built up inside him as he watched the beautiful girl just moments before. All he could feel was compassion for the poor creature that was shivering, standing naked and openly displaying a birth defect for a thrill-hungry audience.

"I can't watch this, Lev, I'm sorry. I'll wait for you outside."

Lev just nodded; he couldn't take his eyes away from the scene in front of him.

Taavi stood in front of the building and lit a cigarette. What he'd just witnessed made him feel a little uneasy, sick to his stomach. The cold wind brushed across his face as a raggedly dressed man walked up to him.

"Can you spare a few coins?"

The man was dirty and wrinkled, his hair disheveled. His body was hunched over like the body of an old man, but looking more closely at him, Taavi realized that he could not have been more than twenty.

"Sorry," Taavi said, turning away from the homeless boy and feeling slightly guilty. He wanted to throw him a coin, but after all, Taavi wasn't earning enough to squander his salary; he was watching every penny. There was no doubt he'd spend a few marks on a beer or two at some point during the evening, but he worked hard and he deserved a little release.

Once Lev came outside, Taavi dropped his cigarette and pressed it into the sidewalk with the toe of his shoe. Then he and Lev began walking. It was recently that Taavi had begun smoking. All of the men at the shop smoked and at first he had refused cigarettes, but then slowly he began to accept when the others offered him a smoke. Now, he went through a half of a package a day.

Again, they continued walking through the strange streets. A large poster advertising a masturbation wheel stood boldly in the window of one of the clubs. *What is a masturbation wheel?* Taavi wondered as he turned away, his face red with shame.

It was getting colder outside. Lev pulled his wool scarf tighter around his neck. "Let's go inside somewhere and have a drink; I'm freezing," he said.

"Yes, that's a good idea," Taavi answered. For some reason, even with all of the excitement to distract him, Taavi could not stop thinking about his wife. He'd hurt Michal last night. He'd never meant to. It didn't matter that she had denied him for so long; he'd acted like a brute, an animal instead of a man. Taavi loved Michal; how could he have been so crass? Looking around him at all of the odd people, he suddenly felt sad and alone. He wished Michal was by his side; he wished his arm was resting on her shoulder. A man wearing a dapper brown uniform, a matching hat, and an armband that bore a strange symbol passed them. The symbol was black, red, and white. It looked like a black widow spider on a red background. For now, Lev and Taavi thought nothing of the man or his uniform. They were innocent of what was to come. But, years later, they would learn the name of that spider-like symbol. It was a swastika.

In many of the alleyways that they passed, they saw war veterans still wearing their old uniforms, huddled over fires that burned in steel trash cans. They were trying to stay warm against the German winter. Many of these veterans were missing limbs. Both Lev and Taavi pretended not to see the broken men who'd been left with their destroyed bodies and loss of self-esteem after defending their country only to lose the war.

There was a tavern a few blocks up. As they passed the window, Taavi asked if Lev wanted to stop for a drink. This place didn't look expensive. There was no show, just men and women sitting at small tables and at the bar. There was a group at the table next to them discussing books they were writing and books they had recently read.

Lev recognized a famous artist sitting in the corner by himself. He mentioned it to Taavi. A couple entered and the bartender acknowledged them loudly as famous performers in the Berlin Philharmonic. Two couples sat at a table on the other side of Taavi and Lev. The women were together and the men were together. They were discussing politics and philosophy.

"Berlin is something, isn't it?" Lev said, as they ordered another beer.

"Yes, it certainly is. I've never seen anything like it," Taavi said, not entirely sure that he liked what he saw.

Taavi was a striking man, far more handsome than Lev, whose looks were pleasant but unmemorable. Tall and well-built, with golden-brown hair streaked blond by the sun, a strong jaw, and high cheekbones, Taavi turned heads everywhere he went. Tonight was no exception. Lev, on the other hand, had dark straight hair that he'd combed back with pomade, a prominent nose, and a weak jawline. The bartender, a wizened looking fellow with a penetrating stare stood behind the bar eyeing them both. Taavi noticed the older man watching him, and wondered what was on the man's mind. In 1920 Berlin, it could be anything. The man might find him attractive and be considering him as a prospective lover, or he might be thinking of a con to pull on Taavi and his friend. Taavi frowned, he was not game for any new adventures that this bartender might have in mind, and he would make it clear if the man should approach him.

But although he kept a clear eye on Taavi, the man did not approach him. He and Lev sat drinking their beer slowly, both of them wanted to enjoy the warmth for awhile before braving the cold on their way back home.

A woman with long lean legs and a shock of short bleached blonde hair that had been bobbed strutted over to the table where Taavi and Lev were drinking. Without asking, she pulled out a chair and sat down next to Lev, facing Taavi. In the dark bar, he could not determine her age, or even if she was pretty. All he could see clearly was her hair, so blonde that it was almost white. She sat boldly like a man with her legs spread apart and her arm draped on the side of the chair. She wore a well-made, fitted man's suit in a dark grey pinstripe. Until Taavi came to Berlin, he'd never seen a woman wearing pants.

"Good evening, gentlemen," she said. "I'm Frieda, and this establishment belongs to me." Frieda looked at Taavi and misinterpreted his facial expression. She barked a harsh laugh. "So? What is it? You find it hard to believe that a woman owns such a place as this? From the way you're dressed, and I mean no disrespect," she giggled a little, winking, "I have a funny but distinct feeling that you're foreign. You're not Berliners. Where are you from?"

"Russia," Taavi answered, giving Frieda a look of disdain. She'd insulted him.

"Don't be so touchy. You're certainly a good looking fellow. You can wear whatever you'd like and it doesn't make a hell of a difference. Women with a good eye can see right through those clothes," she said. Lev watched her, toying with his beer mug.

"Do you have a name?"

"Taavi Margolis," Taavi said.

"Well, that is a good Russian name. You're a communist, perhaps?"

"Did I say I was a red?" Taavi said, unable to contain the anger in his voice. "I don't care at all about politics. In fact, I'm sick of all of the talk of the Red Terror and the White Terror. I'm just trying to make a living and survive here in Germany."

"Relax. It's all right. I wasn't looking to have a fight with you. I don't pass judgment. Plenty of these fine people surrounding you are communists. Some are socialists, eh? I don't care. As long as they come in, drink, and pay their bills. Now that's what I care about." She laughed again.

What a strange woman, Taavi thought. She was bold, coarse and too outspoken. Frieda threw him a book of matches, then put a cigarette into her mouth. "Light it, you silly fool," she said.

He struck the match and watched the end of her cigarette turn orange. Then she drew a long puff and leaned back in her chair. He'd never known a woman who smoked before.

"How would you like a job?" she asked, licking her lips.

"I would," Lev answered.

"Not you." She turned to Taavi and looked directly into his eyes "You."

Taavi took a long breath and sighed. He knew his boss was having a hard time affording to keep his men employed. Money was tight. Business was slow. Part of it was Rivesman's fault; he was difficult and not flexible. He wouldn't even try to compete with the factories. Taavi knew that if he were in charge, he could turn the shop around. But, Rivesman was stubborn and every day when Taavi went to work, he was afraid that the owner of the shop would have to let him go. "A job doing what?" Taavi asked.

"Tending bar. I've been wanting to get rid of that lazy good for nothing behind the bar. You're handsome, and you look strong enough to carry the cases of liquor."

"I don't know anything about tending bar. I'm a carpenter," Taavi said, clearing his throat. She'd taken him by surprise.

"I can have someone come and teach you if you want to do it."

"What kind of money are we talking about?"

"Plenty. More than you earn now; I'll bet on that."

Taavi took a sip of beer and a cigarette out of his pack. He lit it and looked around the room. Working here would not be dull, that was for certain. More money? He would try it. "Yes. I'd like to work for you," he said.

"Good. Can you come in on Saturday afternoon to train with my other bartender?"

Saturday was the Sabbath. He'd never been religious, but even so, he'd never worked on the Sabbath. Taavi realized that this woman didn't know he was Jewish. It was probably best that she didn't know. If she found out he was a Jew, she might renege on her offer. If it was true and he could earn more money at this job than he did working for Rivesman, he could get a nicer apartment outside of the Jewish sector. "Saturday, what time?"

"Three o'clock? You can get settled in and start learning before it gets busy. Then you'll sit on the sidelines and watch as the other bartender works the crowd on Saturday night. Within a week or so, I expect you to be ready to be working on your own. After all, I can't afford to pay two bartenders for the same hours."

"I'll be here," Taavi said.

"Good. Let me buy you both another round of drinks to celebrate."

One round turned to two and then three...

CHAPTER 18

Taavi arrived at home late that night to find the apartment dark and cold. Michal must be asleep he thought. He wanted to talk to her, to apologize, to tell her that he loved her. Quietly, he tiptoed into the bedroom and took off his coat. Then he walked closer to the bed to find it empty. Taavi rushed through the small apartment, turning on the lights, searching for his wife. What he found was a note, scratched in Michal's swirling handwriting on a paper bag that was grease-stained from the bakery.

Taavi,

We have hurt each other enough. I don't blame you entirely for what happened last night. I know in part it was my fault. But because of my past, I am unable to be a proper wife to you. Therefore, I am leaving. The thought of enduring another night like last night leaves me cold and, frankly, shattered. I wish you no harm, but I cannot stay here anymore.

Goodbye, Michal

He read the letter over twice, then sunk down into a chair. He shouldn't have acted the way he did the night before. It was barbaric. However, he couldn't bear to be in her presence for another moment without possessing her. He loved her; he wanted her. He'd always wanted her with a passion that was almost consuming. And now, she was gone. She'd left him and she was alone somewhere in this strange and often terrible city.

Taavi was frightened for her. The only thing that kept him from feeling sheer panic was the effect of the alcohol that still lingered from earlier that night. Michal, how would a girl like her fare in a city like Berlin under the Weimar Republic? A chill shot down his spine. As a man, Taavi had been raised to feel responsible for the women in his life. And now the one he had come to care for the most was in danger, and he had no idea where to begin to look for her.

The room was dark. He lit a cigarette. His mind began racing. The things he'd seen in Berlin, the things that went on outside this small apartment. How would she support herself? Would she end up a prostitute like so many of the women who had lost their husbands in the war and were now alone? Michal, a prostitute? Good God, please not that he thought. Then he pinched the cigarette off and left it in the ashtray. After throwing his coat back on, Taavi headed out into the night to search for the woman he loved.

CHAPTER 19

Taavi walked the entire Jewish quarter. The arctic wind bit his face, but he hardly noticed. He checked the homeless shelters. He navigated the icy walkways through the park. The sun began to rise. Soon Rivesman, his boss, would expect him to be at work. How could he concentrate on anything until he found Michal? Taavi longed to talk to her, but more importantly, he wanted to ensure her safety. If he could just find her, he would ask her to return to the apartment and promise that he would never shame her again. The chill stabbed through his coat and through his skin, burrowing into his insides; his hands were chapped and reddened against the bitter wind, his lips cracked, his eyes watered, leaving frozen tears on his eyelashes, but still he searched.

When Taavi arrived at work at eleven that morning, Rivesman fired him. It was not as if he hadn't expected that to happen, but it still made him feel miserable. He'd hoped to keep the job at the shop until he was sure that everything would work out at the nightclub. But, now he was dependent for his living on a woman who he felt was a little crazy and rather wild. Worse, he had no idea if he would be able to learn everything he needed to know for this new job. He had no idea what would be expected of him. The only apprenticeship he'd ever had was in carpentry. He returned to his apartment and brewed a cup of what passed for coffee. Then he sat down on the used, lumpy sofa that he'd purchased from Rivesman. He had planned to make a new one as soon as he had had time. Now, there was no point. Without Michal, there was no point to any of it. His shoulders slumped and he put his head in his hands.

CHAPTER 20

The house Gerta Fogelman occupied with her husband and a half dozen servants was the most magnificent place Michal had ever seen. The large wooden door to the house was painted deep burgundy and bore a heavy brass knocker that matched the knob. It opened into a world that appeared to Michal to be like a castle from a fairy tale. The foyer was a vast open road with white marble flooring veined with gold that divided into a fork. On one side lay the bedrooms, on the other a massive dining area and several sitting rooms. One of the sitting rooms served as an office, which belonged to Mr. Fogelman.

Gerta showed Michal to her room.

"It's small, I know," Gerta said, almost apologetically. "But you will only have to share a bathroom with Martha; she's the downstairs maid. No one else will use your bathroom."

"There is an upstairs?"

"Oh, yes, upstairs is the ballroom. We use it to entertain."

To Michal, the room that Gerta had given her was not small. In fact, it was almost the size of the entire apartment she'd shared with Taavi.

"It's lovely."

"I want you to be happy here," Gerta said. "I know this sounds rather odd, but I get terribly lonely. I mean, I have friends. If you can call them friends." She smiled a sad, wry smile. "But I don't have anyone I can really talk to … do you know what I mean?"

"I think so," Michal said.

"You remind me of my little sister. She's a few years younger than you. But when we were growing up we were always so close. She's still in Nuremberg. Sometimes she comes to visit, but not often enough."

"You miss her?"

"Very much. She's so lively. The next time she comes, you'll meet her. You'll like her; I'm sure of it. Her name is Deborah, and she's pretty like you." Gerta smiled. "My Debby has long dark hair and big sparkling eyes. Hers are brown, not the color of yours. In fact, I've never seen anyone else with eyes the same color as yours. I'm sure people have told you that you have beautiful eyes." Gerta smiled. "Anyway, you remind me so much of Debby. She is very active in a Jewish youth group. You know how these youth groups are springing up everywhere, most of them are not Jewish, but now the Jews are joining in and creating youth organizations of their own. Deb writes me long letters about how she and her group go hiking and singing in the woods." Gerta giggled. "Sometimes I'm jealous. I sort of miss being single and free. Marriage is certainly not what I thought it would be." Suddenly, Gerta's mood changed. It was as if she had said too much. "Anyway, I shouldn't be boring you with all of this. Why don't you get settled? Later this evening, I'll show you a picture of my sister."

"I would like that," Michal said.

Gerta left and Michal was alone in her new room. Gerta was sweet, Michal thought, but she was consumed with herself. She'd never even asked how Michal's husband had responded to Michal taking this job, moving out and leaving him alone during the week. Gerta didn't even know that Michal had left Taavi. It seemed to Michal that Gerta thought of herself as the center of the world. Perhaps I'm just selfish; I'm just feeling so alone right now, she thought. (If only I could talk to someone who cared, someone who would help me cope.)

Over the next several months, Michal became comfortable in the Fogelman household. She didn't leave on weekends and Gerta never asked why. Sammie was a handful. He kept Michal occupied when he was awake. It seemed as if his little legs and arms were constantly moving. Now that Michal had come to take care of her child, Gerta was free to join several women's clubs. On Tuesdays, she played cards; on Fridays, she joined a book club. When Gerta had said that her husband was rarely home, she had been telling the truth. Michal observed that Richard Fogelman spent long days at his office and sometimes did not return in the evening. In the time that Michal had been staying with Gerta, she'd only seen Richard Fogelman a handful of times, and then only for a few minutes. Gerta confided that she hoped she was wrong, but she thought that her husband was having an affair.

"I should leave him, I know that. But I can't. My parents would be devastated. They would say that I was ruining Sammie's life. So, I'm stuck here."

Michal rubbed her employer's shoulder.

During the day, Michal was too busy with Sammie to think about Taavi, but at night she missed him. She missed having someone who understood her to talk with, someone who knew her past and had lived in the same little village in Siberia. But, more importantly, Michal had not had her menstrual period since the night Taavi had forced himself on her. When she was married to Avram, she had been sure that she was barren; now she knew that she was not. Michal felt small changes begin in her body and she had no doubt that a little life was forming within her womb. At night, as she lay in bed, she talked to the baby. A child was such a wonderful gift, and she was truly happy to be pregnant. But she was afraid that Gerta would let her go once she found out. And, once the baby was born, how could she continue working for the Fogelmans anyway? Sammie required all of her attention. The baby would take up a lot of her time. The only thing to do was to wait until her day off and then take a bus to the Jewish sector and talk to Taavi.

Michal was sure Taavi wondered where she'd gone. How could she face him? What would she say? And after what he'd done, could she really bear to live with him again? Well, she had no other options. This weekend she planned to go back to the apartment, talk to Taavi, and try to work things out.

CHAPTER 21

Because Taavi no longer had the job at the furniture shop to fall back on, he knew that it was essential that he did a good job as a bartender and that he make Frieda happy she had hired him. When he came in on Saturday, Augie, Frieda's other bartender was forced to train him. Although Augie tried to sabotage Taavi at every turn, showing him as little as possible, Taavi was smart and a fast learner. He stood back and watched quietly, so that once the bar got busy, Augie forgot that Taavi was there. That was when he learned the most. By the second week, Taavi was more proficient than his teacher had ever been. Frieda was impressed. Not only was Taavi handsome, but he was smart, quiet, and capable. The hours were long, but Taavi was young and did not tire easily. One night, as the staff was closing the cabaret, Frieda asked Taavi to join her for a drink. He poured them both a shot of whiskey and sat down beside her at the bar. Again, she was dressed like a man. Her black suit, white shirt, and matching tie had been tailored to fit her perfectly.

"You're doing very well here, Taavi. It was a good decision on my part to hire you," Frieda said, lighting a cigarette and offering one to Taavi. He accepted and lit both hers and his own.

"Thank you."

"You're earning nice money; the tips are good?"

"Actually, yes."

She smiled. "You know, I am sometimes a very lonely woman. My husband died last year in the influenza epidemic. It was a terrible thing, that flu. The whole city was paralyzed with fear of contracting it. I caught it too. I was plenty sick, let me tell you, but I was younger and stronger than my husband. He fell so fast and was gone within a week. In fact, the poor man caught the influenza from me when he was trying to take care of me." She looked away. It was the first time he'd ever seen even a trace of emotion on her face. But when Frieda looked back at Taavi, the hardness in her eyes had returned. "Anyway, this club was his, and when he died, he left it to me. He was a much older man, who was well set with plenty of money when I met him. It was a good head for business he had. If he had lived longer and seen the trends that are going on in Berlin right now, my assumption is that he would have expanded the club the same way I have started expanding. He was a good person, my husband was; he was my friend and my mentor. But as a lover, well … he lacked some important things, you understand?"

Taavi shrugged. Until now, he thought Frieda might be a lesbian, but as she sat beside him devouring him with her eyes, he wasn't sure what she wanted.

"I'm not going to make small talk. I'm not a woman who wastes time with small talk. So, I'll get right to the point. I like you. I would like you to move into the apartment in the back of the club. You will be my manager. I have a good feeling about you. I have a hunch I can trust you. Every day, you will be in charge of opening and closing the club. I will come and go. I will count on your good sense and honesty. You will handle everything for me. Of course, you will be paid even better than you are now. What do you say?"

"What is the price of rent to live in the apartment behind the club?"

"No rent. Free. You will live here free. There are plenty of good benefits to this position, but I expect loyalty, and if I ever catch you stealing from me, there will be hell to pay. Do you understand?"

What a strange woman Frieda was. She was nothing like the women he knew growing up in his little village. In fact, she was bold and confident like a man, and she looked at him like he was a woman. Almost like the roles had been reversed. Still, she was offering free rent and an excellent salary. He knew he would earn good tips. How could he refuse?

"I'd love to accept your offer," Taavi said.

"Well, good. You will be responsible for seeing to it that the other employees do their work and that this place runs efficiently. I don't have time for problems. See to it that I don't have any."

"I'm just curious. Why me?"

"Because, quite frankly, as I said before, I feel I can trust you. But, more importantly … I plan on making you my lover."

Taavi was not a shy man, but he had never heard a woman speak so frankly about such an intimate matter. He felt his face go hot and he looked away.

Frieda barked a loud laugh. "I'm sorry to laugh at you, Taavi. But your naivety is so attractive. Especially here amongst all of these characters who have had far too much illicit sex, alcohol, and opium."

She made him feel ashamed. Although he had no desire to take her to his bed, her offer was undeniably beneficial. The money he could save on rent would help him to build his own carpentry shop eventually.

"When can I move in?"

"As soon as you'd like."

"My rent is due at the beginning of next month. How about I move in at the end of this month?"

"That would be perfect. Would you like to see your new place?"

He nodded.

"All right then, follow me."

They walked through the back of the nightclub and found a door to a small office. They went through. On the right side of the office was another door; Frieda took a key out of her pants pocket and opened it. She flipped a light switch that lit the room with a soft pink glow. Taavi was surprised to see an entire apartment unfold behind the cabaret. A small kitchenette with an ice box and a stove, a double bed, a table just large enough for the two chairs that were on either side of it, then a door on the left, which Frieda opened to reveal a private bathroom with a small claw-footed bathtub.

It was cleaner and warmer than the apartment where he was living, as his present landlord was not generous with the heat.

"You like it?" Frieda smiled at him.

He wished that she would wear a dress occasionally. Especially if she expected him to make love to her. Her short hair and manly ways did not appeal to him. When he thought of the perfect woman, he still thought of Michal. Michal, her beauty took his breath away with her dark curls and her slender waist. He should have been more understanding, gentler. After all, she'd been through so much, losing her husband, then being raped by that bear of man.

"Eh?" Frieda said loudly enough to shake him out of his thoughts.

"Yes. Of course I like it."

"Good … Then start moving your things in as soon as possible." She tossed him the key. He caught it. "I have another key in case you lose it." She winked and smiled. "I'll always have a key." He nodded. "Now, enough wasting time, you're on the clock. I'm paying you, so get back to work."

He moved in at the end of the month. On the third night after his arrival, Frieda came to his apartment. She removed her clothing in a businesslike manner and got into Taavi's bed. In the darkness, she was warm and female. He could feel her small breasts press against him and, in his mind, he could make believe that she was Michal. It was only through using his imagination that Taavi was able to achieve an erection. But, Frieda seemed satisfied. In the light of the sun, she looked old and hard. Her face was deeply lined and he could see that grey hair was growing in at the roots.

He was glad that she didn't come to his bed every night. In fact, she only came every couple of weeks. But he saw her come into the club every night. She was always laughing and flirting with men and with women. Then Frieda would disappear for hours. Sometimes she would be gone the entire night; other times, Taavi would see that she'd returned to her regular bar stool.

When Frieda was in the club, she acted as if Taavi was just another employee. She never made any reference to their affair.

Taavi hated the way Frieda made him feel. Yet, he'd never earned so much money, and earned it so easily. The other businesses in town were suffering. However, the cabarets were booming. Every night, people filled the club, drinking to excess. Sometimes there were heated political arguments that exploded into violence, forcing Taavi to intervene. He didn't mind. He was young, strong, and agile. He easily jumped over the bar and broke up the fights. Although Taavi had only been working as a bartender for six months, the police had questioned him twice concerning two murders of different women. They had both been patrons at the bar. The police wanted to know everything about them. Their faces were slightly familiar, but he couldn't remember who they'd left with. There were so many people coming and going every night. And when he mentioned the police questioning him to Frieda, she shrugged her shoulders and said, "There are so many murders in Berlin every night that I've stopped counting. You can expect the police to come in fairly often, asking if you have any information. Many of the murders are sex crimes. Who knows? Things go too far with one of the prostitutes, or maybe crimes of passion. Ehh. The police question every bartender, hoping somebody can give them something to go on. Don't let it get to you."

Taavi had begun drinking excessively. His customers were always buying him shots and his tips depended upon his acceptance of their generosity.

As she'd promised, Frieda had expanded; she'd begun hiring entertainers. All kinds of entertainers, singers who sang provocative songs filled with sarcasm about the government, comedians who told jokes and kept the audience entertained with their political rhetoric, psychics that called up members of the crowd and told them their future, and hypnotists that brought women in the audience to orgasm through hypnosis.

The patrons enjoyed the entertainment, and they loved Taavi, the sexy and mysterious bartender who spoke perfect German with a Russian accent. But, most importantly, Frieda was fortunate because her cabaret attracted a foreign audience of mostly British and Americans. The mark was not worth nearly as much as the pound or the dollar. And because their money was worth so much in Berlin, Taavi's tip jar overflowed. He worked every night, seven nights a week. Every day at noon, Taavi received his salary from Frieda for the night before. Because of the inflation, the prices of and availability of everything were constantly changing, and everyone in Berlin was paid daily. Food was scarce, and people lined up to purchase anything that they thought might be worth trading later. However, through the nightclub, Taavi had made friends in the black market and he used his tips that were often in foreign currency to buy anything his heart desired. He ate well and had more money than he'd ever seen in his life. Frieda bought him gifts of handsome suits and diamond cufflinks. But Taavi felt he had more in common with the prostitutes on the street than he did with the man he knew was still inside of him. Frieda knew no limits when it came to excess of any kind. One night, she brought a woman into their bed. Taavi had never imagined such things. But he'd managed to make love to both women. With Frieda, Taavi had begun to drink to excess. He'd allowed morphine to soothe his angst, and then he'd snort cocaine to keep him awake through the wee hours of the night. He used these substances to help him forget that he was living a life that was against everything he believed. Frieda had introduced him to a world where ordinary lovemaking was only the doorway into her strange sexual appetites. For a while, he endured, even enjoyed some of the overindulgence. But when he awakened in an opium den, surrounded by naked men and women laying sprawled in sexual positions on the floor,

Taavi was sickened by the sight of himself. He got dressed and tripped over one of the nameless bodies on the floor as he raced out into the air. It was fall and the trees had sprinkled the sidewalks of Berlin with an array of deep vivid color. Birds of all kinds sang in the trees. He passed the zoo and the Tiergarten. What had he become? He'd done things that no man should ever experience. Rounding a corner, he passed two gangs having fistfights on the street. By their uniforms, he could see that they were the socialists and the communists. *Battling again*, he thought, pushing one of the men out of his way. The groups were shouting at each other. Taavi walked until he was far enough away to stop and light a cigarette. A girl with long braided hair and high boots with black laces came up and whispered in his ear.

"I can get a child, a boy or a girl who will do anything you want. I mean anything. It will be a child as young as you want, who will look like any film star you fancy. Here, take this number; call and place an order. They'll bring the child right to your flat." She smiled. "Not too expensive either. Although, with that suit, you look like you could afford a good time."

Taavi pushed the girl away from him. He felt like he might vomit in her face. Black boot laces meant something. He'd forgotten what they meant. Frieda had told him once. Different colors meant that the prostitute was willing to engage in different perversions. Taavi was sick of all of the degenerates. He wished he could talk to Michal. He wished he could look into her eyes, which were normally so bright, but the last time he'd seen her they were as dark as charcoal. That was an indication of just how angry she was. How he wished he could tell her that he understood why she was so reluctant and that he would have waited forever. She was worth waiting for if that was what he had to do to prove his love for her.

Taavi went back to his apartment behind the nightclub and locked the door. He didn't go to work that night, and later when Frieda knocked, he didn't answer.

CHAPTER 22

Every weekend, Michal planned to go and talk to Taavi, and every time she got ready to go, she changed her mind. She was too proud to face him, and so she kept putting it off.

When Michal's pregnancy began to show, she'd had to tell Gerta the truth about everything, that she was pregnant, that she was estranged from her husband, and most of all that she was at Gerta's mercy. Michal was afraid that Gerta would fire her, and Michal couldn't blame her. After all, why would she want another child in the house? Michal fell to her knees and took Gerta's hands in hers, begging for help. She cried as she promised Gerta that she would never neglect her duties with Samuel. "Please, I beg you, don't put me out into the street," Michal had said. And Gerta had surprised her. Michal was still holding Gerta's hands. Gerta raised her up until both women were eye to eye. Then Gerta smiled and told Michal how excited she was that a new baby was coming into the house.

"I'm not going to fire you. Sammie loves you and so do I. You'll stay here and have the baby."

"But what about Mr. Fogelman?" Michal asked.

"He won't even know the difference. He's hardly ever here. And when he is, all he cares about is his food and comfort. It will be a long time before he even realizes that there is another child in the house. Just keep the baby in this wing when Richard is at home. The house is so big that he'll never hear him when he cries."

"God bless you," Michal said, kissing Gerta's hands. "Thank you. I don't know what I would have done, where I would have gone." She was crying.

"Stop crying, please," Gerta said, smiling. Michal had never really noticed how pretty Gerta's dancing blue eyes were. "Everything is going to be just fine. In fact, the children will grow up together."

Michal was grateful, very grateful. She kept her promise and even when she was afflicted with the horrible effects of morning sickness, she dragged herself out of bed to make sure that Sammie had his breakfast. In turn, Gerta was very good to Michal. When Gerta saw that Michal was ill, she insisted that Michal go back to bed while she attend to her son.

Michal went into labor early on a Saturday morning in October. Gerta had her driver take Michal to the local hospital, where Michal labored for fourteen hours. On October 22, at 7:30 in the evening, Alina Margolis was born. She was bald and as red as a ripe apple, but Michal thought that she was the most beautiful thing she'd ever seen. As the baby slept in her arms, Michal's thoughts began to wander. She was alone in the white, sterile, hospital room gazing out the window. Alina's head rested on her right arm, which began to feel like tiny pin pricks were traveling through it. She longed to shake her arm, but dared not move for fear of awakening the baby. Never before had Michal felt so close to anyone or anything. And from that moment on, she knew that for the rest of her life she would consider her child more important than herself and make any necessary sacrifices for her precious daughter.

As she looked into the tiny wrinkled face and marveled at the balled up fists, she thought of her own mother. What had her mother felt when she was born? Had she felt the same strong love that Michal felt now? It was so strange how only two days ago she had not even seen this child, yet now, she would easily have given her life to protect this little girl. For some reason, she thought of Avram. Poor, dear Avram. He'd been such a good person, and he would have been so happy had he been the father of this little girl. But fate had not been kind to him. He'd died such a terrible death. It had been a long time since Michal had allowed herself to think about Avram. But the baby was bringing back so many emotions that she'd buried deep inside of her. And then, most of all, as she looked into the little face, she saw traces of Taavi. The way the baby wrinkled her nose even as she slept, the child's full lips. She couldn't tell what color the baby's hair would be yet, and she'd heard that all babies were born with blue eyes. But she wondered if and when the color changed, would it match hers or Taavi's? She missed Taavi. She didn't miss the night he'd hurt her, but in a strange way, she was glad for it. Because if he had not forced himself upon her, she would not have this child lying within her arms. What a strange way of thinking, Michal thought. Her grandmother had once told her that in every curse, there was a blessing and in every blessing there was a curse. Taavi's taking her against her will had been a curse and at the time she'd hated him for it, yet, now, as she held her own child in her arms, she realized that it had also been a blessing. Gently, she leaned down to kiss the top of her daughter's soft head, then turned to glance out the window. The tall buildings surrounding the hospital seemed to engulf her and she wondered where her husband might be in this big frightening city called Berlin.

CHAPTER 23

Although Sammie had always been an active little boy, he took to the baby immediately. Although he was constantly in motion when he was around Alina, he was surprisingly gentle. Both Gerta and Michal had been worried that he would be jealous when the new baby came, but instead, he wanted to hold Alina as soon as he saw her. Michal held the baby in Sammie's arms, supporting her infant, but letting Sammie know at the same time that he would always be a very important part of her life. Gerta became more helpful now that Michal had two children to care for. She and Michal had become more like friends than employer and employee.

One afternoon, Gerta realized that Richard had left some paperwork he'd been working on all night on the kitchen table. She assumed he'd forgotten it and asked Michal to take it to him at the factory. She was being kind, wanting to give Michal a short break from the children.

"He must have put this down as he was getting ready to leave and forgotten to take it. Would you mind please running it over to him? He never leaves his paperwork around the house. It's always in his office. He will probably need it at work today."

Gerta couldn't remember the last time she'd seen Michal take even as little as a half hour for herself. Gerta appreciated how hard Michal worked and how much love she gave both to her own child and to Gerta's son. So, Gerta decided she would watch both children. It would be good for Michal to have some peace.

"Of course I'll take it," Michal said.

"Do you know where the factory is?"

"Yes, you showed me once. I remember."

Gerta handed Michal the papers.

"What about the children? Would you like me to take them with me?"

"No, I'll watch them until you return."

It was a lovely fifteen-minute walk from the house to the factory, through tree-lined streets with large two story houses and well-manicured lawns. Michal tried to put the children out of her mind and just enjoy being outside and having some time alone. But she couldn't, her mind kept drifting back to Alina and Sammie. This was the first time she'd been separated from her daughter.

The factory was a massive place that had poor ventilation. From the arguments Michal had heard between Richard Fogelman and one of his advisers, she'd learned that Fogelman did not provide much heat in the winter and the summers were stifling. She'd been outside Mr. Fogelman's home office, chasing after Sammie, when she'd overheard Fogelman's advisor warn that the communists were trying to form unions in the big factories. The workers were unhappy and planning to band together against the owners. If they were successful in organizing at the Fogelman factory, Richard Fogelman would suffer great financial losses. Michal had not understood much of what she was hearing until today when she visited the factory. This was the first time she'd been there, and now the things the advisor was saying became clearer. As soon as Michal walked into the factory, she began coughing, and her nose felt clogged. She knew from what Gerta had said that the workers worked twelve-hour days without any breaks. And now, as she walked through the endless rows of sewing machines towards Mr. Fogelman's office, she heard the foreman barking orders at the employees. His voice was loud and constant over the thunderous roar of machines. He was demanding that they work faster ... faster. Richard Fogelman's office was on the second floor, and very different from the rest of the factory. She knocked on the door and a pretty young blond with curly bobbed hair answered the door.

"I'm here to see Mr. Fogelman," Michal said.

"Please, sit down. May I tell him who has come to call?"

"Yes, just tell him that his son Sammie's nanny is here." Michal noticed that the office was larger than the apartment she'd once shared with Taavi. Taavi, she allowed herself a moment to indulge in memories of Taavi. Since Alina's birth, she'd been thinking of him more often. Perhaps it was because sometimes Alina reminded her so much of Taavi. When she thought of Taavi, her first thoughts were of the sound of his laughter. He had such contagious laughter with a warm and compelling pitch. Alina had the same contagious giggle, even as a baby. And his eyes, he not only laughed with his voice, but he laughed with his eyes. Taavi. He had a way of making her believe that nothing could harm her. That somehow, some way, even with her world falling apart, he and he alone could find a way to make things right. But ... then ... there had been that night. That night, for the first time Taavi had frightened her. Michal had seen another side of her husband, a side consumed by lust. Before that night, he had always been so kind, loving, patient ... Damn life, damn her own body for being so repulsed by the touch of a man just because of a few minutes of torture by a horrible savage. *Damn that Cossack to hell,* she thought. Then she looked up as Richard Fogelman walked in. They had never been face to face before.

"You forgot these papers, sir. Mrs. Fogelman asked that I bring them to you."

He didn't answer her. Instead, he allowed his eyes to roam her body slowly. Since she'd given birth, her breasts were fuller, larger. She thought that once she'd stopped nursing they would go back to their original size, but it hadn't happened. Her hips were rounded and womanly. And now, Richard Fogelman's eyes were glued to them.

Michal cleared her throat. "Sir," she said, her voice as firm as possible, "I brought these for you." She handed him the papers. As she did, he licked his lips, and Michal saw a smile come over his face. It was a smile that made the skin on the back of her neck feel as if spiders were crawling up into her hair. Michal's hand instinctively went to the back of her head. She ran her fingers through her hair to shake off the feeling.

He took the papers, but as he took them from her, his hand brushed hers and held it. Michal knew that he had taken hold of her hand on purpose and she pulled away. He released easily, but smiled as if he knew for certain that the time would come when he would possess her the same way that he possessed his automobile, his home, and his factory. *I'll be damned if he'll ever take me to his bed,* she thought. Then, in a firm voice, she said, "I'll be going now."

He laughed a little. "Thank you for bringing these to me. And, by the way, what is your name?"

"Michal. I've been working for you for a year."

"Well, how could I have ever missed such a pretty face?"

Michal didn't answer. She left the office and raced through the factory and out into the street. Her heart pounded and she was breathless. All the way back to the house, she thought about Gerta. From the way Richard had looked at her, Michal felt certain that he had been unfaithful to his wife many times. Poor Gerta. Michal began to put the puzzle pieces together. Richard was hardly ever home. Her heart broke for her friend. Gerta had been kind to her, she was a good person; she didn't deserve to be treated so callously. Michal decided to make a special effort to be as invisible as possible when Richard Fogelman was in the house. No matter what happened, even if it cost her the job that she held so dear, she would not betray Gerta. Let Richard be a cad if that was his choice, but she would never be a party to it.

CHAPTER 24

Nights in the bar drinking too much, days when he forgot to come to work because he was lying in opium dens, and waking up beside women whose names he couldn't remember was taking its toll on Taavi. He was tired most of the time, and deep wrinkles were carved into the skin around his eyes. His once-healthy sun-kissed body was now pasty from lack of exposure to the outside. He'd met famous artists, poets, and writers. Many times, his new friends spoke to him in words that were too advanced for his vocabulary. Taavi never told them; he just nodded and let them talk. But he hated being ignorant, so he made a mental note of the word and searched the dictionary as soon as he was alone to find out its meaning. His lack of formal education embarrassed him. He'd had some schooling, but not enough to fit in with the group of intellectuals who had taken him into their crowd. Taavi didn't usually ask many questions of his customers. They came to the nightclub as an escape from their lives, and Taavi had learned to respect their privacy. This was the most crucial part of his job. People learned that they could be comfortable telling him things they would not divulge to anyone else. He never gossiped or shared anyone's secrets and, through his discretion, he earned their trust. Often, they were married and having affairs or involved in some illegal or shameful activity. One of his customers claimed to have had a wild sexual affair with the famous Anita Berber. He even promised to give Taavi tickets to one of Berber's infamous nude performances. But he never came through with his promise.

Taavi just assumed that the man was inventing stories to make himself look important, and Taavi never mentioned the promise. Instead, he allowed the customers to be whoever and whatever they chose to be when they entered his bar. That was why he made more money in tips than most of the bartenders in the local clubs.

One night, a man wearing an ill-fitting black suit sat down at Taavi's bar.

"What can I get you?" Taavi asked the man, wiping the counter.

"A beer," the man said. "You have a Russian accent."

"Yes, I am from Russia, but I live here now," Taavi said, putting the glass of beer in front of the man.

"I'm from Russia too." The man coughed a little then took a sip of his beer. "I'm a professor at the local university. I'm not sure, but I think you're a Jew?"

"Why would you ask?" Taavi looked the man strangely. It was odd to ask such a question without provocation. But Taavi wasn't ashamed of who or what he was. "Yes, I am a Jew ... and what does it matter to you?"

The man laughed bitterly. "I am a Jew too."

Taavi then realized that the man was slightly drunk.

"Do you know that anti-Semitism is on the rise in Germany?" the professor answered. "It's an undercurrent. We Jews see it growing like a strangling vine, but we cover our eyes and refuse to believe that this civilized country, this blessed Germany, would ever turn on us. But it will, just like Russia did."

"That's for sure about Russia. Russia had no qualms about turning on her Jews. Especially the czar, son of a bitch that he was."

"You think it's better now that the czar and his family are dead? You think the communists are better?"

"I don't know. I've been away."

"It's hard to say really what's better or worse. I don't trust Germany and even with the changes in Russia, I still don't trust Russia. For a Jew, I personally believe that the place to live is America."

"Yes, I'm sure it is, but it's not so easy to get there. It takes lots of money. And, besides … my wife is here," Taavi said. It was at that moment that he realized he would never leave Germany without Michal. Somewhere deep in his foolish heart, he believed that they would be together again … someday.

"Take her with you."

"I would. I could probably get by on the money I have. But I don't know where she is. She's left me, and … well … I still love her. America is too far away. If I go, I know that I will never see her again. If I stay, maybe somehow we will find each other."

The old professor shook his head. "I think about leaving. I know that it would be a wise decision, but I have so much here." He took another sip of beer, then smiled a drunken smile at Taavi. "Ah, well, we can only hope that the anti-Semitism will not get out of control. So far, we are lucky. The Weimar Republic is a liberal and accepting government. They pretty much allow us to do as we please. If only there was not such hyper-inflation. But Germany has to pay back her debts, and let's face it, the working class is angry. They don't have enough food … the prices are always going up. I am secretly worried that the country will either go to the communists or socialists, and I'm not sure how the Jews will be affected. But, as you know, we are the chosen people. Chosen by God. For what? I'm not sure. But from what I have seen, in my lifetime anyway, we are chosen for hatred and resentment by the rest of the world. It's sad but true, I am afraid. Do you realize how much the world hates us? Do you?" He was rambling, but even in his drunken stupor, Taavi could hear the wisdom of his words.

"I am well aware that the world hates the Jews. My wife and I escaped from a pogrom in Siberia." Taavi nodded. He wanted to stop this conversation, but the old professor was not allowing him an opportunity to break away. Taavi was scanning the bar for a customer who might be waiting, a reason to break free. But there was no one. It was as if he was destined to hear these words.

"Ahh, so you're from Siberia. You must be a strong man to have lived there. Siberia is an inhospitable home for humans. I've heard about the Jewish settlements in Siberia. It was very kind and generous of the czar to send all of his Jews to a land with such pleasant living conditions. But not unexpected, of course." He winked and smiled a half smile, but his eyes were sad. "But that was not all Russia had in store. Once the Jews were settled in their frozen wonderland, the pogroms began again, just like they have been going on throughout history. As I said before, we are the lucky ones, yes? Right? We are the Jews; we are the chosen people."

"All right, all right, Professor Sapstein, come on now; it's time to go home." A younger man came over and helped the old drunken professor out of the nightclub. But his words still haunted Taavi.

CHAPTER 25

One evening, Taavi was stocking the shelves behind the bar when he heard a familiar voice call his name.

"Tavala," Lev called Taavi by his Yiddish name.

"Lev?"

"How have you been? NU?"

"I'm fine … doing well. And you, how are you?"

"Ehhh, I'm all right. Still building custom furniture for the old bastard."

Taavi laughed and came out from behind the counter to hug his old friend. After Taavi released Lev, he patted Lev's shoulder. "What would Rivesman do without you? He can't do what you can. You are a true artist, a wonder with woodwork. I still remember."

"You look tired, old friend," Lev said.

"I work long hours, but the money is good. Do you need some money?" Taavi said.

"No, I just came to see you."

"We had some good times, didn't we?" Lev said.

"We did. Let me get you a shot of vodka, on me."

"I miss you, Taavi. Let's get together sometime soon."

Taavi poured from the bottle into the shot glass, one for Lev and one for himself.

"L'Chaim."

"L'Chaim."

They chugged their shots. The rich burn of the alcohol gave Taavi the courage to ask, "Have you seen Michal anywhere around the old neighborhood?"

Lev shook his head.

"Never? Not once?"

"I haven't seen her since you left."

Taavi shrugged his shoulders. "I don't know where she went. I hope she's all right."

Lev didn't answer. There was no answer. Murders were not uncommon in Berlin. She could be dead. She may have met another man and left Germany with him. Lev had no idea, so he said nothing. But the pain in his friend's eyes was apparent and he wished he could comfort Taavi in some way.

"We should see each other more," Taavi said. "Come to the club."

"Of course I will."

"No, seriously, come more often."

"I'll try. But, I'm getting married, Taavi. I met someone. A nice girl. She's from Poland. A good girl with a kind heart. She's Jewish, but she has papers that say she's a Christian. With these papers, she got a good job at a factory. It's not easy, but she makes money."

"I'm happy for you."

"Who knows if she'll let me out of her sight."

"Like you're such a catch." Taavi laughed. Then Lev laughed too.

"She's the catch. I'm fortunate. Let's face it, I don't bring much to a marriage."

"You're a good hard working man with a kind heart. You bring plenty."

"You'll come to the wedding?"

"I wouldn't miss it for anything."

Lev left soon after the conversation, but the entire night, Taavi thought about him. Taavi had more money than he'd ever thought he could earn, and he'd done things he had never dreamed were possible, some good, some not so good. But the real man inside of Taavi, the simple man from Siberia, the simple carpenter, longed for a less complicated life. In a strange way, he envied Lev. If all went as planned, Lev would be living the life that Taavi had imagined he and Michal would share. There was no doubt that with Lev's job, he would always be struggling financially, but he would have a wife and perhaps children. And, at night, he would go home to a wholesome meal with a woman he knew was his own.

Taavi had hoped to see Michal when he went to Lev's wedding. He searched the streets and the shops on his way, but he never saw a trace of her. In fact, he even checked the shelters again and knocked on the door to their old apartment, only to find a new couple had moved in with a set of twin boys. After the wedding, although it brought him shame, he walked down to the docks where the Jewish women prostituted themselves to make ends meet. He hoped that Michal had not ended up as one of them, but he would forgive her if she was. It didn't matter to him what she was doing, as long as he was able to find her and to finally open his heart and tell her how he felt. If only he had one more chance, he would beg her to forgive him.

CHAPTER 26

April, 1923, Berlin

The number of nightclubs was growing rapidly and the perversities available for purchase were being hawked by prostitutes all over the streets. The police overlooked the prostitution; it was no longer a crime and most of the prostitutes were registered with the police department and checked regularly for disease. The sexually driven killings continued and would come to be referred to as *Lustmord*. Inflation had been a problem since the end of the First World War and the signing of the treatise of Versailles, but now it was even more rapidly on the rise, and the middle class was quickly disintegrating. An entire life's savings might be eaten up by the price of a sandwich. Sometimes, one of the poor citizens of Germany who had lost everything would go mad and act as a sniper, shooting from the rooftops. On the main streets, one might well see very wealthy women in lovely dresses out shopping or big business owners in well-made suits hurrying along the thoroughfare. However, behind the façade, in the back streets off the main drag, were the pathetic, the poor, and the sick. Tuberculosis was rampant, especially in children. One might pass them, coughing into bloody handkerchiefs, but still selling their young bodies for one more meal. However, for foreigners who brought francs, American dollars, or pounds, Berlin was a free for all, the most exciting city in Europe.

Anything, no matter what it was, could be bought at a very low price.

The poor and the middle class German people were frustrated, starving to death, and desperately searching for a change.

CHAPTER 27

Mid-July, 1923, Berlin

Richard and Gerta Fogelman had begun to argue loudly whenever he was at home. Michal could hear their constant bickering, but she never mentioned what had happened that day she'd gone to the factory. However, after that visit, she'd been fairly certain that Richard was unfaithful to his wife. She was sorry for her friend, but didn't have the heart or the words to tell her, so she remained quiet. If there was an argument during the night, Michal lay quietly in her room, listening, her heart breaking for Gerta. But when the fighting took place in the morning, as it did on this particular day, Michal would take the children out for a walk, sometimes to the park or the zoo. Gerta had expressed her gratitude to Michal for taking Sammie away when she and Richard were yelling at each other. Although he was only five, he had already begun to show signs that his parents' problems were affecting him. He'd begun wetting his bed, which infuriated his father. Richard would holler at the boy and shake him if he discovered the mess. However, when Michal found the wet sheets, she quickly changed them without telling the housekeeper, to prevent her from reporting Sammie's behavior to his father.

It was early on a Sunday morning; Gerta and Richard were at the breakfast table when a heated argument broke out. Michal was dressing the children before taking them downstairs to eat their first meal of the day.

"It's Sunday, Richard. There is no reason that you have to leave. Why can't you ever spend any time with us? Your son hardly knows you."

"You have no right to question what I do. There are problems at the factory. The unions are closing in on me, commies that they are. Damn the workers; they should be happy they have a job at all. They are never satisfied. I'm being destroyed...."

"I know all about your problems, Richard, you've told me a hundred times, but it's Sunday. Can't you spend some time here with us, with your son and your wife? You can't do much about the unions on Sunday."

"Stop questioning my decisions. Don't you have everything you need and want? Isn't this house and all of these servants enough for you? You have beautiful clothes; you redecorate the house every other month. What else could you possibly want?"

"You, Richard. I want you ... I don't have a husband. You haven't touched me in over a year."

Upstairs, Michal wondered how much little Sammie understood.

There was no answer from Richard. All Michal heard next was the slamming of the front door. She knew that he had left. Then she heard the slamming of Gerta's bedroom door, and she assumed that Gerta was probably crying in her bed as she had been doing so often lately. Michal had begun to worry about Gerta. Gerta had grown very thin; in fact, she hardly ate. Her once thick healthy hair had grown limp and lackluster.

Michal stood outside the door to Gerta's room and tapped gently. Gerta didn't answer.

"I'm going to take the children to the park. Is that all right with you?"

"Yes." It was just loud enough for Michal to hear.

"I'll give them some breakfast first. Then we should be back sometime around lunch."

There was no answer, but Michal was sure that Gerta had heard her. Sammie was standing beside Michal, while Alina was playing on the floor. Michal looked down at Sammie; his little face was pale with worry. His mouth hung open. She gave him a big smile, kissed his cheek, and took his hand. Then she helped Alina to her feet.

"We're going to the park," Michal said to Sammie. "We'll have lots of fun." The little boy looked up at her and she felt her heart breaking for him. "Come on ... let's put Alina into her stroller. She's still too little to walk. But you, Sammie, are a big boy now."

"I am and I'm getting bigger every day. Someday soon I'm going to be all grown up and I'll be a famous movie star like the ones we see on the screen when you take us to the cinema," he said. Michal was glad he was distracted from his mother's misery.

Michal felt her face grow hot. She knew she shouldn't take the children to the cinema. They were too young, and most of the time Alina became so bored that she'd start crying so loudly that they'd have to leave. But Michal loved the theater, and she enjoyed the enchantment of the silver screen. Berlin was exploding with new film techniques and, as she sat in the dark and the curtain rose, she was swept into the magic.

Sammie held the side bar of the stroller while Michal pushed. As they walked further from the Fogelman home, Sammie became more at ease. It was obvious to Michal that Sammie felt closer to her than he did to his mother. That was because poor

Gerta was always so distracted by her own problems. Michal knew that Gerta was distraught because of Richard's lack of interest, and she was sure that Gerta sensed the presence of another woman. Michal could not be sure that Richard was cheating on his wife, but she assumed from everything she knew of him and the marriage that he was.

The park was alive with the singing of birds ... birds of all colors and sizes. The leaves on the trees were different shades of green and yellow and dandelions grew along the edge of the park. They entered and walked along the walkway until Sammie saw a group of children and their mothers gathered around a man who was sitting cross-legged in the center of the crowd.

"Come on, Michal, let's go and see what's going on there," he said, smiling up at Michal. He was such a handsome little boy that Michal found she had to smile and nod.

"All right, Sammie, just don't run. I don't want you to fall and hurt yourself."

He started by walking, but the momentum of curiosity overtook him and the child began to run. Michal shook her head and pushed the stroller a little faster to catch up.

The man who sat in the center of the group was telling a story. Michal put her finger over her lips, signaling Sammie to be quiet. Alina had fallen asleep in the stroller from the motion of the ride. Gently, Michal pushed the stroller back and forth in a slow continuous motion to keep Alina from awakening.

Sammie loved stories. Michal knew how much he enjoyed it when she came into his room at night to put him to bed and told him a story. Hopefully, Alina would sleep long enough for the storyteller to finish. Sammie sat down quietly on the cool grass and blended right in with the other children, while the mothers stood in the back, watching and whispering softly to each other. Michal didn't know any of the women, so she stood alone.

"And the evil giant controlled all of the good people who worked to keep him happy. They did everything he asked, and yet they were hungry and their children were starving," the man who was telling the story said, as he looked into the wide of eyes of all of the children. Then he continued.

"All the people asked of the giant was that he treat them fairly, but he was greedy and he was rich."

Michal leaned against a tree and listened. She had stopped pushing the stroller, but she glanced at Alina, who was still sleeping soundly. Then she looked up to catch the storyteller watching her. His eyes were the deepest shade of blue she had ever seen, not light blue, but midnight blue. His hair was dark, thick, wavy, and unkempt. He was slender and his clothes fell about his frame haphazardly. But he was filled with passion, and something about the fire that exuded from him reached deep inside of Michal. He smiled at her as he pushed his hair away from his face. She returned his smile. Then ... he smiled even brighter.

"The poor people had no choice but to fight the giant. They knew that if they didn't, the giant would take everything they had, and work them until they died of starvation. But the giant was so much bigger than they were, and the only way that the people in the village could even hope to defeat such a force was if they joined together."

Michal heard Alina stir in her buggy. She glanced at the baby, who had awakened. Alina could go from a deep sleep to running at top speed in seconds. Once Alina was awake, she was a handful. Michal tried rocking the stroller gently. Often the motion would send her back to sleep. Alina stretched, then her eyes closed softly and she drifted off again. By this time, the performance was over. Sammie was talking to another little boy. Since the problems had begun in the Fogelman household, Sammie had not been interested in playing with other children. He'd withdrawn. So, rather than discourage him from talking to the other child, Michal stood back and waited. The two boys were playing with stones they'd found on the ground.

"I am Otto Keihn, and I thank you for listening. My book, *Fables to Build a New World*, is available for purchase at Merek's books, which is right on the corner." He pointed towards the shop and the heads of the audience turned. Then, Otto Keihn got up and stretched his long legs and arched his back. Then, without hesitation, he walked over to Michal. In his hand, he held a book.

"Hello," He smiled.

"Hello," she answered, still keeping an eye on Sammie.

"Would you like to have this? It's a copy of my book." He held the book out to her.

"No, thank you … I don't have any money with me," she said, but just as she did, Sammie left his new friend and came running over to them.

"Did you like my story?" Otto asked Sammie.

"Very much, sir."

Otto smiled. "I don't want you to pay for my book. I would like to offer it to you as a gift for your son. You can read it to him. He seems to enjoy the tales."

"Thank you, but no," she said, "and, he isn't my son. This is Sammie. I'm his nanny."

"And, who is this?" he said, looking at the bright eyes that were now open in the stroller.

"This is Alina; she's my daughter."

"Hello, Alina."

"Your husband is a lucky man…"

She looked away. "I haven't seen my husband in many years."

"I would like to say that I'm sorry, but I'm not. I'm glad."

She frowned, feeling awkward and not knowing what to say.

"Please, don't be offended. I mean no harm. I only wanted to ask if maybe you would like to go for a walk with me sometime, or perhaps have a meal?"

"I am still a married woman. I cannot accept a date with a strange man."

"Again, please, I am sorry I had no intention of being disrespectful. You are just so lovely and, well, and…."

"And?" she said, raising her eyebrows. "I think we should be going. Come along, Sammie."

"Please, don't be offended. I just wanted to get to know you better," Otto said, throwing his hands up in the air.

"You should come to our house and tell us more stories," Sammie said. "Can I have the book?"

"Yes, of course you can," Otto said, handing the book to Sammie.

"I don't think it's a good idea for him to come to the house," Michal shook her head at Sammie.

"But can I keep the book, please Michal?"

"I suppose," she said. Then she turned to Otto. "Thank you for the book. We'll be going now," she said and began to walk away.

Just as Michal was wheeling her carriage around the corner of a tree-lined street across from a row of shops, she saw a man come out of the dry goods store and begin running. The owner was on his heels, wearing a white apron, and shouting obscenities. The owner gained upon the thief and pulled him down from a fence, throwing him to the ground. The thief pulled a gun and shot the store owner point blank in the forehead. The owner fell, his apron turning red with blood as crowds of people came rushing outside at the noise of the gunshot. Two men tried to grab the man with the gun, who was now frightened by what he'd just done. He writhed in their grasp and when he was unable to break free and unable to aim directly at either man, he shot wildly into the crowd. People were scattering to hide and screaming as the man with the gun began running. Otto raced over and pushed Michal and Sammie to the ground. Then he threw his own body over Alina, who was wailing in her stroller from the loud sounds of the gunshots. There were more squabbles in the street. Michal heard them, but from where she was lying on the ground, she could not see them. It was several minutes, but seemed like hours before three police officers arrived. One of the officers tended to the man with the apron, who lay in a pool of blood on the sidewalk, while the other two chased the criminal. The police had arrived too late; the man escaped into the crowd and disappeared. Gingerly, Otto rose from his position of protecting Alina.

"Are you hurt?" he asked Michal.

She shook her head. "I'm fine."

"I'm not fine, I hurt my knee when I fell and my elbow too." Sammie was crying.

"Let me see," Otto said. He looked at Sammie's injuries, then he smiled at the boy. "You're a man. Men don't cry when they fall down. You're not hurt, just a little scratched up. An injury like that is nothing to a real grown up man."

Sammie stopped crying. "I'm growing up very fast," he said.

"Of course you are." Otto nodded and patted Sammie's shoulder.

Michal mouthed the words, "Thank you for everything."

Otto smiled. "I'm glad I was here."

"I have to admit, so am I," she said.

"Let me go into the store and get you something cold to drink."

Michal nodded. "Thank you." She was out of breath and overwhelmed.

Otto returned with a large glass of water. He handed it to Michal, who took a sip and then gave a sip to Sammie. Then she held the cup to Alina's lips.

"Are you all right?" Otto said.

"I think so, just a little shaken up."

"I know that what just happened here on the street was terrible, but this is what happens when people are starving. That man stole food. Then he panicked when he felt surrounded. How can you blame him?"

"He killed a man … he could have killed all of us."

"Don't you see? Our money here in Germany is practically worthless; the man was only trying to feed his family."

"That's still no way to behave. There are other options."

"Like what? You mean the charities? Or those terrible shelters filled with tuberculosis? We don't know anything about the shooter's situation. Besides, with money being as tight as it is, he would be lucky to get a meal at a shelter. I can't judge other people when I am faced with the poverty in Germany right now. The rich have everything and the poor are starving. This is a climate for disaster."

She finished the water and handed the glass back to Otto. He took it. "I'm going to return this glass to the restaurant. The manager was kind enough to allow me to take it with a promise that I would return it. I'll be right back."

He returned. "Let me walk you back home. I want to be sure that you're all right," Otto said.

"Yes, please do," Sammie said. He took Otto's hand. Michal bit her lower lip in contemplation. She shouldn't be surprised that Sammie took to Otto so quickly. The child was starved for a father's love. Her own child would be the same when she got a little older. Having no male role models in their lives to look up to, of course they would grasp on to any man who treated them as though they mattered. Michal glanced over at Sammie and thought about Taavi. Poor Sammie had never really had a father's love. But Michal wondered how Taavi would have been as a father to Alina. If only she could swallow her pride, go, and talk to Taavi, let him know he has a daughter. She owed it to Alina. The child deserved a chance at a normal life. Right now, she was growing up as the nanny's daughter in the home of her employer. Michal had to admit to herself that the Fogelmans had everything the world could offer materially, and living in the Fogelman home, Alina never wanted for nutritious food, warmth, clean clothing, or a safe neighborhood. With the state of things in Berlin right now, Alina might not have these things if it were not for Michal's employers. Still, would it be better for Alina if she had a family of her own? If she had a father who she could look up to? Or was Michal putting too much stock in Taavi? When she and Taavi were together, they barely had enough food for the two of them. Perhaps things were better for Alina just as they were.

Otto walked quietly beside the stroller, holding Sammie's hand. He caught Michal's eye and smiled. "Are you doing all right?"

She nodded.

"What you just went through was terrible. If there is anything I can do…."

She shook her head. "No, thank you. But I am glad you were there at the right time. It was quite frightening."

"I know this is bold, but I would really like to get to know you better. Let me take you out for a meal. Lunch? Dinner, perhaps?"

"I don't know."

"Just as friends. We would be having a meal just as friends. How can that be wrong? It's only a meal, and it would mean so much to me."

She laughed a light giggle. "I saw the way all of the mothers were looking at you; it hardly seems to me that you are wanting for company."

"But you're wrong. I am. I want to spend my time with someone who I feel I might be able to talk to."

"And you feel that you can talk to me?"

"I don't know. I will be quite honest with you. I like your eyes. I like the serious look in your eyes. You seem different from other women. You have a depth about you."

"All of this information you gathered about me just from looking at me across the park?" She laughed, then looked at him sideways. "Ahhh, I know, let me guess … perhaps you are one of the famous psychics of Berlin. You would have to be, to know so much about me without ever even speaking to me."

"You're laughing at me. I'm not joking. I feel that you're different. I might be wrong. But my gut tells me I'm not wrong. And I believe it would be worth the time and trouble for both of us to find out."

"You are incredibly bold."

"Yes, most revolutionaries are," he said. "And, I, my dear, am a revolutionary. I am determined to make a difference in the world."

She laughed. He mock bowed. Then he laughed too.

"I am serious, though. We do need a change here. The wealth has to be distributed more fairly."

"Please don't tell me that you're a member of that National Socialist group that everyone is talking so much about. They are anti-Semitic and, you might as well know right now, I am a Jew."

"I am not a member of that Jew-hating party of miserable bastards. In fact, I am quite the opposite; I'm a communist."

166

"Oh, a troublemaker on the other side of the fence," she said.

"I don't want to make trouble. I want to see the world become a better place. A better place for all people, not just the rich. I want to help those who are too weak or underprivileged to help themselves."

"A lofty goal indeed."

"Indeed." He smiled. "But a goal that my conscience insists that I must pursue."

They walked for a while in silence. Then Otto cleared his throat. "You know, I don't even know your name."

"Her name is Michal, I'm Sammie, and the baby is Alina."

"I'm not a baby," Alina said. "I'm three."

"Of course you're not," Otto said, then he winked conspiratorially at Sammie. Michal saw Sammie wink back.

This Otto fellow seemed to be a nice man, Michal thought. So what could be the harm in having dinner with him on her day off on Sunday? After all, she and Taavi were separated. Perhaps she could pay a sitter to watch Alina.

"So, now you know my name," she said.

"Yes, and we have been officially introduced." Again, Otto winked at Sammie. "Perhaps you will have dinner with me."

"Sunday is my day off. I'll have to arrange a babysitter."

"That should be easy. I have a sister; she's almost fifteen. She would be happy to watch your daughter while we went out for a quick dinner."

"How do you know? You haven't asked her."

"I can guarantee it. She loves children and she doesn't have any younger brothers or sisters ... so, I am sure this would be a treat for her. What time can I come by for you?"

"Would seven be alright?"

"Perfect." He smiled.

CHAPTER 28

Otto picked Michal up at the Fogelman's home and they took the subway back to the house where Otto lived with his sister. It was closer to town, but not directly in town.

It turned out that Otto's sister was a sprite of a girl. Bridget was short with an athletic build, light brown, almost blonde hair, and an endless supply of energy. Michal was surprised to see that Alina took to her right away.

"Are you sure that you want to watch Alina while we go out for dinner?" Michal asked Bridget.

"Of course. Don't worry, she'll be fine with me."

Michal had never left her daughter with a stranger before and, even though Otto's sister seemed sweet and friendly, Michal was a little apprehensive.

Otto and Michal walked for several blocks to a quiet little restaurant with worn but clean eggshell-colored tablecloths.

"Feel free to sit anywhere you'd like," a heavy-set man with a thick black mustache said.

They chose a table near the window. There were no menus. A young girl with a tooth missing in the front of her mouth came to take their order. She seemed bored as she recited what was available for dinner that night.

"We don't have menus," she said, "because we never know what we're going to be able to get on any particular day. Sometimes maybe we can get fish, sometimes if we are very fortunate chicken, or cheese. Most times we try to have bread. You understand; everything is scarce."

"Of course," Otto said with a charming smile. Then he turned to Michal, who seemed to be feeling a little awkward. "Would you like me to order for you?"

"Yes." She was relieved. She had no idea what to order or what to do. Was he going to pay the check? Would she be expected to pay some of it? She'd never been out for dinner with a man who was not her husband or betrothed before. It was all so strange and new. But Otto was so comfortable that he put her at ease.

"So, tell me a little about yourself, Michal."

She took a breath and sighed. "Well, as you know, I am Jewish. I don't think you are."

"No, I am not."

"Does it bother you that I am?"

"Nothing about you bothers me. In fact, I have a little secret to tell you. Do you promise not to tell anyone?"

She straightened her back as if she was worried that he might reveal something she would rather not know.

Otto laughed. "It's all right. It's nothing that would get you into trouble in any way. I promise."

She cocked her head to the side. "Tell me then," Her curiosity was getting the better of her.

"Well..." He hesitated for effect. She moved forward in her chair, waiting for him to speak. "Well ... I have been thinking about you every day since the first time I saw you. And..." He cleared his throat for effect. "I wrote you a poem. A poem just for you ... Would you like to hear it?"

"Yes." A poem just for her?

Otto took a folded piece of paper out of his pocket, but before he could begin reading, the food arrived.

CHAPTER 29

It became a ritual. Every Sunday evening, Otto came to the Fogelman home at seven-thirty. He and Michal would take the subway back to his apartment, where they would leave Alina with Bridget. Then the two of them would walk through the streets as the sun was setting. They usually went to the same café to share their dinner and all of the events that had taken place during the week.

One Monday morning, Otto was being featured at a book signing for children's literature at the little bookshop where he sold his books. He'd invited Michal the night before when they were having dinner. Then, to his surprise and delight, she'd arrived with both children. He couldn't take his eyes off her. Otto was known to be promiscuous amongst his friends in the art world. When people spoke about him, they used words like suave and debonair, passionate and handsome. It was well known amongst his peers that Otto was bisexual, but he had never felt about a woman the way he felt about Michal. When he thought of her, he would smile to himself with the realization that opposites do attract, in the same manner that opposing sides of a magnet hold together tightly. He adored the way that she was so proper, but at the same time it made him reluctant to try to take her to bed. In fact, he had not even kissed her yet. And for Otto, this was strange behavior indeed. He thought that she liked him, but he wasn't sure. Perhaps he was intrigued by the way that he could never be sure of her; she always kept him guessing. In the past, Otto was a confirmed bachelor. He never wanted to marry, but he had actually begun to consider the possibility with Michal. And if she didn't have a husband in some faraway place, he would already have proposed. It was hard to be around her and not want to take her into his arms and plant a kiss on those soft lips.

Michal noticed how the mothers who'd brought their children to the book signing looked at Otto with desire. Some of the women made crude sexual innuendos to him as he signed their children's books, while others just stared shyly. After the book signing, Otto gave Alina and Sammie each a piece of candy, and then he accompanied them home on the S-Bahn.

Richard Fogelman was out of town again. He was supposed to be selecting fabrics for the fashions of the coming year. Gerta stopped mentioning the fact that her husband was staying away overnight more and more. But Michal knew that Gerta was distressed over the way that Richard had distanced himself from his family.

When Michal and Otto returned with the children to the Fogelman house, Gerta invited Otto to join them for dinner. It was unusual for the mistress of the house to extend an invitation to her nanny's boyfriend, but Michal and Gerta had become such close friends that it wasn't awkward for either of them. Otto was unsure and uncomfortable. He had reservations about making friends with anyone who was rich but not an artist. He hated businessmen and the Fogelmans were owners of one of the biggest garment factories in Berlin. In Otto's mind, these were the type of people that he considered the enemy. They were ruining Germany with their greed. But Michal looked so pretty when she told him that she really wished he would stay, that he couldn't refuse her.

All through dinner, Otto had to hold his tongue. The waste and entitlement of the upper class was repugnant to him. Servants served heaping platters of food. Food like this was unattainable to the poor and disappearing middle class. As he ate, he felt his throat close. It was hard to enjoy such luxuries while others suffered. To anyone else, Gerta would have been considered a charming hostess. But to Otto, she was a spoiled woman who was blind to the coming doom that he saw clearly. Right now, the Weimar Republic was a democracy, fair to all. But just lurking in the shadows was a group that he knew was intent upon destroying the entire Jewish population in Germany. Before Otto had become emotionally invested in Michal, he'd hated the National Socialist Party with its hatred-spewing doctrine, but he'd not taken them seriously. Yes, of course, he'd gotten into street fights with them on occasion. Their demonstrations irked him. But, now he was taking their threats to heart. Michal's Jewish heritage frightened him. He was smart enough to realize that Germany was unstable, and he feared for her safety. That weird little crippled fellow, Joseph Goebbels, was both brilliant and terrifying. He followed his leader, Adolf Hitler, around like a puppy and was determined to have him appointed chancellor of Germany. Goebbels was using the anger and hatred of the underprivileged Germans toward Jews like the Fogelmans to create a following for his leader. People were not taking Hitler seriously, but Otto was not able to dismiss the little man with the silly mustache so easily. Especially when the woman he was falling in love with was in question. Indeed, they were on the precipice of a time of grave danger.

After dinner, Gerta retired to her room, and Michal asked Otto to remain in the parlor while she put the children to bed. He agreed to wait while she got them ready, but then offered to

174

tell them both a story. Michal was delighted and so were the children.

The excitement of the day had exhausted Alina and she was asleep before she could hear any of the folk tale that Otto was telling. But not Sammie. His eyes were wide as Otto sat on the edge of his bed and told the little boy a story in his melodious voice.

Michal stood in the doorway of the bedroom and watched. Sammie was enthralled. Otto was gentle and engaging. She saw the need for a father in Sammie's life and she knew that Alina would have a better chance at a good life if she had one too. Especially a father like Otto.

Sammie began laughing. Otto was saying something, his arms raised over his head animatedly.

It was at that moment that Michal decided that she wanted to be free of Taavi and to spend her life with Otto. She decided that he would be a good father for Alina. But to divorce Taavi would mean she would have to see him, talk to him. She dreaded the very idea of telling Taavi that she'd found another man. It unnerved her. There was something about Taavi that she just couldn't let go. Worse, if she did want to break up the marriage, she would have to go to a rabbi and talk to him in order to be awarded her "Get" her Jewish divorce. Yet, how could she spend her life married to a man whom she never saw? Michal was confused, but as she watched Otto with Sammie, she was starting to care for Otto.

Sammie didn't want to go to sleep, but Otto was firm and insistent until Sammie finally agreed.

Once both children were in bed, Otto and Michal were sitting alone in the parlor.

"Would you like a cup of tea?" she asked him. The moonlight filtered through the window and caught her eyes, which sparkled like gray diamonds. Her hair was lit by the moon as well.

"No, thank you," he said. There was so much he wanted to say, so much he needed to say. But he dared not speak, lest he spoil the moment.

For the first time, he touched her hand. She did not move it away. His heart swelled. Dare he try to kiss her? She gazed into his eyes. Neither of them spoke. Otto swallowed hard as he touched her face ever so lightly. She smiled. He hoped he was reading her signals correctly. In slow motion, he leaned over and kissed her.

Michal kissed him back.

CHAPTER 30

Michal had never felt so guilty and happy at the same time. She spent all week in eager anticipation of Otto's arrival on Sunday. He took her to dinner. They spent hours walking. As they walked, he asked her about her life, and unlike most men she'd known, he listened. He not only listened, but he cared, he asked questions. Otto was interested in everything she had to say. Her views on politics, art, and music were just as important to him as her likes and dislikes in fashion. Nothing was off limits in their conversations. Taavi had been harder to talk to; he was more practical. If she began rambling about things that didn't matter, he would hear her, but not listen the way Otto did. Otto was always attentive. He made her feel as if everything she had to say was important to him. However, not only did they discuss general things, but they conversed about her deepest feelings. Michal told him about her marriage to Avram, then to Taavi, and finally on one evening when the sky was lit with stars they sat together on a bench, she told him about the rape. She hung her head and wept until her slender shoulders shook. He didn't attempt to touch her. He just sat beside her and listened, waiting until she reached for his hand. Then gently he brought her palm to his lips.

"He could have killed me. And sometimes I wish he had," she said in a small voice.

"And then what of Alina? She would never have been born. You gave her life, Michal. Life is a wonderful gift to give someone."

"Yes. I suppose. Mine hasn't been easy, that's for sure. I was wrong; I should have made things work with her father. I owed her that much. My marriage to Taavi failed because I couldn't be a wife to him after the rape. When he tried to touch me, all I could think about was that horrible man and that he'd soiled the inside of my body."

"But he didn't. He was there, it's true. But if he had really soiled you, you could never have had such a beautiful child. He hurt you. I understand that. But because you can't let go of what he did, you keep reliving it, and it is keeping you from ever finding happiness. As long as you keep the Cossack alive in your mind, he will continue to destroy you. He is gone … nothing but a ghost from the past. Let him be gone. Do you understand me?"

She nodded. "So what can I do? How do I ever get over this?"

"We are friends, right?"

"Yes."

"Good friends. You trust me, don't you?"

"I do."

"I am not saying this to seduce you, although I want you. I have wanted you from the first moment I saw you. But, it's more than that, Michal. You need me too. I understand you. I know what you've been through. This may sound self-serving, and in a way, it is, but not completely." Her hair had fallen over her eye. Gently, he moved it away. "Let me kiss you. Let me love you. Let me show you how much a man can adore and worship a woman."

Her heart was beating fast. She was terrified, but when she looked at Otto, she didn't see the Cossack's face. For a moment, she felt a pang of guilt over Taavi. "I don't know, Otto. I am still married."

"Yes, but you can't talk to your husband the way we talk to each other. He can't help you. I can."

Michal felt slightly dizzy. She couldn't believe her own needs. She wanted Otto to kiss her. She was willing to try with him. In fact, she actually wanted to go to his bed, even if it was a sin. It felt natural and it had been so long since she'd felt comfortable in her own skin as a woman. "Yes," she whispered, clearing her throat. "Yes, let's try."

He took her hand. Silently, they walked back to his flat. His sister, Bridget, and Alina had become very close. Alina was the sister Bridget had always longed for, and she loved the way Alina emulated her. When Otto and Michal were out, Bridget allowed Alina to play dress up with her clothes and even try the lipstick that she'd stolen from the general store. They baked cookies that were terrible because they never had enough sugar to make them properly. Then Bridget would lay out the good china that her parents had left to her and Otto. Bridget would boil water and she and Alina would have tea parties. Alina spoke well enough to say things that made Bridget laugh. And Bridget loved reading to her. When Otto and Michal walked in, they saw that the two girls had fallen asleep together on the sofa. Otto raised his finger to his lips. "Shhh…" he whispered, leading Michal to his room.

She was trembling so hard that for a moment he just held her in his arms. Michal pushed all thoughts of guilt and fear from her mind. Instead, she laid her head on Otto's shoulder. He kissed the top of her hair and whispered, "It will be alright."

Slowly, very slowly. Gently, very gently. He raised her face to meet his and kissed her lips. His hand tenderly caressed her body, and then finally with his gentle heart, he loved her back into the world of the living.

CHAPTER 31

November 10th, 1923

Michal raced past the tree-lined houses until she arrived at the small café where Otto waited for her. His thick dark hair hung in a heavy wave over his eye as he sat sipping his coffee. When he saw her, he lifted his head and a smile warmed his face. She felt the warmth caress her like a blanket on a winter night. She sat down across from him and rubbed her hands together to combat the chill that had set in outside. He took her hands in his and then brought them to his lips, blowing on them and rubbing them.

"Your hands are freezing." He gently turned her hands over and kissed the palms.

"I know … It's getting cold; the winter is coming."

"Where are the children?" Otto asked.

"Would you believe that Gerta insisted on watching them so that I could meet you? You see, not all employers are bad," she said.

"Not all, just most."

She shook her head "You're incorrigible."

"Am I?"

"Mmhmm."

He laughed.

"What are you reading?" she asked.

"Oh, I was reading the newspaper while I waited for you."

"Anything interesting?" She picked up the newspaper. On the cover was a group of men wearing brown uniforms with red armbands with strange black spider-like insignias on the bands.

"You see that silly looking little fellow in the middle of the group? The one with the comical mustache?"

"Yes ... I see him."

"His name is Adolf Hitler. For the last two days, he's been causing all sorts of trouble in Munich. I've been watching him for a while now. He tried to take over the government."

"Is he a communist?"

"Not at all. He's a bastard. A power hungry son of a bitch. Besides all that, he hates Jews, blames the Jews for everything that's wrong with Germany. It's a good thing that they threw him in jail or he might have come to Berlin, and who knows what he and his cronies would do? There would be fights in the streets, that's for sure."

"Do you think these people are anything to worry about?"

"No, they have the leader under control. The government will toss him in jail for a while; by the time he gets out, everyone will have forgotten him. Nothing to worry about, my love."

"Are you sure?"

"Of course." He smiled. "By the way, the cold air suits you. It makes your cheeks a lovely shade of pink. You are far too fetching today to worry about anything."

"I do worry, Otto. It's hard not to worry. I have a child and the economy is so bad."

"Yes, but you have a wonderful employer. Remember?"

"Yes, she is a wonderful person. Even if she is rich. And I know how you hate the rich."

"I only hate the businesspeople who take advantage of the workers."

"Yes, Otto. But Gerta doesn't take advantage of anyone. I work for her and she treats me very well."

"Yes, of course she does. But her husband, now he owns a factory and he treats his employees like they aren't even human. I know you don't want to blame her for this, but where do you think all the money she has is coming from?"

"I don't want to think about it, Otto. I can't change things. I'm happy that Gerta is taking care of my daughter and me. It's nice of her to allow my child to live with me in her house. I'm grateful to her. But I do have worries. It's a long time away, but I don't know how I will ever have enough money to provide a decent dowry for my daughter. I save every penny, but every day our money is worth less and less."

"There will be a change, my love, but it will be a good change. When the communists take over, there will be plenty for everyone. The rich will be forced to share what they have."

"Otto, I don't know. I went through this in Russia. I'm not sure what happened after the communists came in, but while the White Army was leaving, it was terrible for the Jews. You

183

don't understand because you aren't Jewish. But it's always been this way for Jews. We have been hated throughout history. And a change of government usually means danger for us."

"Sweetheart, please, don't worry … not today. A friend of mine is reading from his new novel at the library this afternoon. I was hoping we might go … His books are very good."

"I would love to, but I have to get back to the house. I can't expect Gerta to watch my child all day while I'm out with you. She's paying me to watch my daughter. It doesn't seem fair."

"All right, then just sit with me for a few more minutes and let me look at you. That in itself is a gift."

She shook her head. "Otto, you are so silly sometimes."

"I'm not. I'm an artist and an artist can't help but be lost in your beauty."

She was flattered. How could she resist? He made her feel beautiful and it had been so many years since she'd been with a man, so many years since Taavi had said sweet words to her.

CHAPTER 32

Otto didn't want to alarm Michal, but although everyone said that the National Socialist Party had no chance of ever being elected, he was worried. Every time he read or saw something featuring the escapades of the little man with the small mustache and his cohort limping beside him, Otto felt uneasy.

CHAPTER 33

February 1924

Winter swept in with a gust of snow a week before Hanukkah that year. Gerta Fogelman bought gifts for Alina as well as her own son. Michal was so grateful for the kindness. Gerta had become a true friend. And to Gerta, Michal was the only person whom she could trust. She could not speak honestly to any of her family or friends. Gerta had begun to express great concern to Michal over Richard's constant disappearances.

At night, when Richard was in town, Michal would hear Gerta and Richard fighting as she lay in bed. She knew that Gerta was still in love with Richard and she felt sorry for her friend.

Then the inevitable came. Richard wanted a divorce. It happened on a brisk morning in February. Michal was upstairs dressing the children for breakfast when she heard the door slam. The noise was loud enough to startle Alina and she began to cry. Michal picked her up and held her.

"Baby," Sammie said.

"That's not nice," Michal said.

Alina stuck her tongue out at Sammie.

Just then, Gerta came upstairs, her face red with tears.

"I need to talk to you," Gerta said to Michal.

"You two, go into Sammie's room and play. We'll go downstairs for breakfast in a few minutes," Michal said.

"But I'm hungry," Sammie said.

"Please? Just this once, Sammie. Take Alina into your room and play for a few minutes. Do it for me?" Michal said.

Sammie's shoulders slumped "Come on, Alina," he said and took her hand.

Once the children were in Sammie's room and the door was closed, Gerta sat down on Michal's bed.

"Richard wants a divorce. He has another woman. They've been seeing each other for over a year and he wants to marry her." Gerta was sobbing as she spoke. She wiped her nose with the back of her hand and continued. "My heart is broken. I'm going home to my family in Frankfurt. He says I can keep the house. But I can't stay here. The whole town will be talking about it and everyone will stare at me wherever I go. They'll know that my husband left me and they will think it's because I'm not good enough. They'll think I'm pathetic."

"You are good enough. It isn't you. It's him. You are a beautiful woman, smart...."

"I am not. I'm a failure."

"But--"

"Please, no more. I don't want to discuss this any further; I am leaving Berlin."

"Gerta, are you sure you want to do this? What about Sammie? He has friends here. He's starting school."

"I have to go home; I'm sorry, Michal. I don't know where you're going to go. I can give you a little money. I don't have much. Most of everything I have belongs to Richard. But, I've put a little away, and I'll give you what I can."

"Of course. I wasn't even thinking about Alina and me. But, I understand," Michal said. She knew that Richard gave Gerta an allowance every week for her frivolities, her clothing, gifts, and any other trinkets she might desire. He kept control of all of the real money, and he paid all of the bills. Michal's heart sank. She realized that she was in trouble. Where was she to go now? What was she to do? "I will need to make some arrangements for Alina and me. How soon are you going home?"

"I want to leave next week."

Michal sighed. She would have to talk to Otto on Sunday and see if she and Alina could stay with him until she was able to find another job. She would miss Gerta and Sammie. Michal was ashamed to admit it, even to herself, but she would miss the lovely home, the good quality food, and Gerta's endless generosity. Even if all of it was actually from Richard.

Otto arrived on time on Sunday evening. He brought two red roses tied with a black velvet ribbon and handed them to Michal. She excused herself, took them to her room, and put them in a vase with water. Then she and Otto went about their regular routine. All week, Michal had been fretting about discussing what had happened between Richard and Gerta with Otto. She was afraid that moving in with Otto would put a strain on their relationship. She had no doubt he would take them in, but she wondered if it would be out of obligation. However, right now, her only other option was to search for Taavi. She could ask him for financial help to raise his daughter.

He should be helping her, but her feelings towards Taavi were so confused that she just couldn't face him right now.

"I have something to talk to you about," Michal said, as she sipped a cup of turnip coffee and looked out the window of the cafe at the snow dusted sidewalk.

"Of course, love, you can talk to me about anything."

She cleared her throat. "Richard is divorcing Gerta and she is going home to Frankfurt, leaving Berlin. I am losing my job and until I can find another one, Alina and I have no place to go. Worse yet, I don't know who is going to hire me as a live in nanny when I have to bring my daughter with me."

He was silent.

"I'm sorry. I didn't mean to throw this problem into your lap. It's not your concern at all."

"Of course it's my concern. I was just sorting it all out, that's all. You and Alina will move into my flat. You'll both share my sister's room."

"Otto…"

"Don't look so troubled. It will be fine. And … late at night when both of the girls are asleep … if you would like … you can sneak into my room and I will tell you bedtime stories."

"Oh, Otto…" she had hoped he would say yes, and he had come through. "I will try to find employment as quickly as possible. I know that it will be crowded.…"

"Nonsense. I'm actually looking forward to having you around all the time."

He was a tender lover, a romantic, with the gentleness of Avram and the passion of Taavi, but there was something about him that neither of the other two had possessed. He was an experienced lover. Michal had no doubt that many women had been to his bed. But he had given her a great gift, gently, carefully, with loving hands, he taught her body to feel again, and to feel more than she'd ever thought possible.

The landlord in the building where Otto lived was not generous with the heat, and that winter was exceptionally cold. Once the pipes froze and there was no running water for several days. But Otto never let anything upset him. And for Michal, the joy she felt in Otto's arms made up for all of the comforts that she'd once had at the Fogelman house and had now given up.

Before Michal and Gerta Fogelman parted, Gerta gave Michal several of her old dresses. To Michal, they were lovely, like new. Although she never had the occasion to wear them, she cherished them.

One night, Otto bought a candle on the black market. He insisted that Michal dress up in one of Gerta's old gowns that she kept in her closet. He too dressed in a suit and then he lit the candle and sang to her as they waltzed in the small living room. Both of the girls watched them dance. Otto was a wonderful dancer, and he looked breathtakingly handsome in his suit. His voice, a tenor, was clear and he carried a tune well. In fact, with just a candle, Otto had transformed the dim and dull apartment into a ballroom. There was some special spark that lived deep in the core of him that dreams were built upon.

Bridget and Alina were like sisters. Alina missed Sammie. She asked for him several times, and every time Michal had to explain that he went to live far away with his grandparents. Alina wanted to know where her grandparents were. Michal tried to explain that she thought they might be in Heaven. Alina wanted to know where that was. She was at that age where she was constantly asking why. Michal thanked God for Bridget, who had the patience to answer Alina for hours at a time. Food was not nearly as plentiful as it had been at the Fogelman's, and the quality was certainly not as good. But, they enjoyed what they had and at night, every night, before bed, Otto told one of his stories. The girls sat quietly, spellbound, listening to his mesmerizing voice, watching the deep expression in his eyes, and losing themselves in the song of his words. Michal knew that beneath the surface, all of Otto's stories held fast to his communist leanings. She understood his feelings about the rich and poor, but she didn't care enough to be politically active. Michal was happy in the simple joy of loving and being loved, and of having a home where her child was safe and wanted. To Michal, these were the things that mattered in life.

On two occasions, Otto brought Michal along with him to the Communist Party meetings that he attended, but they made her nervous. The members were passionate, their voices were loud, and the whole meeting felt like a bomb ready to explode. She didn't want to think about all of the political unrest in Germany. And since Otto could see that the meetings distressed Michal, he stopped asking her to accompany him.

But Otto had friends everywhere, actors, painters, musicians, writers, and playwrights. He was well known and well liked in all of the artistic circles. They attended theatrical openings, art exhibits, and concerts. Otto took Michal to groundbreaking releases at the cinema. She loved the enormous screen and the beautiful movie stars. Michal had never experienced anything like this before and through Otto, she learned that she loved the arts.

CHAPTER 34

Spring 1924

The weather was breaking. The bitter cold of the winter months was finally loosening her grip on Germany. Otto had begun asking Michal to seek out a meeting with Taavi and ask him for a divorce. He wanted to marry her, he said. Otto explained that he'd never wanted a family before, but he wanted one now. She avoided the subject as much as possible. There was no telling how Taavi would react. It had been such a long time since she'd last seen him. Taavi might be angry; he would definitely ask a million questions, and worst of all, she would have to look into his eyes and know that she'd sinned with another man while she was still Taavi's wife. The idea of a meeting made her anxious; she was still not sure what she felt for Taavi. He had hurt her, but he had also rescued her. If she saw him, she wasn't sure what she would say or how she would feel. So every time Otto brought it up, she avoided discussing the subject.

Otto was a passionate man, filled with grand ideas. He loved to talk, to tell Michal how the world would be once the communists took over. She smiled and listened. One afternoon, Bridget had taken Alina to the park. Otto was sitting in his room writing a story when there was a knock at the door. Michal answered to find Ivan, one of Otto's friends, and a wild Russian painter waiting on the other side.

"Is Otto at home?"

"He's here, but he's working."

Otto came out of his room, his hair disheveled. Michal smiled when she saw him; she was still struck by how handsome he was.

"Sit, please, sit," Otto said to his friend.

"I came to tell you that there is to be a demonstration tonight. I trust you will be there?"

"When and where?"

"We will meet at the club and then we plan to walk down Alexanderplatz. I expect there will be some trouble with the National Socialists. But at least we will make some noise."

"I'd rather you didn't go..." Michal said. "You might get hurt and there's no reason that you need to be there."

"I need to support what I believe in."

"You're such an idealist. Be happy we can live here in Berlin in peace. I know what it is to be hunted by a government. It was that way in Russia. We never knew if tomorrow would bring a pogrom on our entire village that would leave people dead and houses burnt to the ground."

"But, don't you see? How can you not see? The rich have everything. If we don't bring them down, they will starve us all to death."

"It's true we don't have the kind of luxuries I had when I worked for the Fogelman's, but we have plenty. We don't go to bed hungry and we have a roof over our heads. Most of all, we are safe. You are safe to write what you please, to say what you want. Believe me, Otto, it is good here in Berlin."

"Do we have plenty, Michal? Food is becoming scarcer every day. We are struggling to survive. Yesterday you stood in line for four hours just to buy a pair of shoes that are too big for either of the girls. And, you were lucky to be able to buy any shoes at all. Our money is worth less and less every day. Don't you see? Something has to be done, and soon. I must do what I believe is right."

"The girls will grow into the shoes."

"Is that your only answer? Look at them, look at the girls ... their clothes are ragged, their shoes have holes, our food is not healthy food. My friends are rummaging through the garbage trying to find bits and pieces that they can eat to survive another day. I refuse to do that. I'd rather starve."

"You are a fool. Is it better to be dead? Is it better for the police or some other political group to shoot you dead on the street? Is that better, Otto?" She glared at him, then she turned her deadly gaze on Ivan. "And you too are a fool." Michal got up and walked out of the living room and into the children's room. She locked the door behind her.

That night, Otto went to the demonstration. He returned several hours later, a little beaten up, but exhilarated. Michal was asleep in bed with the girls. Otto tiptoed into the room and gently nudged her shoulder. She awoke and saw him. In the dark, she could not see the dried blood around his nostrils.

Michal got out of bed and went into the kitchen. She put a pot of water on the stove to boil for tea. Still she had not looked at Otto or spoken to him.

"Michal, please don't be angry. Try to understand me…"

When she turned to tell him how angry she was, she saw the blood on his face and the beginning of bruising around one of his eyes. Her shoulders slumped and her anger faded to concern. "Oh, Otto, don't you understand? I care about you. I don't want to see you hurt or, God forbid, killed."

"Just hearing you say that made it worth my while to get hurt." He smiled.

"Stop playing. To you, all of life is a game. It's not a game, Otto. What you are doing is dangerous. Very dangerous. I saw someone I cared about killed right in front of me. I don't want to go through that again."

"I know. I'm sorry that I caused you so much distress. Forgive me?" His eyes were so soft and he spoke so tenderly that she could not help but forgive him.

Michal shook her head and turned on the water. At least it was getting warm, but that was because the winter was over. She dipped a rag in the warm water and began to clean the blood from his handsome face. He touched her hand with his slender almost delicate fingers, and she felt a pain in her heart. How unlike Taavi he was. Taavi was a mountain of a man, a man other men would be afraid to challenge. If Otto were forced to defend himself physically, he would easily be killed. His strength came from the beauty of his soul and the brilliance of his mind. Otto was a poet, a writer, a dreamer, but not a fighter. She feared for him.

CHAPTER 35

June, 1925

Michal had found a part-time job working at the hospital as an aide. It was not an easy job, cleaning bedpans and changing sheets that had been splattered with blood, urine, or feces. Many times she gagged uncontrollably, but still she continued to work. Alina was only five years old, and she must be fed and cared for. Michal had no real skills. When she'd gone to the hospital to apply for work, she'd told the woman she'd met with in personnel of her experience with Bepa. The woman had listened, but it was obvious that she didn't acknowledge Michal's past work as a midwife as qualifying her for any real medical position. But the woman had felt sorry for Michal; she had looked at her well-worn clothes and knew how badly Michal was in need of work.

"I'm afraid I can't offer you a job as a midwife or a nurse," she said, tapping her pencil. "I wish I was able to help you, but, quite frankly, you aren't qualified."

Michal felt the tears well up in her eyes, but she looked away and nodded her head. "Thank you anyway; thank you for interviewing me," she said and got up to leave.

"Wait. I know it's not much of a job. But if you want to work, I can offer you a position as a part-time aide. It's not easy work. You will be under the command of all of the nurses on the floor.

You will be there to help them with whatever they need. However, if you want the job, it's yours."

Michal didn't hesitate. "Yes, yes, I want it. Thank you so much."

The nurses were demanding and demeaning towards Michal and many times when they were exceptionally humiliating, she ran to the bathroom and locked herself in a stall where she leaned against the wall and cried until she had no tears left. Then she washed her face, took a deep breath, and went back to the nurses' station. Instead of showing the nurses that she was hurt, Michal picked up right where she'd left off.

Michal didn't earn much money, but combined with Otto's book sales, they were surviving, but just barely. The couple had already gone through all of the money that Bepa had given Michal, and there was nothing left to fall back on. But Otto didn't seem to notice. He'd spent fifty marks on a tube of crimson lipstick for Michal, just because he said it would look lovely on her. She had wanted to scream when he gave her the gift. In fact, she wanted to tell him to get his head out of the clouds, but she couldn't. He'd meant so well. He'd wanted to make her happy, even if it took food out of their mouths. What Michal had originally found deliciously attractive in Otto was turning sour. Life was hard and it seemed to her that she was the one carrying the burden. One afternoon when Bridget and Alina were at school, Michal took the dresses Gerta had given her to a resale shop. If Otto knew she was selling her dresses, he would have been distraught. More than once he'd made it clear that, to him, luxuries came before necessities. Even with the little that they had, he'd brought her roses once. It was a sweet gesture, but the money would have been better spent on food. Michal had a hard time understanding him because he was such a contradiction. On one hand, he was passionately

197

spouting the rhetoric of communism. Otto made speeches to the family about how the world was going to become equal. There would be no rich or poor; everyone would have to relinquish their material goods and share the world's wealth. He was fervent about his hatred for the rich, and yet in everything he did, he fashioned his life like a man who had more than enough money and loved the things that money could buy.

When Otto was getting ready to go to one of his communist meetings, he spent hours getting ready. His hair was carefully disheveled, as was his clothing. He made the perfect picture of the handsome, charming, Revolutionary. And it made Michal sick to her stomach to watch the hypocrisy. But when he made love to her, she forgot all of his faults. He was romantic and experienced in love, and he'd changed her feelings about sex completely.

The resale store had a strong odor of perfume that covered a stench of old unclean clothes. A shrewd looking woman, thin with bony fingers and silver white hair pulled into a tight bun, sat at a counter.

"I'd like to sell these dresses," Michal said.

"Not good quality," the woman said, trying to hide the true worth of the garments, but her face betrayed her.

Michal knew better. She was well aware of the high quality of the material and the beading on the gowns "You're wrong. They are excellent quality."

"Hmmm," the woman said, running her hands over the fabric. "I will give you one-hundred marks for all of them. That's a good price. More than I usually pay for anything."

"A hundred marks for all of them? They are worth ten times that, if not more."

"Too bad for you. A hundred marks, take it or leave it. I don't care. I can't sell them for very much in this economy … and if I can't make money, then what do I need them for? Eh?"

Michal sighed. A hundred marks. Not much. But, the rent was due, and they needed food. Otto hadn't earned much this month. She had no other choice. Michal nodded.

"All right. One hundred marks."

Michal tucked the money into her handbag and noticed that the stitching was unraveling. Then she began walking back home. It was a beautiful day. Little buds had begun forming on the trees and the beautiful birds that Berlin was known for were singing in glorious harmony. A butterfly soared in front of her. It was a magnificent monarch. Michal marveled at its exquisiteness. She longed to buy a cup of tea and sit in the park for a while, but she dared not spend the money, and she didn't have time. She had to hurry home to get ready for work.

When she got back to the apartment, she went upstairs and paid the landlord the rent that was due. Then she went into her apartment. It was very quiet, so she assumed that Otto was working on a new book. She put up a pot of water to boil for coffee and quietly knocked on his door to see if he wanted a cup. He didn't answer, but she heard voices on the other side of the door.

"Otto? Are you alright?"

"Yes, I'm fine," he said. "But don't come in."

"Why? What's going on?" Without thinking, she opened the door.

Then she knew why he'd not wanted her to enter. Otto was in bed with another man. A man as handsome as himself. A man Michal recognized from one of the theatrical productions they'd seen. Both Otto and the actor were naked. Michal was confused, hurt, and betrayed. She slammed the door to the room and leaned her head against the wall, trying to catch her breath … trying to take in what she'd just seen and make sense of it. If Otto was a homosexual, how could he have been such a wonderful lover to her? And, if he cared for her, how could he be unfaithful?

All she could think of was getting away … taking Alina and leaving. The thought of looking at Otto sickened her right now. Michal began packing her things and Alina's. She was tossing them into her old suitcase. There was not much to pack. The shelter was the only place to go. If she had not just paid the landlord, she'd have a little more money to find a place to stay. But she knew it was pointless to explain anything to her landlord. He wouldn't refund anything. The money was gone.

The door to the apartment slammed. The man Otto had been in bed with left and Otto came into the bedroom where Michal was packing.

"I'm so sorry," he said. "I never meant to hurt you. It was the last thing in the world I ever wanted to do."

"I don't understand any of this," she said, still not looking at him. "But I am taking Alina and leaving."

"But, I love you."

"YOU love me? You love me? What you did in there with that man tells me that you don't love me."

"It's not all black and white, Michal. Life is not all black and white; that's only the way that you see it. Life is shades of gray, some darker some lighter. I can't help myself. It doesn't mean I don't love you."

"Go to hell with your poetic philosophy. I am sick and tired of you. I am working myself to death while you are living in a fantasy world. And now this … I can't understand this at all."

"I love you. I've always loved you. But Eric and I share something that you can't understand … something I need, like food or water. Just because I can fuck Eric doesn't mean I love him."

"Please, don't say another word. And don't use that vulgar language with me. I am a good girl, a religious woman from a fine family. I know I have sinned, and I have fallen. My relationship with you should not ever have happened. Taavi and I are still married. What I did with you is a terrible sin, and perhaps that's why all of this is happening to me." Her whole body was shaking. "Leaving my country and coming here to Berlin was a mistake. I can see that now. Somehow, because everyone around me has no morals, I began to think that it was all right to do whatever I wanted. I allowed Berlin to change me. The innocent girl who married Avram in Siberia no longer exists. Berlin, you, the madness surrounding all of us, has jaded my views. I've lost sight of right and wrong." She was tossing the last piece of Alina's clothing into the suitcase. "Otto, I don't know who you are, I don't understand you, and I don't care to try anymore. I am done with you. Done, do you hear me? Done."

She picked up the suitcase and walked out the front door, leaving it open. Tears spilled down her cheeks. Otto didn't follow her.

Michal stood outside the school waiting for Alina. The black suitcase sat on the ground beside her on the white concrete sidewalk. With the sleeve of her blouse, Michal wiped the tears from her face. She didn't want Alina to see she'd been crying.

As she did every day since Alina and Michal had moved in, Bridget walked two blocks from her own school to meet with Alina and walk her home safely. The two girls came strolling by, holding hands.

"Michal. What are you doing here?" Bridget said.

"Bridget … go home. I'm sorry. Alina and I are going to have to go away."

"What? Why? Did I do something wrong? What happened?"

"We just have to go; that's all. It's nothing you did."

"Where are you going?"

"We're going to go to the shelter for a while."

"The shelter? That's terrible. Why, why don't you just come home? Did Otto say something?"

"I'm sorry, Bridget. I really am. I can't explain. I know it's upsetting, but we have to go."

Bridget was crying. Alina felt the angst and began to cry and grip Bridget's hand.

"I'm really sorry," Michal said, and she was sorry for Bridget. The two girls had become so close and now they were going to be separated. "You can come and see Alina at the shelter if you would like. It's on Weisenstrasse."

"I know the place. I've seen it. It's horrible. Please, Michal, don't take Alina there."

"There are things I can't explain to you, Bridget. I am sorry; I wish I could. Go home. Please."

Then Michal took Alina's hand and led her away. Alina turned around and stopped. Michal lifted her daughter into her arms and, as she did, she saw Bridget still standing a few feet away waving with tears streaming down her face.

CHAPTER 36

The conditions at the shelter seemed to be worse than Michal remembered. It was filled with degenerate men and women who shuffled around with the look of lost souls in their empty eyes. The rooms were cramped and smelled of too many unwashed bodies.

Michal checked in and was given a single bed to share with Alina. A woman at the desk filled out papers for her and informed her that she could stay in the shelter for two weeks, but then she must find another place to live. That night, Alina fell into the deep sleep of a child with her head on her mother's bosom. But Michal couldn't sleep; she was exhausted, but if she drifted off, Michal was sure that their suitcase would be stolen. The people in the shelter were poor and desperate looking for anything they could use or sell. Michal insisted that Alina keep her shoes on while she slept. She complained a little about being uncomfortable, but Michal insisted that they were on an adventure. "Look, Mommy is going to keep her shoes on too. It will be a special night," Michal said, and her words seemed to appease Alina, at least for the moment.

What was left of the money that she'd gotten for her dresses Michal had tucked deeply into her bra. There wasn't much, but it was all she had, and she knew she'd need every cent.

Morning came, and Michal was worn out. But she dressed Alina and, carrying the suitcase containing all of their belongings, she walked her daughter to school.

After she dropped Alina off, Michal went to work. She had a locker in the staff changing room where she could lock up her suitcase. Her things would be safe if she left them there for the next two weeks, when she would receive her paycheck. Once she got her check, she would be able to find a small apartment. The work schedule for the coming two weeks was posted on the wall as it was every Monday. She read her hours over twice. When Michal had lived with Otto and Bridget, she was available to work any hours. But now, she couldn't leave Alina alone in the shelter, so she had to work when Alina was at school. She had been working days for over a month and had no reason to believe that her hours would change, but as she read the schedule, her heart sank. She was expected to work the midnight shift. How could she leave her daughter alone in the shelter all night? Anything could happen. Anything at all. Michal couldn't trust anyone she'd met in that shelter. Not even the woman at the desk, who had far too much on her mind to be bothered watching Michal's child. Alina was a five-year-old girl. Children were being sold into prostitution every day. That meant that Alina would be worth money to someone. Very dangerous, very frightening. Michal's mind was racing; she had to think. If she asked Bridget, she knew that Bridget would be more than happy to watch Alina. But she couldn't expect Bridget to come to the shelter and stay with Alina, and she wouldn't take Alina to the apartment, because the idea of seeing Otto repelled her.

There was nothing to do except talk with her boss and ask if she could please put her on days. Michal planned to beg for mercy and understanding. What else could she do? She took a deep breath and knocked on the door of the head nurse's office.

"Yes, Michal?"

"I have a problem…" Michal explained her situation.

The head nurse continued doing her paperwork while Michal was talking.

"There are plenty of people looking for jobs who would be willing to work any hours just to have an income. I am too busy taking care of more important matters to spend my time worrying about whether we will have an aid on the floor or not. If you can't be reliable, then I am going to have to let you go."

"Please, I need this job." Michal felt her eyes sting with tears.

"I understand, but the good of the hospital has to come first. You are the newest hire; therefore, when nobody wants to work midnights, you are the one who is scheduled to work them. If you can't do it, I am forced to find someone who can." When it came right down to it, right now, Michal was not able to work nights. At least not until she found someone who she could trust to watch her child.

"I'm terribly sorry," the head nurse said.

Michal left the office and leaned against the wall. She sank down until she was practically on her knees and began praying.

Two orderlies walked by and stared at her. "Are you all right, miss?" one of them asked.

"Yes, yes, I'm fine." Michal stood up and walked back to get her things from the locker. Then, with suitcase in hand, she left the building.

Now Michal was out of work. There would be no income at all. She walked back to the shelter to wait until it was time for Alina to be released from school. Then she would walk to the school and meet her. For the next two weeks, they would have food and a place to sleep, even if it was horrible. But then what? For her daughter's sake, Michal would have to crawl on her knees and go back to the apartment she shared with Otto. After all, she'd paid the rent. She was entitled to stay. If she could find work, she might never have to go back. And she had two weeks to try her hardest.

Every day, Michal walked Alina to school, then went into every restaurant, hotel, and factory she could find looking for work. Everywhere she went, she carried the suitcase. And everyone she met with said that there were no jobs available.

Three days passed before Michal saw a familiar face. It was Yana, the girl she'd met at the shelter when she and Taavi had first arrived in Berlin.

"You look so familiar to me," Yana said.

"Yes, I remember you. We met several years ago when I first came to Germany from Russia."

"Oh yes … you're the one with the handsome husband. So, where is he?"

"We are not together."

"I'm sorry to hear that. But, take it from me, men aren't worth troubling yourself over." Yana flipped her hand.

"You're not married?"

"No, and I have no plans of ever getting married."

"Do you know of any work? Anyone who might be hiring? I need a job. I have a child. She's in school right now. But..." Michal asked.

"Well, I've been working the docks. It's easy money as long as you don't think too hard about it. I go from shelter to shelter. When my time runs out at this one, I go to another one. Winters are rough, but it's June and summer is on its way. Things are much easier in the summer."

"You mean you work as a prostitute?"

"Don't make it sound so terrible. Everyone is doing it. Even the snobby housewives who just want a little extra money. To be quite honest with you, it's a hell of a lot easier than being married. At least when they're done doing their business, they pay you and go away. There's something to be said for that."

"I could never. I'm sorry. I don't mean to judge you, but it's not something I could ever do."

Yana laughed. "We all say that at first. Then, when there is no money and you are sent out of the shelter..."

"No, not that ... not me ... I can't, I couldn't."

Every day when Michal dropped Alina off at school, she walked from business to business, only to hear the same answer. "No." The desperation was swallowing her up and she was drowning in an ocean of misery. She begged every one of the company owners for any kind of work; she offered to wash floors, to clean bathrooms, to do anything to earn money, anything but sell her body.

Before Michal realized it, a week had passed. Her heart beat with panic and she was beginning to find it hard to catch her breath. Only seven more days here and she and Alina would have to go to another shelter. Then there was no guarantee that there would be space available. Or, if not a shelter, then the inevitable slap in the face, she would have to go back to Otto. As Michal waited outside the school for Alina, Bridget came around the corner.

"I knew you'd be here," Bridget said.

"I'm here to pick up Alina."

"Yes, I know. I came here to find you. I thought you might want to know that my brother is very sick. He has a bad infection; he needs a doctor, but we can't afford one. Otto is burning up with fever; he's delirious. This morning before I left for school, I went in to check on him and he didn't even know me. My teacher at school thinks it's probably influenza. I'm terribly afraid he might die, Michal."

Michal felt her heart crumble into small pieces and bleed out. Otto had hurt her deeply and, in many ways, she hated him. But she still loved him too. And thinking of him sick, very sick, was distressing. A tenderness came over her. Could he have stopped whatever it was inside of him that drove him to do what he did? Had she not suspected it all along? Not even just a little? She'd been confused because he'd made love to her as if he adored her and it brought her body and soul back to life. For that, she had to be grateful to him, and somehow she knew that in his own way, he really did love her. But, all along, he'd needed something more, something she just was not able to give him.

"I want to see him. As soon as Alina comes out, we will all go to the apartment."

"I knew you would help me. I knew you would know what to do; that's why I came to find you. Thank God you're willing to come and see him."

CHAPTER 37

Otto lay on the bed, his body cold, but covered in a film of sweat that had completely drenched his hair. His eyes were open but unseeing and his skin was the light gray color of the sky as a storm had begun to lift.

"It's me, Otto, Michal…"

He didn't respond. "How long has he been like this?" she asked Bridget.

"Two days. He went to bed the night before last complaining of a terrible headache and stomach cramps. When I got home from school the following day he was in bed, but he could talk to me. Then this morning, he was like this."

"Go and find the doctor. Tell him to come right away."

"But we have no money to pay him. My brother hasn't earned much this month and what we had we spent on food."

"I have some money. Go Bridget … get the doctor."

CHAPTER 38

Otto died without ever awakening. In fact, he was already dead when the doctor arrived. Still, the physician insisted on payment and since he'd made the house call he was entitled to it. Michal was too drained and shocked by Otto's death to argue. And even though it was the last of the money that she had, she paid the doctor. After the doctor left, Michal was alone with Otto's body. He didn't look the same. Without the strong energetic life force he'd always had, he seemed small and pitiful. Looking at him lying there covered to his chin with a sheet, his eyes closed forever, his smile gone forever, Michal forgave him. Then she leaned her head on his chest and wept softly. In a whisper that only she could hear, she spoke to him.

"Otto. If you can hear me, I want you to know that I understand. You never meant to hurt me. In your own way, in the only way that you could, you loved me … And, I loved you in my own way too. Goodbye, Otto, my dear friend, my Otto."

There would be no funeral. Only a pauper's grave. Bridget was sitting on the sofa crying softly. Alina was cuddled into Bridget's arms.

Inside her heart, Michal was distraught. But she knew she must appear strong for the sake of the girls. She wanted to keep Bridget with her, but she could hardly afford to take care of Alina.

"Bridget, do you have any family that you can live with?"

"Yes, I have an aunt and uncle in Nuremburg. It's my father's sister and her husband. They hated Otto because my uncle is very involved with the National Socialist party. My uncle knew that my brother was a communist and whenever they saw each other they would argue. But they don't hate me. Many times they have asked me to leave Otto and come and live with them. They thought my brother was a bad influence," she said. "But I loved my brother. He had faults, lots of them … but he was a good person too. After our parents died, all we had was each other. As long as Otto was alive, I couldn't leave him; he was my brother."

"I know … I understand. I do. Let's send a wire to your aunt and uncle and see what they say. The rent is paid on this apartment until the end of the month, so we have a little time to wait for their answer."

"Do you have any money to send a wire?"

"I'll get it. You wait here with Alina. I'll be back later tonight."

Michal went to the shelter and found Yana sitting on a cot near the window.

"I got a bed in a good location this time," Yana said with a smile. "Where's your kid?"

"My daughter is with a friend." Michal smiled. "I need to ask you for a very big favor. I won't blame you if you say no, but frankly, I am frantic. A friend of mine passed away. I need to send a wire to his family and I don't have the money to send it. If you loan me the money, I swear to you on my life I will get it back to you as soon as I can find work."

Yana shook her head. "I don't usually lend money. It's not easy to come by ... but I feel sorry for you. So ... a few marks? What's a few marks?"

"You'll do it?" Michal was on edge waiting for Yana's answer. Her only other option was to do what Yana did to earn some cash.

"Yes, here ... take this." Yana handed her a couple of marks "It should be enough."

"Thank you, thank you so much, Yana. God bless you ... God bless you for helping me. I will get this money back to you; I swear it."

"Yes, well, I won't count on it. But still, you would make a lousy prostitute, so what other choice do I have? Go now," she said with a wry smile.

They sent the wire and waited. Meanwhile, Alina had begun scratching her body and crying. Michal lifted her shirt to see that angry red bumps had swelled on Alina's skin and tiny little mites were running across her midsection.

"Oh, dear God," Michal said, as she looked at the infestation.

"What is it?" Bridget asked.

"I'm not sure. But there are bugs all over her. I'm going to take her to the pharmacy and ask the pharmacist what this is. I can't afford to have the doctor come back. We don't have any money. I'm not even sure how I am ever going to get the medicine to help Alina. All I can do is beg the pharmacist to help us and pray he will take pity on my child."

"Body lice," the pharmacist said, after he lifted Alina's shirt and studied the rash.

"What is that? How can we get rid of it?" Michal asked, close to hysteria.

"It comes from other people who have it and also from poor hygiene. Did she sleep on dirty sheets where someone who might have had this could have slept?"

The shelter, Michal thought, but why my daughter, why not me? I slept there too. Maybe she got it at school? "Yes, she might have. What can I do to help her? Is there a medicine? Is it expensive? I don't have any money."

The pharmacist was an elderly man with thinning gray hair and blue eyes that still danced like the eyes of a much younger man. He stretched as if his back was stiff, then smiled at Michal.

"You don't need any medication. Just give her a very warm bath. Let her soak. Boil the sheets where she has been sleeping. Get rid of her pillows. Make sure you clean all of her clothes in the same way. Now, don't be alarmed, just be aware. I want you to watch her for any signs of infection. Body lice can cause serious diseases, so although I think she'll be fine, keep an eye on her. Try to keep her from scratching, because if she causes open sores on her skin, that will make her more prone to infection. If she seems to be getting lethargic or starts running a fever, come back here and see me. Do you understand all of my instructions?"

Michal nodded. "Thank you. I'll do as you say."

"Here ... take this." The pharmacist handed her a bar of laundry soap. "I don't often give this away, soap is expensive, but you should wash her with it every day. Besides, you're such a pretty young thing that I want to see you smile."

She smiled at him. "Really, thank you."

"Remember, keep an eye on her. It's very important. Sometimes body lice can cause tuberculosis. So, please don't take it lightly."

Tuberculosis. My God, please, not this,…Michal thought. But she nodded to the pharmacist and thanked him again. Then she rushed home with Alina and began to boil water.

It was a lot of work to make sure everything was boiled and cleaned, but it took her mind off of Otto. She was consumed with making sure she'd not left any eggs or insects. Because if even one was left alive, this entire process would have to be done all over again. And, in between boiling and bathing, she continued to watch Alina for any problems that might arise.

Michal scrubbed her child with the laundry soap until Alina's skin turned red. There was no trace of the insects after Alina's bath, but she was still scratching the red angry bumps. Michal put mittens on her hands and bound them with tape to stop her from attacking the sores. Alina wailed at not being able to scratch the constant irritating itch. Helpless, Michal sat by her daughter's bedside and finally Alina cried herself to sleep. Bridget, too, had finally fallen asleep. The apartment was finally silent. Michal walked into the dark living room and sat down in her favorite chair. Memories of Otto and the hours they'd spent here in this very room came flooding back to her. Evidence of his impeccable taste was everywhere. From the paintings he'd received as gifts from his artist friends, to the second hand furniture that he'd recovered with matching fabric. How many nights had they all sat together, she in this same chair, Bridget and Alina on the sofa, and Otto on a hardback chair in the center? They had all been enthralled as Otto told the stories he'd written. If she tried hard enough, she could still hear Otto's voice in her mind. Michal sighed. She thought of Avram, of her parents and her brother and sister, of Siberia. How simple life had been before the pogrom. She knew right from wrong, and had no doubts as to what she would be doing the next day and the day after that. Now, however, she was alone, frightened and confused. Even with all she'd seen, done, and been through, even after the sin she'd committed by falling in love with the romance of Otto and sharing his bed while she was still Taavi's wife, even after all of the changes she had gone through, she still could not bring herself to sell her body to strangers. Her precious child who slept in the room right down the hall depended upon her for food and shelter and, God forbid maybe even medical care. How could she provide all of this? Finding a job was impossible, and even if she found one, they barely paid enough to buy a few morsels of food. More importantly, she was only available to work when Alina was in school. If Bridget did not go to live with her aunt and uncle, she could watch Alina while Michal went to work. Of course, that is if she was able to find work. But, when she and Otto had lived together, he had brought home some money, not much, but some, and together they were barely scraping by. Now, she would carry the entire burden. It felt as if a boulder had fallen on her shoulders. She had only one viable option. Michal had to swallow her pride and search for Taavi, who had no idea that he had a child. She had no way of knowing if he had found someone else, or even if he'd left Berlin. All she knew was that once the rent for the month ran out, she and Alina would be homeless again. If Bridget's aunt and uncle were not willing to take her, then Bridget would have nowhere to go. Michal would never put Bridget out on the street. But, how could Michal explain Bridget to Taavi without telling him about Otto? And once she told him about Otto, would he ever forgive her? Well, for now, she would take the girls to the shelter to eat. There they could get at least one meal a day. She had another week at the apartment before they had to leave. Hopefully, she would hear from Bridget's aunt and uncle before that. Once she knew whether she was going to be responsible for Bridget or not, she could decide what her next move would be. She wasn't sure how to go about looking for work as a nanny. But, even so, if she had two children with her, it would be more difficult to find domestic employment. And even with only one, Michal was not sure that anyone would hire her as a live in maid or nanny. She'd been fortunate to find Gerta Fogelman, but how many Gerta Fogelmans were out looking for household help? Probably not many. She had just been lucky. The opportunity to work for Gerta had fallen into her lap at just the right time. But now? What now? Her back ached and felt heavy with all of the responsibility and decisions.

She thought about Siberia. Michal tried, but she realized she could no longer remember any of the faces of the people she'd known before she came to Berlin. Not clearly anyway. Not even Avram, dear tender Avram. He'd been such a sweet man, and he'd tried so hard to be a good husband. It was hard to think of the good times she'd had with him, even harder than to remember his terrible end. The beautiful moments hurt far more. She could ask Yana to lend her the money to return to Russia. Then, if by some miracle, Yana was willing to give her the money, she could take Alina to live with Bepa, but she had been so old when Michal had last seen her that Michal wondered if she was still alive. But even if she were alive, how could Michal take Alina and go back to a deserted cabin in Siberia? Her daughter had been born in Berlin, where she'd already started school. If they stayed in the city, Alina would grow up reading and writing, and she would have opportunities that Michal had never even dreamed possible as a child. Besides, how could she expect Yana to help her? Yana had enough trouble just trying to stay alive. Michal realized she was doing nothing more than weighing every possible option, and nothing seemed feasible except Taavi. It was hard for Michal to believe how much the years had changed her. Somewhere along the line, she'd shed her headscarf, her conservative clothing, her morals, and her modesty. She'd allowed a man who was not her husband to hold her and touch her in a way that was unholy for an unmarried couple. It was a sin, and yet it had saved her; it had broken the barrier that had kept her from having a healthy marriage with Taavi. Michal bit her lower lip. Now she could go back to Taavi and try again. Otto had given her that. Life was confusing.

However, until she had an answer from Bridget's family, she could not make any decisions. Bridget had always been kind to Alina. She'd been like Alina's sister. Every night, Michal watched as Bridget sat with Alina on her lap, telling the child a story and twisting Alina's dark spiral curled hair between her fingers gently. Michal could not, would not, abandon Bridget. If her aunt and uncle were not willing to take her, Michal would have to find a way to take care of all of them. And, without Taavi, there was only one way to do that … prostitution. Michal shivered.

CHAPTER 39

They did not have long to wait. A wire from Bridget's uncle came two days later. He was terribly sorry to learn of her brother's death, but of course he was more than happy to take his niece in to live with him and his wife. They had never had any children and they welcomed the idea of having Bridget in their home. Along with the wire came enough marks for a train ticket. Bridget gripped the money in her hand and looked at Michal.

"I don't want to leave you and Alina. I hardly know my uncle. The only thing I really remember about him is that he hated my brother. Whenever we saw my aunt and uncle, he and my brother always fought. You know how silly Otto was with all of his political stuff? Well, my uncle is the same way, except he is fascinated with the National Socialist Party. He's quite convinced that the ridiculous little man with the half mustache is going to save Germany from all of her problems. In fact, the last time I saw him, he'd grown the same foolish looking mustache as that Hitler fellow. I don't care about politics; I could live with his nonsense about the Socialist Party, but I feel so at home here with you and Alina."

"I know, Bridget. I do know. And I wish to God that I could keep you and take care of you. But, the truth is, I have no choice but to contact Alina's father and ask him to take us in. If I have another child with me, well, I don't know how he'll react. I don't even know if he has taken on another woman or if he has any money to help care for us. But I can't see any other way. I can't find any work and I don't know where else to search for a job."

"You want me to go to Nuremberg?"

"Of course I don't want you to go. In fact, I wish we could all stay together." Michal put her arms around Bridget, who was trembling, still holding the letter and money in her hand. "But I think it is best."

"I'm seventeen, Michal. I could get a job and live on my own. Or I could work and help with the bills, then we could all stay together."

"Bridget, Berlin is a dangerous city. You are a young beautiful girl. Anything could happen to you here. I wish I could guarantee your safety. I wish I could promise that I would take care of you. But the truth is, I am not sure that I will be able to take care of Alina and myself. At least if you go to live with your uncle, you will be safe. You will have a place to live, and food, and … most of all … you won't end up like some of the young girls that we see on the street every day selling your body and compromising yourself."

"Do you care about me?"

"Yes, very much. And I know how close you and Alina are."

"We are."

"Oh, Bridget. I wish I had a better solution."

Bridget nodded. "I understand." There were tears in her eyes. "You're right. I will miss you both."

Alina was crying and gripping onto Bridget, who held her tightly. "I don't want you to go … Please, don't go," Alina said.

"Shhh," Bridget whispered. "You are going to be just fine, and when you are old enough, you will come to visit me in Nuremburg if your mother will allow you to."

"I want to go with you now."

"I know … I know. I want to take you with me. You've been the only sister I've ever had. But I can't take you, Alina."

"I love you, Bridget."

"I know, I love you too, Alina." Bridget kissed the top of Alina's head. "I will always remember you."

"Who will curl my hair at night if you go?"

"Your mommy will."

Alina shook her head. Her eyes were red with tears "NO … I hate Mommy. I hate her for making you go."

"Don't hate Mommy; she loves you."

"I want you to stay. Please?"

"I'm sorry. I'm so sorry, Alina, but I have to go," Bridget said, hugging the little girl close to her breast.

"We will miss you too. I will write to you and until Alina can read and write, I'll read your letters to her. One day, with God's help, we will be together again," Michal said, gripping Bridget's hand. "Can you ever forgive me?"

"I already do. I know you wouldn't do this if you didn't have to."

"I've thought it over a thousand times. I can't see any other way."

"Will you take me to the train station tomorrow morning so that I can see when the next train is leaving for Nuremburg?"

"Of course," Michal said, but she felt heartsick and filled with guilt.

CHAPTER 40

Alina didn't stop crying until the train carrying Bridget away had gone far enough out of the terminal that it could no longer be seen. Then she wiped her eyes with the back of her hand and gave her mother an angry look.

"I hate you, Mommy. I wish you were dead."

Michal felt her heart sink. But she couldn't say anything except, "I am sorry, Alina … I had no choice."

Alina refused to hold Michal's hand as they left the station and headed back to the apartment. The wicked frozen winds of February froze Alina's tears onto her eyelashes and because it was wet, the skin on her face turned very red and irritated. Well, at least Alina had survived the body lice and had not gotten an infection. Alina wrapped her arms around her body. She walked alone like a little soldier, so brave that Michal felt her heart break. She wished that she could shield her daughter from the pain of life, but she'd learned that was not possible.

Michal decided to wait until the following morning to go to the carpentry shop and search for Taavi. She hoped that Alina would be calmer and easier to manage by then. It was going to be difficult enough to face Taavi and to tell him the truth about where she'd been without Alina throwing a tantrum. Anything could happen. He might walk away from her and deny that Alina was his child. Taavi could very well be involved with another woman by now. It was best not to think of what might happen. All she could do was clear her mind and go forward. Taavi was her last hope.

CHAPTER 41

After Bridget left, Alina was sulky and difficult. Michal decided it was best to wait for at least another day before taking Alina to see Taavi. Of course, the clock was ticking and she only had a little over a week paid for in the apartment. If she avoided the landlord, she might be able to stay an extra day or two before he evicted them. The last thing she wanted was to take Alina back to stay at the shelter. However, it was probably best if Alina appeared to be a delightful child rather than a burden when Taavi saw her for the first time. Well, she had to pray because if Taavi wasn't receptive, her only choice was to return to the shelter, penniless, jobless, and alone in her responsibility for Alina's well-being.

There was not much food left. Michal had not eaten for a day and a half. She'd given all that was left to Alina. That night, with Alina throwing a tantrum because she didn't want to go, Michal took Alina to the shelter to eat. The main room smelled of sweat and dirty clothes. Alina folded her arms and demanded to go home, but Michal held tight to her daughter's hand and led her through the cafeteria line. After their trays were filled with a bowl of soup and a slice of bread, Michal led Alina to a long table. They sat down and began to eat.

"It stinks in here, Mama--"

"Shhh. Eat your food and we'll go back to the apartment as soon as you finish."

The elderly woman who had been sitting on the other side of Alina stood up and took her tray to the clean-up area, leaving the seat beside the child vacant. A man with a scruffy gray beard and thin greasy hair sat down. Alina took a bite of her bread.

"Don't," Alina said.

"What?" Michal asked.

"That man touched me under my dress."

Michal stood up and glared at the filthy disheveled man. "How dare you do that to a child? Are you a demon of some kind?"

The man started laughing. It was a sly and bitter laugh. Michal tried to get the attention of someone in authority, but there were too many people in the room. No one heard or noticed her calling for help. She could not leave Alina alone with this man while she tried to find some way to report him. And if she took Alina with her, they would have to take their food because if they left it for even a moment it would be stolen. Looking around frantically, Michal realized that there was nowhere that two seats were open together. She would not leave Alina anywhere alone. It looked like there was nothing she could do except push Alina to the other side and sit beside the disgusting lout herself.

"You swine," she said.

"I don't care what you think of me." The man shrugged his shoulders. His breath stunk of alcohol, his hands were filthy, and when she thought of those hands touching her child's body, she shivered. What was left of his graying hair was stuck to his head with grease and sprinkles of yellow dandruff.

Michal gagged. But she knew she must eat. There was no food at the house. She tucked the bread into her coat pocket and picked up the bowl to gulp the soup. She'd never eaten without utensils before, but she wanted to finish as quickly as possible.

Once Alina had finished her last bite, Michal grabbed her child's hand and pulled her out of the shelter into the dark cold night air.

Derelicts hovered in the alleyways, some of them just broken men who'd returned from the Great War as invalids, but others were pimps and drug pushers. Michal was afraid of the pimps. They smiled fetchingly at her. But she knew that she and Alina were worth money to them and they were trying to lure her and her child into their circle.

Dear God, Michal thought, (it is only by your grace that Alina and I are still alive. Please watch over us and help us to get home safely.

"Come on, Alina, walk faster." Michal pulled Alina's hand.

"I can't, Mommy."

Michal sighed. What was she doing? She knew that the child was moving as quickly as her little legs would carry her. A chill went down Michal's spine. The quicker they got home, the sooner they would be out of danger.

"Want to earn some quick cash?" a man with a fedora and a cheap suit said, as he leaned out from between two buildings and smiled at Michal. He reeked of men's cologne. "I know a lot of men who would pay a good sum for a mother and daughter. Especially such a young child. Too young not to be a virgin."

Michal picked Alina up into her arms and began to run. The child was heavy for Michal's small frame. But even though her arms ached and her legs were quivering with the weight,

Michal didn't dare put Alina down until they arrived at the door to the apartment.

Michal's heart was pounding so hard she thought she might have a heart attack. Her hands were shaking, but she found the keys. It was hard for her to steady her fingers enough to get the key into the lock. Slow down, she thought. Breathe deeply. Open the door. As soon as they were both safely inside the little flat, Michal slammed the door behind her and turned the lock to assure that no one who might have followed them could get in. Then she flipped on the light switch. For now, they were safe. Michal fell to her knees, holding her daughter in her arms and weeping.

What had the world come to? How had things ever gotten so out of hand?

Because Michal was crying, Alina began to cry as well. Then she began screaming for Bridget. Michal was exhausted. Tonight had made things clear; they were in a very bad position. Survival in Berlin without any money was dangerous business. Alina sensed her mother's angst and responded by being fussy and unwilling to go to bed. Michal knew it was because Alina was afraid. How could she not be? Her life was so unstable. She'd lost her surrogate sister and the funny man who told her stories all within a few weeks. Alina had slept in a shelter and had recovered from insects crawling all over her body. And now she'd been molested by a filthy monster. There was never enough to eat, and it seemed that Alina was always hungry. Michal couldn't blame Alina; she was just a little girl. How could she understand the enormity of what her mother was facing? Alina was whining and crying, refusing to sleep, holding on to Michal. "I want Bridget. Why did Bridget have to go away?" Michal was trembling; she had to quiet Alina or she feared she would lose her mind. She had explained countless times that Bridget had gone to live with her aunt and uncle. It would seem that Alina understood what Michal was telling her, then an hour or so later, she would begin asking for Bridget again. If only Alina would fall asleep. Michal needed a few hours of peace and quiet. Then she became afraid. What if Alina was so fussy because she was getting sick? Michal said a silent prayer, begging God to forgive her for wanting Alina to fall asleep. She loved her daughter. "Please, God, keep her healthy and strong. Help us to find a way out of this."

In order to quiet Alina's constant crying and questions about Bridget, Michal gave Alina the last lump of sugar that they had. Before popping the small kernel into the child's mouth, she exacted a promise from Alina that Alina would stop fussing. It didn't work. So much for a promise from a five-year-old, Michal thought. But she couldn't blame Alina for feeling abandoned. Bridget had really formed a bond with the child, and Alina missed her surrogate sister terribly. Finally, at a little after eleven that night, the child was spent, and she fell into a fitful sleep. She slept beside her mother that night, curling into Michal like a lost lamb.

Michal awakened at four in the morning. The room was totally dark, but she could feel Alina still asleep beside her. When she slept, Alina looked blissful, sucking gently and rhythmically on her thumb. Soon, Michal would have to start breaking that habit. It wasn't good for Alina's teeth. But the little girl had been through so much that Michal couldn't bear the thought of taking anything away from her daughter that might give Alina even a small drop of comfort. Careful not to awaken Alina, Michal slipped out of bed and covered her child, then she went into the living room to contemplate her meeting with Taavi that would take place later today.

Not much was left of the turnip coffee; it was mostly bitter water, but at least it was hot. At night, the landlord turned the heat down even lower and did not raise it until much later in the morning. Michal wrapped a blanket around her shoulders against the cool night air and sipped the flavored water. In only a few hours, she would face Taavi. She would have to swallow her pride and beg him to take care of his child. Taavi. Handsome, arrogant Taavi. She'd walked out on him, and now she was about to return on her knees as a failure.

Michal curled her legs under her body to stay warm and waited until the sun rose. Then Alina came shuffling out of bed.

"I'm hungry, Mama."

"I know. I don't have anything to give you."

"Mama?"

Michal bit her lower lip. Then she remembered the bread in her coat pocket. "Wait, I do have something." Michal handed the small heel of bread to Alina, who ate it quickly.

"I'm still hungry," she said.

"All right then. Let's get dressed. We have to go over to the shelter and see if we can't get you something to eat."

"I don't want to go there. That man that was there yesterday scared me."

"I know. But we have to go today. We don't have any more food. If you're still hungry, there is no other place for us to get anything to eat."

Alina stuck out her lower lip. "I hate it there, Mama. Why can't we go back to Sammie's house?"

"Don't you remember? Sammie and his mommy had to move to Frankfurt to live with Sammie's grandparents. So, let's just go over to the shelter. We can eat something quickly. Then we have a special errand to run."

Alina pouted, but she allowed Michal to help her get dressed. Then Michal quickly dressed herself and took a quick look in the mirror. She was only twenty-one, but her eyes had lost their sparkle. If only she had some lipstick to rub on her lips and cheeks before she saw Taavi. That might make her look a little more attractive. But she had none. Lipstick cost money, and she didn't have money to waste on frivolities. Right now, she didn't even have a few marks for a slice of bread to give Alina.

"Come on, let's get you into some warm clothes. It's very cold outside."

Alina allowed Michal to put her hand through the sleeves of her coat, then bundle her with warm gloves and thick stockings under.

"Today is a very special day. I need you to be an exceptionally good girl today. Please do this for me, Alina?"

Alina looked up at Michal. She nodded her head. "I will, Mama." Alina's eyes looked so sad, far too sad for such a young child. It broke Michal's heart.

Snow was falling as they made their way to the shelter to join the rest of the crowd waiting for a crust of bread. Alina complained of the cold as they stood in line. Michal picked her daughter up and held her in her arms as long as she was able to sustain the weight in order to keep Alina a little warmer. Their breath rose like white smoke against the crystal blue sky.

Finally, they reached the front of the line, where they each received a crust of bread, a thin slice of cheese, and some hot water. At least it was warmer inside the shelter. Alina gobbled her food down quickly.

"Are you still hungry?" Michal asked. She'd saved her share to give to Alina if Alina was still hungry.

"Yes."

"Here, eat this." Michal gave her food to her daughter.

"Then what are you going to eat?"

"I'm not hungry, sweetheart."

"Are you sure?"

"Yes, of course I'm sure." Michal was starving. All she'd had to eat was a bowl of watery soup the night before. But she couldn't eat while Alina was still hungry.

Alina took the food and ate it quickly. Once they'd finished, Michal took Alina's hand and led her out of the shelter.

"Where are we going?"

"Remember I told you that today we are going on a very special outing? And remember you promised me that you would be very good today?"

"Yes. I will," Alina said. She gripped tightly to Michal's hand with one hand and with the other she popped her thumb into her mouth.

It was an eight block walk and the sidewalk had frozen patches of ice covered with snow. Alina's nose was running and she slipped twice on the ice. If she hadn't been holding Michal's hand, she would have fallen and possibly scraped her knee or elbow. As it was, she was cold, and demanding to go home. For a while, Michal carried Alina in her arms. But she was too heavy and finally Michal had to put her down to walk on her own. She began complaining about being tired and her feet hurting, but Michal urged her on until finally they arrived at the carpentry shop where Taavi worked.

Michal wiped Alina's nose with a handkerchief and then smiled at her daughter. "You're doing so well. I am so proud of you for walking all this way like a big girl." Michal smiled at Alina. "Now, don't forget your promise to me to be a good girl, please? And if you're really good. I will take Otto's old socks with the holes in them and together we can sew buttons on them and make puppets. What do you think? Doesn't that sound like fun?"

Alina nodded.

"So remember, if you're very good … I promise we'll make puppets."

"Can we make up a puppet play?"

"Of course we will. You think about the play you want to do and be very good and very quiet until we're done here."

"Okay, Mommy."

They entered the shop. This was the first time Michal had been inside of Taavi's place of employment. There were blocks of wood leaning against walls and shavings on the ground. Beautiful hand carved pieces awaited pick up by their new owners. She glanced around the shop and saw several men, but not Taavi.

A man wearing a heavy flannel coat and wool hat walked up to her "Can I help you?" he said.

"I'm looking for Taavi Margolis."

"I'm sorry, he doesn't work here anymore."

Michal's heart sank. Where could he have gone? If she couldn't find Taavi, she had no choice but to join the other women who stood at the docks hoping for a man's attention. The thought made her shudder.

"But ... do you know where he is? Where I can find him?"

"I'm sorry, I don't."

"Please, you have to help me," Michal heard the panic in her own voice, but she couldn't control it, and now Alina was looking around the room frightened.

"Hold on a minute. Now, don't cry. Let's see ... I think he was pretty good friends with Lev. I can't say whether Lev knows what happened to him. But I'll ask him to come and talk to you. The man turned to the workers in the shop, "Where's Lev?"

"In the back," one of the men answered.

"Go and bring him up here."

It was a few minutes before Lev came walking up "Yes, sir?" Lev asked skeptically. "Did you call for me?"

"You were friends with Taavi, weren't you?"

Lev shrugged, not wanting to commit to anything until he knew where the conversation was leading. Lev had lost his wife recently. She'd died in an accident at the factory where she worked. The loss had devastated him, and since her death he'd become withdrawn and quiet.

"This lady is looking for him ... You go on and talk to her. But don't be too long, I need you to get back to work," the man with the flannel coat said and walked away.

Lev sighed and went up to the front of the shop to meet with the visitor.

"Are you looking for Taavi?"

"Yes, I'm Michal Margolis. I'm Taavi's wife. This is his daughter. We have to find him. We have to...."

Lev raised his eyebrows. Taavi had mentioned a wife, but he'd never mentioned that he had a child. Would he want this woman to find him? Lev didn't want to betray his friend, yet the woman looked so lost, desperate, pathetic....

"Please," Michal said, her lips quivering. "I need to find him. If you know where he is...."

Lev couldn't give this woman the address to the night club where Taavi was working. It was obvious to him that she wasn't the night club type. Besides, he didn't feel right giving her any information without Taavi's permission; yet he felt he must do something.

"All right," Lev said. "I can't tell you where he is. But if you give me an address that I can give to Taavi, an address where he can find you, I'll see to it that he gets it."

"Oh, thank you. Thank you." Michal took Lev's hand in both of hers.

"I can't guarantee anything."

"I know. I understand. Let me give you my address. Do you have a pencil and paper?"

Lev walked away and came back, handing a dirty torn sheet of paper and a crudely sharpened pencil to Michal. She wrote her address.

"I heard the man call you Lev? Your name is Lev?"

"Yes, my name is Lev."

"I am grateful to you, Lev. But I have to tell you that I only have about a week left to stay at this address. Then the rent will be due and I have no money. We have been eating at the shelter for the homeless. I am begging you, please do a mitzvah and give this address to Taavi as soon as possible. Tell him please … please … tell him that we need him." The tears spilled down her cheeks.

Lev nodded "I will. I promise." Then he took a few marks out of his pocket. "Take this money and feed the child," he said.

"I couldn't.…"

"You can and you will." He stuffed the money into her coat pocket and walked away.

CHAPTER 42

On the way home, Michal stopped in the bakery to see if there was anything available to purchase. Even the baker had lost weight. That was truly evidence that there wasn't much food to be had.

"How can I help you, pretty lady?" he said, winking at Michal.

"I have a few marks … do you have anything that I can buy to eat?" Michal held out the money that Lev had given her.

"Let me see what I can do. For such a beautiful woman, I have something that I have been saving in the back." He brought out three rolls. They were a bit stale and hard, but at least there was no visible mold.

"I'll take them," Michal said. Now, she and Alina would have something to eat and they would be able to avoid going to the shelter tonight.

By the time they got back to the apartment, Michal was drained from pulling Alina along while Alina complained about everything she could possibly complain about.

Until recently, Alina had been a happy child. When they lived with the Fogelmans, she'd been an easygoing baby. With Bridget and Otto, she'd been a curious and fun loving child. But Alina was changing and, although she was only five years old, Michal could see that Alina resented and blamed her mother for everything. Especially for Bridget's leaving. Michal knew how close the two girls had grown over the year that they'd spent together. And she couldn't blame Alina for her anger and her difficult behavior. It seemed that Alina was always hungry, always. Her constant nagging for food was driving Michal crazy. She gave everything she could to Alina. In fact, Michal had lost so much weight that her hip bones jutted out of her body.

"It's cold in here," Alina said, as Michal removed her coat.

"I know, let me wrap you up in a blanket and then I'll read you a story. How would you like that?"

"I'd like Bridget to read me a story."

Michal wanted to scream, to tell Alina to shut up already, that she was doing the best she could. She wanted to strike the child. To hit her hard. (My dear God, help me, Michal thought. She had to walk away from Alina. She couldn't trust herself not to hit her child. Michal's body was trembling with anger and frustration. She went into the bedroom and slammed the door. She threw herself on the bed and pounded the mattress with her fists until she'd spent all of her rage. Then she sat up and took several deep breaths. Better to hit a mattress than to hurt her precious daughter.

"Mama?" Alina was standing in the doorway, her dark eyes wide with fear.

"Yes, sweetheart ... come here. Mama's all right. I'm going to read you a story."

Gingerly, Alina crawled up on the bed and sat beside Michal, who leaned over and kissed the top of her daughter's head.

"I'm sorry if I scared you. Mama is just having a very hard time right now."

Alina just stared up at Michal, who knew the child didn't understand.

"But Mama loves you very much. And I'm so sorry about Bridget, sweetheart. With God's help, we will see her again."

"I know I will see her again. She and I made a promise that no matter how far away we were from each other, we would always be sisters."

Michal felt the tears well in her eyes as she stroked Alina's hair. Alina was miserable. And Michal blamed herself. She was the mother; it was her fault that her daughter was hungry, fatherless, and had just lost her best friend.

"Here, let's get you into your pajamas."

For once, Alina didn't argue. Michal got her ready for bed, helped her to wash her face and brush her teeth, then Alina went to the shelf to get her favorite book. She handed it to her mother, put her thumb in her mouth, and laid her head in Michal's lap.

"Once upon a time … a long time ago … in a faraway kingdom.…" Michal began. She was relieved to feel her daughter grow quiet and calm as Alina listened to the story that Otto had written. Perhaps it was the walk or lack of nutrition, but Alina quickly drifted off to sleep. When Michal was sure by her even breathing that Alina was in deep slumber, she lay the book down and covered her child. Then she went into the living room.

She threw herself into a chair and put her hands over her face. All she could think of was, *What if Taavi never came? What was her next move?*

CHAPTER 43

"Lev? It's always good to see you. How have you been? What brings you here?" Taavi was opening a bottle of beer for a customer on the other side of the bar. "Can I get you a beer? On me?"

"Sure," Lev said. He studied his friend. Taavi wore a white shirt, open at the neck, with the sleeves rolled up to reveal his muscular arms.

Taavi set the mug in front of Lev and wiped his hands with the rag he had wrapped around his belt. "How are you?"

"As well as I can be, Taavi. I lost my wife. She died," Lev said, as he looked at Taavi's face more closely. Although his body was in wonderful shape, Taavi had aged. He had dark circles under his eyes and deep wrinkles had formed between his brows.

"Oh, my God. I am sorry, Lev."

"Yes, me too. I miss her more than I can say. So, Nu? How are you?"

"Fine. Tired."

"Taavi. Listen, I came to talk to you about something important. Your wife came to see me today at the shop. She was looking for you."

"Michal?" Taavi felt his breath catch in his throat. "Michal came looking for me? Is she all right? Where is she? How is she?"

"She seems all right, but I think she needs your help."

"My help? I haven't seen her for six years." Taavi looked away. He didn't want Lev to see the range of emotions reflected in his face.

"I have an address where she is staying." Lev handed the paper to Taavi. Taavi looked at Michal's familiar handwriting and his heart swelled.

"You have a child, Taavi. I saw her. A little girl. Did you know?"

Taavi's shoulders dropped. He shook his head. "No. I had no idea..." Taavi poured a vodka for himself and drank it in a single swig. "A child? Who has been taking care of her and the child?"

"I don't know what she's been doing. She came to me this morning. That was the first time I have ever met her. I have no idea where she has been all this time. She didn't say."

"What can I do? I am assuming that Michal gave you this address because she wants to see me, is that right? Does she need money?"

"Yes, both. She wants to see you and she desperately needs money. They have no food, and soon they will have no place to live."

"Did she say when she wants me to come to this address?"

"She didn't say an exact time or day. All she said was that she needs to see you as soon as possible. If you can, why don't you go there in the morning when you get off work?"

"I get off at about four a.m. I'll go home and clean up. Then I can go to see her at about six. Do you think that's too early?"

"No, go as soon as you can."

"She knows I'm coming? You told her you would find me and tell me to come?"

"Yes, Taavi, she knows."

CHAPTER 44

A comedian was performing at the club that night, but Taavi never heard a word of his act. Taavi was too busy thinking about Michal. What if she wanted a divorce? What if she'd found another man? What if she only wanted money? And why the hell did he still care so much?

After the bar closed that night, Taavi went back to his room. He was laying out his clothes when Frieda knocked at his door.

"Liebchen … it's me," she whispered.

He opened the door. "Look what I've got," she said, pulling an opium pipe out of the pocket of her silk robe.

"Not tonight," he said.

"It will help you sleep."

"Not tonight. I don't want to go to sleep. I have somewhere I have to go."

"Taavi, come on. Where do you have to go that you can't go later this afternoon? It's four in the morning."

He stared directly at her. It had been a long time since he'd really looked at her. She was weathered, worn, and hard. He had become the same. When Taavi had first come to Berlin, he was proud of the man he was. Now, he had lost his self-respect. He was doing things he'd never dreamed he would have agreed to do, acting in shameful ways he'd never thought he was capable of.

"Frieda ... not tonight." His voice was firm. He could see by the look on her face that she was disappointed and perhaps even a little worried that she had done something to offend him. It seemed she was always holding on to him so tight, always trying to keep control; she was so afraid that she would lose him.

"You want to just maybe make love tonight? No opium, no morphine?"

"I want to be left alone. I'm not feeling well." He felt sorry for her. "Look, Frieda, I am sorry. But not tonight. All right?"

"Are you sick? Do you need to go and see a doctor? I can have one come here."

"No, Frieda. I need you to leave me alone for now."

She nodded. "Yes, of course." Her voice cracked, but she turned and walked out of the apartment. He didn't go after her.

CHAPTER 45

Taavi's emotions were a mixture of contrasts as he walked up to the entranceway of the apartment at the address on the paper Lev had given him. He was furious with Michal for leaving him, for denying him her love, which had turned him into an animal that last night. He was shocked, but deeply touched that he had a child, and at the same time he was angry that Michal had kept his daughter away from him for so long. But, most of all, Taavi missed the only woman he'd ever really loved. In his mind's eye, he could still see her smile, feel the warmth of her hand in his own. How could a man hate and love a woman so much and all at the same time? His hand trembled as he knocked on the door. Part of him wanted to flee like a child to escape the uncertainty of what awaited him. But he was frozen to the ground ... waiting ... waiting for her to answer the door.

Michal opened the door.

"Taavi?" Michal looked up into his eyes "Come in."

She was perhaps even more beautiful than he remembered. Her long curls hung about her waist and she wore only a simple house dress, but her eyes, those smoldering charcoal eyes....

"How are you?" he asked, feeling foolish, clumsy, and at a loss for words.

"I'm surviving," she said, and he saw her lower lip tremble just slightly.

"You asked Lev to find me and tell me to come here?" he said.

"Yes, Taavi."

He cocked his head and waited. She turned away from him and cleared her throat. "I've done some terrible things since we have been separated. Things I am ashamed of. But, I wanted to see you. I have so much to say…" She couldn't look at him. "Sit down, please."

He sat.

"I don't know where to begin."

"You need money?" he interrupted her.

"Yes, I do. But that isn't the only reason that I sent for you. Not by far."

"Then, what is it, Michal?" He knew he sounded harsh, but if he allowed himself to be at all vulnerable, he might crack.

"I'm sorry, Taavi. I'm sorry for everything. I was a terrible wife to you and then after I left I was too proud to come to you and tell you that we have a child…."

"I know. Lev told me … you should have come."

"Yes, you're right. I should have. But that isn't all, Taavi. I've sinned. I've sinned in the worst possible way…."

Taavi felt his stomach churn. Had she resorted to prostitution to support herself and his child?

"I was with another man for a while. You can walk away from me and ask for a divorce; I will understand. But I couldn't lie to you; I had to tell you the truth."

Taavi nodded his head. He took a wad of bills out of his pants pocket and placed it on the coffee table. Then he got up and walked to the door. "Goodbye, Michal."

"Taavi … don't you even want to see your daughter?"

He did. He wanted to turn back and take Michal into his arms, but she'd been with another man. Taavi felt sick to his stomach at the very thought of her in someone else's arms. "I think it's best that I leave. It's probably better for all of us if I never see my child."

"Taavi…" he was walking down the hall towards the door to the outside of the building. Once he was gone, Michal was sure she would never see him again. "Taavi … please, please don't go. Give me another chance."

He turned all the way around to look at her. She looked so small, so slender, so alone. He felt an invisible thread come from her and tug at his heart. When they were apart he was willing to accept her back on any terms. But then he hadn't realized how hard it would be to think of another man kissing her, holding her. She was looking at him begging him to forgive her. His eyes connected directly to hers and he felt his heart breaking. Although it hurt him and he felt betrayed, he loved her. And, hadn't he done far worse things? If he walked away now it would be the end and he couldn't bear to lose her, not again.

"I love you, Taavi."

Those words broke through and collapsed all of his resistance like rushing water through a hole in a dam. Taavi couldn't move. Instead, he stood and stared at her. Then, in a whisper, he said, "I love you too, Michal. I loved you from the first time I saw you and I've never stopped."

"Forgive me, Taavi. Please, I've made so many mistakes."

She ran into his arms. Tears slipped down her cheeks as he held her tightly. "Michal, I have sinned too. I have sinned plenty. But if you are willing, maybe we can start over. We can both find it in our hearts to forgive." He could no longer hold back; a single tear fell upon her hair.

"Thank God, Taavi. Thank God you're here. Thank God you have forgiven me and we are together again."

He kissed her lips and sighed. "I have longed to hold you like this."

She gripped him tighter. For several minutes, they stood in the hallway of the apartment building, until a man came out of the door of his flat. He was carrying a lunch pail and looked as if he might be on his way to work. He stared at Michal and Taavi. Then they both realized that they were standing outside in the cold. Michal was only wearing a thin housedress, but until now she hadn't even felt chilled.

"Can I come in? I would love to see my daughter."

She nodded. "Yes, I think it's a good idea. Come in, Taavi."

CHAPTER 46

That night, Taavi stayed for dinner. He went to his friends on the black market and bought plenty of food. Michal prepared the meal, while Taavi sat on the floor and entertained Alina, whose laughter filled the small rooms with joy. It warmed Michal's heart to see Alina smiling, and not hungry.

After Alina went to sleep in her own bed, Michal took Taavi's hand and led him to her bedroom. It was awkward at first. So much had happened in the time they were apart.

"Taavi, our breakup was my fault. I know that now. Here, sit down on the bed." She sat beside him and took his hand in hers. "I want you to make love to me. I know now that this is the way it should have been before," she said. "And, I am sorry. I wasn't ready. The rape during the pogrom had damaged me. I couldn't get it out of my mind."

"I know that. That terrible night when I forced you. God, Michal, I've regretted that night. But I only did it because somehow I believed that if I could just make love to you once, you would be all right. You would see that what we shared was love, and it was nothing like what happened to you with the Cossack. And then, I guess it turned out to be just like what happened with the rape. I made mistakes too. Believe me, Michal, I didn't want it to work out that way."

"We were young and inexperienced. I know I had too much pride and I had to overcome that before I could be a good wife to you. But I believe that God has given us a second chance. This time I want us to have a real marriage. I'm ready."

"Is this something that you came to realize when you were away from me? I mean, is this something that you learned in the arms of another man?" He swallowed hard.

"Does it matter? Does it really matter, Taavi? Is this what you want or not?" She looked up into his eyes. "I don't want to tell you what happened; it would only hurt you. And it's over now. If you want me, if you will give me another chance, from this day forward I will be the best wife you could ever imagine." Tears welled up in the corners of her eyes.

"I just want to say that if it was another man … then as hard as this is for me … I have to thank him. He has given me my wife."

"Taavi, you never stop surprising me. I love you. I really love you."

"I want our marriage to work. I want you. I want you more than I've ever wanted anything. Whatever you did while we were apart is over now. I did some bad things too. All that matters is today, our future together … we have each other now. And this time we have a better understanding of how to love each other. I am willing to lay down my heart, my soul, and my pride to make this work between us, to build a family with you."

"And so am I," she whispered.

Taavi kissed Michal and then slowly and gently he made love to her. At first, he felt clumsy, his hands trembled, and sweat formed at his brow. He didn't want to make a mistake and repel her again. Even with all the women he'd made love to in the past, there was something inside of him that assured him that this was different. This time, every move he made really mattered. And, truth be told, Taavi was nothing like the arrogant man he'd been five years ago when he demanded that Michal be a wife to him. Taavi had learned; he'd learned the value of true feelings, and he'd experienced enough empty sexual encounters for a lifetime. He wanted a family, a home, and a woman who would be his best friend and his partner in life. Although he'd been surrounded by people while he worked at the cabaret, he'd always felt a deep emptiness in the pit of his stomach. When he saw Michal, he knew that she was the only one who could fill that void inside of him, and he didn't want to lose her again. For Michal, the Cossack was forgotten. That had been Otto's gift to her. And no matter what else he'd done, he'd saved her from a life of fear and haunting memories. Michal was grateful. She had always loved Taavi, but they had begun with a dark cloud hanging over them. It was time to begin again. Michal allowed herself to be swept up with emotion; her lovemaking with Taavi was more magical than anything she'd ever experienced with Otto or Avram. For Taavi, the joining together with his wife erased from his heart and mind any trace of the years he'd spent living a life of debauchery. They were like two pieces of a puzzle that had been lost for ages, and were finally united together. Now they had cemented together and were indivisible.

CHAPTER 47

Taavi knew that he had to leave his job at the nightclub if he wanted to be a good husband and father. The only way that he could change his life was to completely break free of Frieda, the alcohol, the drugs, and the endless sexual encounters with nameless, faceless people who he hardly recognized in the morning.

At least he'd saved a nice sum of money working at the bar. If he took that money, he would be able to open his own custom carpentry shop. There were still plenty of rich people who would admire his craftsmanship and purchase his hand-made pieces. He'd become accustomed to his nocturnal, overindulgent lifestyle, but he also knew that it was taking a toll on him. And, if he continued, he had a good chance of dying young. But most importantly, he loved Michal. And the moment he saw Alina, he knew that she belonged to both of them. She had his nose and his smile, her mother's hair and tiny hands. Taavi was in awe. He couldn't believe the miracle that he was a father. A father had responsibilities. He planned to take good care of his family. If he had to work day and night as long as he lived, his wife and daughter would never want for anything again.

Taavi had missed a night of work. He knew Frieda would be looking for him, so he returned to the club the following day to collect his things and tell her that he was quitting. There was a possibility that Frieda had slept in his bed awaiting his return. It would be terrible if that were the case. If she was there waiting for him, he would have to tell her his plans before he had a chance to pack up his belongings. He was glad he had not told her where he was going when he left, because he was sure she would have scanned his rooms until she found the cardboard cigar box in his drawer filled with all of his savings. There was no doubt in Taavi's mind that if Frieda found his money, she would take it. Not because she wanted or needed it, but as long as he had no money, she would have control over him. Taavi turned the key to the door of his rooms and silently went inside. Quietly, he peeked into his bedroom and was thankful to find that Frieda was not there. The next thing he did was look for his money. And he sighed with relief to find it just as he had left it. After placing the piles of bills in the bottom of the old suitcase he'd brought when he'd arrived five years earlier, he began packing the things he'd acquired while he'd lived in these rooms behind the club. It was early in the morning and he'd come early on purpose. From what he knew of her, Frieda would have just gone to sleep. Once he was all packed and was ready to leave, he went into the empty club. It was silent. All of the chairs were stacked up on the tables. The bar was clean. He wondered who had worked it the night before when he hadn't shown up for work. Taavi assumed that she'd probably gone to check his rooms, but he wasn't sure if she was angry, worried, or both. It was possible that Frieda could have called the police and reported him missing. Taavi sighed. One thing was for sure, Frieda was going to be angry when she found out his plans to leave forever. If he was a coward, he would walk out right now without another word, without even an explanation. But that wouldn't be fair to her. She had been kind to him. And even though he was sure she would be wild with fury and shout obscenities at him, he would do right by her. He would wait until she came in and thank her for everything that she had done for him before he left.

Taavi sat in the empty club until eleven that morning, when Frieda finally arrived.

"Are you all right?" She ran over to him. Frieda was a hard woman, and he had never before seen such concern in her face about anyone or anything. Looking at her now, he felt guilty for what he was about to do.

"Yes, no need to be worried. I'm fine."

She cocked her head to the side, as if she couldn't understand what he'd just said. Then she trembled slightly and her eyes glared at him.

"Where were you last night?"

"I'm sorry. I couldn't come in."

"You couldn't call? You should have at least let me know. This is my business, my livelihood. Have you no respect for me or for your job?"

"I'm sorry. You're right. I should have called you."

"It was a disaster here last night without you … Nobody was available to take your place. I had to step in. I don't even know how to tend bar. It was a disaster, I tell you. We lost money and maybe we even lost customers last night. This was very irresponsible of you, Taavi. I expected more from you. I'll grant you that you have been a pain in the ass, but …"

"Frieda." He cut her off in mid-sentence. "I have something to tell you."

Her face turned from anger to worry and, for the first time, he realized that she really did care deeply for him. In fact, she might even be in love with him. "What is it? Are you ill?"

He shook his head. "No, Frieda. I'm all right. But, I have to leave this job. I want to thank you for everything you've done for me--"

"Leave? You can't just leave? What is it that's wrong; do you want more money? Do you need something?"

"Frieda, let's just say that it's just time for me to go."

"This doesn't make any sense to me."

"I know. I knew it wouldn't, but I couldn't leave without letting you know how much I appreciate--"

It was her turn to cut him off. Her face looked as if she'd just chewed on glass. "Shut your mouth, Taavi. Shut your mouth right now. You were nothing when I found you. A poor Russian Jew with no education, no class, nothing, nothing to offer anyone. Without me, you would be laying on the street someplace and begging for food. I brought you here to my club and it was me, do you understand that? It was me who introduced you to some of the most influential people in Berlin society. And now this? You stand here and tell me you're leaving. Just like that, no reason? Don't I deserve more? At least an explanation?" She grunted. "I should have expected this from a dirty Jew. That's right, a dirty Jew. That's all you are. I gave you everything, money, everything. And ... this is how you thank me? You desert me? Just like that?"

He felt bad and, for a moment, he wished he'd just disappeared and avoided this confrontation altogether.

"I wish you the best of everything--"

"Take your wishes and go to Hell with them, Taavi ... Go to Hell, you bastard, do you hear me?"

He nodded, then picked up his valise and walked out of his previous life forever.

As he headed down the street, he heard her yelling behind him, "You son of a bitch. Everyone told me not to trust a Jew. You are worthless. Worthless, do you hear me?"

He never turned around.

CHAPTER 48

Taavi took no time off before starting his new business. There was a lot to be done. First, he rented a space, then purchased equipment and supplies. Once he'd set everything up, he asked Lev to come and work with him. Lev was afraid that there wouldn't be enough business for both of them, but Taavi promised Lev that he would not fail. Lev finally agreed and joined Taavi in his venture. Next, Taavi put advertisements in the local paper. Michal was nervous about all of the money Taavi was spending. She had been so poor for so long, and seeing all of this money being spent at once frightened her. But Taavi was confident in his plans. When she told him how worried she was, he smiled and winked at her. Then he begged her to trust him. So, she swallowed her fears and did as he asked.

Michal was elated that Taavi had friends in the black market who were able to get their hands on decent food. And she was even more excited that she and Taavi were able to afford the food. Tears came to her eyes when, one afternoon, Taavi brought home a warm coat for Alina. Alina tried it on; it was a little too big, but Michal assured Taavi that Alina would grow into it.

Of course, Taavi had no idea that the apartment where they were living was the same place that Michal had shared with Otto. In fact, he knew very little about Otto. All he knew was that there had been another man when he and Michal were separated. He didn't ask and Michal didn't volunteer any information. But the flat was not really to Taavi's liking. It had limited heat and hot water. So, he asked Michal if she would be willing to live above his shop. "There is a nice apartment upstairs. It will be easy for me to come and go to work. There is plenty of hot water and the landlord understands that I will pay extra for heat in the winter. Michal was glad to leave the past behind with all of its memories, so she readily agreed.

"I will make you the most beautiful furniture for this apartment that you have ever seen," he said, smiling. "Only the best for my beautiful wife."

Alina had never been so contented. The child stopped sulking because her father spent time playing games with her and reading to her. Eventually, Alina even stopped asking for Bridget.

The apartment above the furniture store was lovely, well-maintained, and even had its own bathroom with a white porcelain claw-foot tub. As promised, the landlords were generous with the heat because Taavi paid them extra to assure that the place would be warm in the winter. No matter what time of year, they always had hot water, and every night Michal enjoyed a warm bath. She felt as if she had died and gone to straight to Heaven.

If Taavi had been in love with Michal before, his love had grown ten-fold in the time they were apart. Being reunited with his wife brought Taavi a sense of purpose and stability that he'd begun to believe he'd lost forever. For a long time, Taavi had been feeling lost. Now he was on the road to becoming the man he had always known he was meant to be.

Michal and Taavi were like young lovers. They wanted so much to make up for lost time, to please each other in ways that they had never even attempted before the breakup. Michal went to great lengths to prepare Taavi's favorite foods, to surprise him when he got home for dinner. After a long day at work, Taavi often stopped at the florist and bought a bouquet for his love.

It was only one month after the couple had reunited that Michal felt her breasts begin to swell. She was sick in the morning and again in the evenings. Her menstrual flow was late. There was no doubt in her mind that they had been blessed with another child. That night after dinner, when Alina had gone off to bed, Taavi took Michal in his arms and pulled her gently onto his lap.

She giggled. "I have some news for you."

"Oh?"

"I think you are going to have to build a crib. I'm having a baby."

He hugged her tightly, taking in the sweet floral scent of her hair. Michal had been happy to have laundry soap to wash her hair, but Taavi insisted on buying her the finest shampoo. It had the faint smell of a rose garden. When Taavi had first given her the shampoo, Michal had tried to save it for a special occasion. But Taavi told her that every day since they had reunited was a special occasion and he insisted on indulging her. As he took in the fragrance, he felt overwhelmed with love.

"Michal ... another baby?" Taavi asked.

"Another blessing."

"You know, when I was young and arrogant I used to doubt the existence of God. But it took a miracle to bring us back together. It was not a coincidence. I am sure of it. Only something as powerful as God could have made such a miracle."

"And now we will have two children, Taavi. We are so blessed; we have a wonderful place to live and plenty to eat. People are starving."

"I know that. In fact, I've begun to give thanks every day."

"Have you ever wished that we had enough to help others?"

"I have wished that. And sometimes I give to the poor who beg on the street. I don't know if it makes a difference in their lives, but I would like to think that it does."

She snuggled into his chest and they sat like that for a long time before he lifted her in his arms and carried her to bed.

CHAPTER 49

It is said that word of mouth is the best advertising, and it was through this method that Taavi's business began to flourish. He became known throughout Germany and Austria as an amazingly talented carpenter. He paid Lev well, and together they built a thriving shop, but they also built an even deeper friendship. When Taavi first opened the store, he was worried that he would not be able to earn as much money as he'd earned at the bar. He never told anyone of his concerns, especially not Michal. He didn't want her to fret. But he was wrong to be afraid of that failure. There were still plenty of wealthy people who loved his pieces, each of which was a work of art with plenty of attention to detail.

Taavi and Michal were not rich like the Fogelmans had been, but they had everything they needed, and, most importantly, they were happy. There was nothing Taavi would not do to make Michal smile. Whenever he went to meet with his friends from the black market, he always brought special gifts for Michal. He brought cookies filled with apricot jam and real coffee. For Alina, he always brought lumps of sugar and once he came home with a baby doll with two changeable outfits.

CHAPTER 50

Gilde Margolis decided she was ready to make her entrance into the world in the middle of the frigid December of 1926. It was the fourth night of Hanukkah, right after dinner, while Michal was cleaning the kitchen that her water broke. Alina, as she did every night of Hanukkah, carefully set up the menorah and filled it with candles on the kitchen table. This was Alina's favorite holiday and she was eagerly waiting for Taavi to say the prayers and light the candles, because every night for eight nights, Alina knew that she would receive a beautifully wrapped gift.

"Come on, Papa, let's start the prayers."

"Yes, Alina, we will." He smiled. "I know you're excited, but I'm waiting for your mama."

Michal did not come for a long time.

Taavi went into the kitchen, but Michal wasn't there. Then he looked around the apartment for her and found the bathroom door locked.

"Michal?"

"Taavi … I'm in labor," Michal whispered. "Get the doctor."

"Open the door."

She did.

He saw the liquid on the floor. "Is everything all right?"

She nodded. "I need the doctor."

Taavi ran out without his coat and raced down the street, slipping on the ice that coated the sidewalk. He almost fell, but caught himself, skinning his knuckles against the bricks of a building, but he didn't stop to look at his injury. When he got to the doctor's office, there were patients still waiting.

"I need the doctor."

"We're trying to close the office. As you can see, we have a lot of people waiting, so we aren't taking any more patients tonight. Come back in the morning."

"I need to see the doctor now," Taavi said.

"I'm sorry; that's just not possible," the nurse at the desk answered.

Taavi pushed the door to the office open. When Taavi extended his chest and stood tall, he looked like the human version of a lion. He walked right into an examining room, where he found a man sitting on a table with the doctor studying a red boil on the man's chest.

"I need you. I need you right now. My wife is in labor."

"Take her over to the hospital."

"I can't get her there. I need you to come to the house."

"I'm sorry. I have an office full of patients. It's Hanukkah and I want to go home to spend some time with my own family. But I can't leave until I've finished here. You'll have to find someone else."

Taavi pulled a thick wad of marks from his pocket and threw them down on the table. "I am willing to pay you very well."

The doctor looked at the pile of money. Then he turned to the patient, handed him a tube of cream, and said, "Use this twice a day for a week. The swelling should come down. Then drain it with hot towels. Come and see me to recheck it."

"Let's go," the doctor said to Taavi, as he grabbed his coat.

CHAPTER 51

Alina was worried about her mother; she asked Taavi over and over when she would be allowed to go into the room to see Michal. Taavi tried to remain patient with her, but he was on edge with worry and snapped at her, telling her to please be quiet. She started crying and he immediately felt guilty and took her into his arms and held her.

"Mama will be all right. But please stop asking me when we can go in and see her."

Alina nodded, slipping her thumb into her mouth. Michal had broken her of the habit, but when she was nervous, Alina still sucked her thumb. She lay quietly in her father's arms for almost an hour before she asked again.

"When can we go in to see Mommy?"

Taavi shrugged his shoulders and said, "I don't know."

"I'm hungry, Daddy; can we have something to eat? Please."

Taavi was exhausted and didn't want to leave the house, but he reminded himself that Alina was only a child and her needs must not be ignored. He went to the kitchen and found that there was nothing to feed the child.

"Stay here and be very good. I'm going to run down to the store to get you something to eat."

"I want to go with you, Daddy. Please don't leave me here alone. I'm afraid."

Taavi was frustrated. He was anxious. It would be so much easier if he could just go and get something for Alina to eat, instead of dragging her along with him. He wanted to get back as quickly as possible. But when he looked at his five-year-old daughter, he saw that she was trembling. Taavi took a deep breath.

"All right, all right," he said as calmly as he was able. "Don't be afraid. I'll take you with me."

Taavi took Alina's small coat, hat, and scarf down from the hook on the wall and dressed her calmly. Then he mustered a smile and took his daughter's hand. Everything was closed except for the newsstand. He would have to purchase some snacks like crackers there until the regular stores opened in the morning.

Alina held fast to her father's hand as he waited for the man at the newspaper stand to give him change.

"What's that, Papa?" she said, looking down at what looked like a cartoon. Taavi glanced down. At first, it didn't register in his mind, because his mind was too filled with worry about Michal. But then he realized that what he was looking at was not a cartoon at all; it was anti-Semitic propaganda.

That was when Taavi realized that it was a newspaper with the words *Der Strummer* printed in black letters across the top of the front page. Under the heading was a picture of a doctor with a large exaggerated nose and thick hungry-looking lips. Sitting on the examining table was a young innocent looking blonde female. The caption below read, "A German virgin girl at the hands of her devious Jewish doctor." Taavi picked up the paper and opened it to another page. There he saw two youngsters being lured by a man wearing a yarmulke and pe'ot. The caption read, "We must protect our children. The Jews are our misfortune." Taavi had endured anti-Semitism all of his life, but seeing it in black and white newsprint was even more unsettling.

Alina was eating the crackers and holding her father's hand as they walked back home together. Taavi was trying to control his desire to pull Alina along more quickly. He wanted to get back in case Michal needed him. But as much as he tried to shake the memory of the newspaper he'd just seen, he was haunted by it. Taavi could not help but remember something a rabbi had once told him. Unlike the other boys in the settlement where Taavi grew up, he had not taken many religious classes, but the one he did attend was given by Rabbi Rothman, a German who had moved to Russia to marry and start his congregation. Rothman had told the boys in class, "When people see something in print, they tend to believe it is true, regardless of whether it is or not." Taavi wondered what kind of effect the *Der Strummer* had on the Germans who saw it and what kind of hatred it would bring upon the Jews.

When they arrived back at the house, nothing had changed. But at least Alina had something in her stomach, so she was willing to sit quietly beside her father and wait.

Eight hours passed this way. Alina drifted in and out of sleep. Each time she awakened, she asked Taavi the same question.

"Can we go in and see Mommy yet?"

"Not yet, sweetheart," he would say and pat her head gently. It took all the patience he could muster to give her the same answer. Then in the early hours as the sun was rising, they heard the hearty cry of an infant. Taavi jumped to his feet.

"Stay here ... I'll be right back," Taavi said to Alina.

"I want to go with you."

"No, not yet. Stay here."

Taavi knocked on the bedroom door. "Doctor?"

"Yes, she's fine. You have a daughter. Give me a minute in here and then you can come in."

Taavi paced in front of the door like a panther in a cage until the doctor came out of the room.

"You can go in now."

Taavi had not been present at Alina's birth. In fact, he'd never seen a woman right after childbirth. Seeing Michal with her hair stuck to her face with sweat, her eyes half closed with exhaustion, holding a tiny bundle in her arms, made his heart swell. If he'd thought, she was beautiful before, now he thought she was not only beautiful, but angelic. He bent and kissed her forehead. Then he turned the blanket that covered the baby. For the first time, Taavi saw his new daughter, and was taken aback by how much the small face resembled his own.

"What should we call her?"

Michal shrugged. "What would you like to call her?"

"Gilde. It was my mother's name. Would that be all right?"

"Of course. Gilde is a beautiful name."

"I love you," he said, and sat on the bed beside her.

"I love you too."

Alina was standing at the doorway, her thumb still in her mouth. "Mama? Can I come in?" she asked in a small voice.

"Yes, of course, come in and meet your new sister."

Michal was afraid that Alina would be jealous. But Alina had never failed to surprise Michal. Not only was she not jealous, but she took to little Gilde immediately, claiming her as her own. From the moment Alina saw her sister, she took over and decided to become Gilde's second mother.

CHAPTER 52

In the very beginning, Gilde slept in Michal and Taavi's room. It was easier for Michal to breastfeed her that way. Alina was filled with delight when Michal would hold the baby in Alina's arms, giving Alina the feeling that she was holding her sister. But it was late December and far too cold to take a baby outside, and Alina soon became bored with being housebound. When she went to school, it was a relief to have her out of the house for a few hours. Taavi brought home toys for Alina, and tried to give Michal a break by taking her to the park on Saturdays when the shop was closed. Even though he'd found God, he still had not found religion, and never spent his Saturdays in shul like Lev and so many of his other Jewish friends.

At the end of April, the weather, although still cold, was mild enough for Michal and Alina to take Gilde for short walks outside. Alina wanted to push the stroller. Michal allowed her to do so, but only with careful supervision.

Gilde was growing rapidly and so was her relationship with her sister. Alina was busy trying to teach Gilde to crawl. It was a relief that the two children kept each other amused. Michal still had to watch them carefully, because although Alina would never purposely hurt Gilde, she was still a child herself and could be overzealous.

At night, Taavi sat on the floor with Gilde and Alina. Michal watched him as Gilde climbed on him, laughing and trying to tickle him under his arms. He turned her over and then tickled her instead. Alina was laughing too. Michal smiled. She listened as Taavi sang to the girls.

"You've got to have a little Mazel, because Mazel means good luck."

Both girls sang along with Taavi. He'd taught them the little song and they loved it. In fact, this was a song Michal remembered from her own childhood. Her mother used to sing it sometimes when she was alone with Michal and her father was not around.

They continued singing, "If you have a little Mazel, you'll always have good luck."

Taavi ruffled Gilde's golden hair, then he put his arm around Alina and gave her a hug. The three of them collapsed into giggles.

Gilde tried to stand up but she fell back on her bottom. Her lower lip jutted out and she was about to cry. Taavi smiled at her and said "You're not hurt. You did a very good job of standing up. Pretty soon you'll be running." Then he hugged Gilde and she smiled.

"I got a good mark on my history exam," Alina said.

"You are a smart girl. You both make me so proud."

Michal could see that the girls adored their father.

She'd lost track of time as she was standing in the doorway, watching her husband and children play. This was a home. This was the way a family should be.

Michal walked back into the kitchen to finish cleaning. She smiled to herself. It was good to have Taavi back.

The days were golden with laughter and love, and Michal should have been in constant bliss. But, she had a debt to pay and that debt was haunting her. Until she repaid it, she would not be at peace. So, one Sunday she asked Taavi to watch the girls. She refused to tell him where she was going, as she knew he would try to stop her. As she left the flat, she turned to him and smiled.

"Don't worry. I'll be back very soon."

Taavi shook his head. "I really wish you would talk to me and tell me what you're up to."

"I promise I'll tell you when I get back."

Michal kept her wits about her as she headed down to the docks. Even though it was a Sunday afternoon, the streets were filled with both male and female prostitutes of all ages. Pimps still hovered in alleyways. She took a deep breath and stood up as straight and tall as she could and tried to look unapproachable. Still, she was solicited by men and women continuously. Finally, Michal could not bear to walk the streets anymore looking for her old friend. She found a young woman who looked too sweet and young to be a prostitute. However, Michal was quite sure that she was one.

"Do you know a girl; her name is Yana? The last I saw her, she was working out here by the docks?"

"Of course, everyone knew Yana. She was young, right?"

"Yes."

"So?"

"Do you know where I can find her? I have something for her." Michal had taken a few marks from her grocery money to give to Yana. She remembered how Yana had once helped her and she wanted to pay Yana back her money.

"You won't find her here. She's dead. They found her in the river. I guess one of her customers liked to play rough. Cut her up real bad."

Michal felt sick. She thought she might vomit. Her hand gripped the side of the building and she tried to breathe deeply.

"Yeah, it was terrible. Everyone who saw it said it was horrible what he done to her. I felt bad. But them things happen on the street," the young girl said.

Michal took the money out of her pocket and put it into the girl's palm. "Go and have a good meal," she said, squeezing the young prostitute's hand.

Then Michal turned and walked quickly back to the safety of her life. Tears welled up behind her eyes as she raced through the section of town where the lost came to sell all that they had left that had any worth. Poor Yana. As tough as Yana had tried to be, Michal knew that the girl had a kind heart. After all, Yana had given her money when Yana had barely enough for herself. Michal was sorry for all of them. But she was filled with gratitude and even a little guilt that she'd been spared.

CHAPTER 53

Two years later, Lev got married for the second time. He met a Gentile girl with an easy smile and a quick wit, who he brought to meet Taavi and Michal one evening. It was an unexpected visit, but Lev and his fiancée, Lotti, brought a bottle of wine and a cake. As soon as Lev introduced Lotti, she gave Michal a hug. Both children were asleep, so the two couples were able to sit on the sofa and talk. "How did you meet?" Michal asked Lotti.

"I work in a factory around the corner from your store. Lev and I would see each other in the park during our lunch hours. We began talking and one thing led to another … and he asked me to have dinner with him."

"At first, she said no," Lev said and reached for Lotti's hand. "I think maybe it's this mezuzah that I wear?"

"Yes, well, please don't be offended; I mean no harm. But, I am ashamed to say that my father is anti-Semitic; he was afraid for me to date a Jewish man. We never had long discussions about it; it was just something I always knew growing up. You see, he is still stuck in the middle ages. And he is afraid for me...."

"We have lived with the hatred of our people our entire lives," Taavi said.

"I don't hate your people. I love Lev and I wanted to become a Jew. I told Lev I wanted to go to a rabbi and be converted. Lev refused. He thinks it's unnecessary. He isn't that religious, he says, and there's no reason to alienate my father. It's a sad thing to watch Lev trying to make friends with my dad. I know that my parents will never accept us. But it doesn't matter. I've lost them; they've disowned me. Even so…I wouldn't change a thing. If I could go back to the time before Lev and I met, I would want to meet him, fall in love with him, and be his wife. Like I said, I wouldn't change a thing."

"Being in love is the greatest feeling in the world," Taavi said. "I know. I have lived with it and without it, and let me tell you … to love and be loved is the most wonderful feeling in the world."

Lev smiled at Lotti.

They were sharing a second glass of wine, when Lotti noticed the children's book on the playroom table that Taavi had built. It was a miniature table and chairs that he'd painted pink and white. "Is that a book by Otto Keihn?"

Just hearing Otto's name rattled Michal. It took her right back to a time she'd not thought about for many years. She'd seen that children's book every day. She hadn't noticed it for a long time amongst the other toys and books that Taavi had gotten for the girls. Because it had been there so long, Michal no longer noticed it. The children had so many other books, and Michal could not remember the last time Alina had requested a story to be read from Otto's book, "Yes, it's a children's fable book by Otto Keihn."

"Oh, I've heard a lot about him. I'm pretty sure that I heard that he died a few years ago. I think I read something about it in the paper. From what I understand, he was a raging communist."

Michal shrugged. "I don't know much about him. I can't even remember where I got that book," she said. She didn't want to discuss Otto. In fact, she was surprised that he was well known enough for his death to have been posted in the newspapers. When they were together, she'd never realized that he was famous outside of his little community of artists.

"That doesn't surprise me," Taavi said. "Berlin is full of communists. It's jam packed with people who are devoted to all kinds of political parties. I don't worry about the commies as much as I do the National Socialist Party. I'm keeping an eye on them."

"I don't think they're anything to worry about. They're a small group of lunatics without much influence on anybody or anything. Just troublemakers," Lev said.

"Yes, but again, they are very anti-Semitic. Michal and I are from Russia; we know the dangers of anti-Semitism. We have seen pogroms first hand."

"That could never happen here," Lev said. "Berlin is too civilized for something as barbaric as a pogrom."

"I would have to agree," Lotti said. "People are too educated and intelligent here to allow for that to happen."

"Maybe," Taavi said. "Let's just say that I hope you're right."

"What do you think, Michal?" Lotti asked.

Michal shook her head and shrugged her shoulders. She didn't want to talk about pogroms in Siberia or the possibility of them happening in Germany. She wanted to forget that such terrible things could happen. For a moment, she was lost in a memory. Otto, dear, sweet but confused Otto. He had given her all he had to give. His bisexuality had hurt her at the time. In fact, she was angry with him for what she had considered a betrayal of her trust, but now, as she looked at Taavi, she knew that she'd found her one true *bashert* … her destiny. And in a very strange but important way, Otto had helped her.

Taavi studied Michal's face. He misinterpreted what she was thinking. He was afraid that all this talk of pogroms was leading her thoughts back to that fateful day when the Cossack … He decided that it was best to change the subject quickly. The less time Michal spent dwelling on the past, the better.

"So," Taavi said. "Lev told me about your new apartment. It sounds nice."

"Yes, you will have to bring the children and come for dinner," Lotti said.

"My Lotti is a wonderful cook." Lev smiled.

"He's lying. I'm a terrible cook. But I try very hard. Maybe you can help me learn, Michal."

"Yes, of course," she said, snapping out of her thoughts and back into the present moment.

"I'd love to learn to bake too."

"That would be a good idea, my darling. You're not such a good baker," Lev said.

"You, be quiet," she said, teasing him. Then she winked at Michal. "He's telling the truth. I'm a terrible baker."

"Come over and we'll bake. The girls will love it."

"I adore children, so it should be a lot of fun."

They talked about building furniture for Lotti and Lev's new apartment. Lotti blushed when Lev mentioned that they wanted to have children as soon as possible because of his age.

"I'm ten years older than Lotti," he said. "I ask myself every day, "What would such a beautiful young woman want with an old man like me?"

"Oh, you are so silly. You're not an old man. You're only thirty-one, for goodness sake. That's not old."

Lev smiled. "You see? Nu? I am lucky?"

Michal and Lotti became fast friends. For Michal, it was wonderful to have a friend. It had been years since Michal had last seen Gerta, who, until Lotti, had been the closest thing Michal had ever known to a lady friend. Lotti spent many afternoons with Michal and the girls. She told Michal that she wanted to have a child as soon as possible, given Lev's age. And, to her delight, three months after the wedding, Lotti told Michal that she was pregnant.

Unlike Michal, Lotti had a rough pregnancy. In her second trimester, she found spots of blood on her underwear. Her stomach was cramping. She didn't want to alarm Lev. Perhaps it would stop soon. After all, she'd never been pregnant before, and she wasn't sure what to expect. Lotti called Michal.

"I'm bleeding a little," Lotti said. "Is it normal to bleed when you're pregnant?"

Michal knew that blood during a pregnancy was not a good sign. "Why don't I come over? I have to bring the girls with me; I have no place to leave them. Would that be alright with you?"

"Yes, of course. Please, come."

"I'll be right over."

"Michal?"

"Yes?"

"Am I having a miscarriage?"

"I don't know, Lotti. But, hold tight. I'm on my way." Michal sat beside Lotti as she lay in bed, terrified that she would lose the child. Alina and Gilde ran around the apartment playing, while Michal spoke softly to Lotti, trying to reassure her.

An hour later, Michal insisted that Lotti go to the bathroom and check to see if she was still losing blood. "If you are, we are going to have to call the doctor," Michal said.

Michal could hardly breathe as she waited for Lotti to return. She remembered helping women who were having miscarriages when she was with Bepa.

"It seems to have stopped," Lotti said.

"Are you sure?"

"Yes. I used a menstrual rag to wipe myself and it came back clean."

"Thank God," Michal said. "Still, you should lie down and rest. Keep your feet up."

Lotti was trembling when she got into bed. "I'm scared, Michal."

"I know," Michal said, and she rubbed Lotti's head like Lotti was one of her children.

Finally, Lotti fell asleep. Michal looked at her friend and remembered how she had longed to become pregnant with Avram and how she'd been unable to conceive. She understood how much this baby meant to Lotti and she prayed that Lotti would not miscarry.

Gilde was a toddler now, she was two and had begun to assert her independence from everyone except for Alina, who she followed around like a puppy. Michal longed for another baby, for the sweet smell of powder and milk that surrounded a tiny infant. But she and Taavi had decided they didn't want any more until they were able to purchase a home. He wanted his children to have their own house, with a yard where they could play. It was his dream.

CHAPTER 54

In her seventh month, Lotti woke up with a headache, slight nausea, and occasional stomach cramps. Since her body had behaved so strangely throughout the pregnancy, she thought nothing of it. She got out of bed and began cleaning her house as she did every morning. By noon, she was feeling very ill. Her head ached and she had vomited twice; sharp pains were shooting through her belly. By the time Lev got home from work, she was spotting heavily.

Lev took Lotti to the hospital, then telephoned Michal. She left the children with Taavi and took a streetcar to meet Lev. When she arrived, she found Lev in the waiting room. His face was pale. She sat down beside him.

"How is she?"

He shrugged. "I don't know. No one has told me anything. I am waiting."

Michal and Lev sat silently in the waiting room, both of them silently praying.

Three hours later, the doctor came down the hall and walked towards them. Michal felt the breath catch in her throat and she coughed.

"Mr. Glassman? You are the husband of Lotti Glassman?" the doctor said.

"Yes," Lev said. "How is my wife?"

"I'm afraid that she has lost a lot of blood. I can't promise anything, but because she is young and strong ... I believe she will survive. As far as the baby is concerned ... I am sorry. I was not able to save the child."

Lev's shoulders dropped and his head hung low.

"Thank God she's alive." Michal rubbed Lev's arm.

"It would be wise to notify her parents ... just in case ... things take a turn for the worse ... you understand?" the doctor said to both Michal and Lev.

Lev nodded. "Can I go in and see her?"

"Give the nurses a few minutes. They'll call you in when she's ready."

Lev and Michal sat on the hard wooden chairs and watched the big round clock on the wall. Fifteen minutes that seemed like hours passed, and still the nurses had not come out to allow them to go into the room.

"I think I should call her parents," Lev said. "I know they hate me. But they should know."

"Can I call them for you?" Michal asked.

Lev shook his head. "No, they don't know you. I'm going to have to call them and tell them everything. I'll be right back." Lev went to the public phone. He was gone a very short time, but when he returned, it appeared that the blood had drained from his face.

"They're coming here," he said to Michal. "They blame me." He began pacing. "I wish someone would come out and tell us that we could see her already. I have to see her."

A nurse with a crisp white uniform and matching white hat came towards them. "You can go in now. Don't stay long. She's very weak and tired. It's best if she gets some rest."

Lev rushed into the room. He put his face next to Lotti's on the pillow and whispered something that Michal could not hear. Lotti's eyes flickered open and she tried to smile, but tears began to form and roll down her cheeks. Her voice was a hoarse whisper, "I lost the baby, didn't I?"

"There will be other babies," Lev said. "You're young. We'll try again." He took her hand and squeezed it gently. "I love you. I am grateful to God that you are alive and you are going to be all right. You are my world, Lotti."

"Michal? You're here too? Taavi is watching the children?"

"Yes," Michal whispered. "He's watching the girls so that I can be here with you."

"It's so kind of you to come…"

"Don't be silly, Lotti. You're my best friend."

Lotti smiled, then her head slipped to the side and she fell asleep.

There was only one chair in Lotti's room. "You sit," Lev whispered. I'll stand here by the bed.

Michal sat. A half hour passed.

A nurse peeked her head inside the room "You two, it's time to go. Let her sleep. She needs to regain her strength."

Lev and Michal went back into the waiting room just as Lotti's parents came rushing into the ward.

"Where's my daughter?" Lotti's father, a heavy-set man with a head of wavy golden brown hair and a red weather-beaten face said to Lev.

"She's resting."

Lotti's mother didn't say a word, but Michal watched her as she continually twisted the handle of her handbag.

"I want to see her. NOW!" Lotti's father said. "Come with me," he said to his wife, who followed him. "What room is she in?"

"Two-thirty-four," Lev answered.

Lotti's parents walked towards the room, but the nurse stopped them. "I'm sorry, the patient in this room is resting. You'll have to come back later."

Lotti's father was beet red with anger. He walked back to the waiting room with Lotti's mother following behind him. "I never wanted her to marry you," he said to Lev. "This miscarriage is a curse from God for her marrying a Jew. Of course you realize this, I'm sure?"

Lev didn't answer.

"You should realize it. If you care at all for Lotti, let her go. Get out of her life."

"I'm not going anywhere," Lev said.

Lotti's father pushed Lev. Lev pushed him back. Three chairs in the waiting room were knocked over before two nurses came and threatened to call the police if they didn't all leave.

The entire group was escorted out of the hospital. Lotti's parents went home without saying goodbye to either Lev or Michal. There was nothing to do but go home and wait. So

Michal returned to her family with a promise from Lev that he would call her and keep her updated on Lotti's condition. Lev walked towards the train, giving the impression that he too was going back to his apartment. But once everyone else had gone, Lev slipped back into the hospital and tiptoed into his wife's room. No one heard him. He sat quietly on the chair beside her bed and waited for her to awaken.

Lotti spent two weeks in the hospital. During this time, she was given strict orders never to attempt another pregnancy. The doctor said that she was not able to carry full term and if she got pregnant again, it could threaten her life. Lev held her as she wept. Her sadness broke his heart. Lev was powerless; there was nothing that he could do to change the situation. Over and over again, he told her that it didn't matter to him if they had children or not. He felt so grateful that she had survived. But Lotti had always wanted children and now she knew she would never be able to have her own. Taavi called and told Lev to stay with his wife, and not to worry about coming into work. Michal visited the hospital several times during Lotti's stay, but even she was not able to lift Lotti out of her depression.

When Lotti returned home, she spoke very little. Most of the time, she stayed in her room and barely ate. Lev was worried. He discussed the situation with Taavi at work. Taavi insisted that Lotti was young and would recover. But, as the months passed and Lotti grew thinner and more lethargic, Lev began to worry. Michal came at least twice a week to visit. She came in the evening when she was able to leave the girls with Taavi, because she was afraid that they were too active and loud for Lotti to tolerate. One afternoon Michal had baked bread. She made two beautiful braided challahs. She thought maybe if she brought one over, Lotti might be willing to eat a slice of fresh bread. It was late March and, although the weather was still cold, it was a lot warmer than it had been a month earlier. Michal thought that perhaps she would wait until Alina got home from school, then take the girls with her to Lotti's house, drop off the bread, and then go to the library. They had not gone to the library all winter, mostly because of the cold, but also because Gilde was only three and she didn't behave well at the library. But Michal knew that Alina loved the shelves of books. She was nine years old and already an avid reader. It was not fair that Alina had to forgo this pleasure. The last time they had gone to the library was the previous fall, when Michal had left Gilde with Taavi and taken Alina alone. She and Michal had spent several hours reading and deciding which books she would borrow. It was a great afternoon. Michal still remembered how close she felt to Alina that day.

Taavi was working, so Michal would have to take both girls, but she decided that it would be good for them to get out, even if they only stayed at the library for a short time. It had been a long winter. Michal dressed the girls warmly and wrapped the bread in a clean kitchen towel. Then the three walked together to Lotti's apartment.

Lotti welcomed them, but Michal could see that Lotti was still melancholy. Immediately, Gilde wanted a slice of the bread.

"I want a slice with butter," she said. "Do you have any butter?" Gilde asked Lotti.

"No, sweetie, that's a gift for Lotti. We have some at home," Michal said.

"But, I want a piece now!"

"You're being very rude," Michal said.

"It's all right," Lotti said, and cut a slice for Gilde. "Here, let me put some butter on this." After the bread was buttered, she handed it to Gilde, who stuffed it into her mouth.

"Gilde! Eat like a lady," Michal said.

"Would you like a slice too?" Lotti asked Alina.

Alina shook her head. "No, thank you."

"Would you like one, Michal?"

"No, thanks."

Lotti smiled and wrapped the bread in the towel again.

"How are you feeling?" Michal asked.

"I'm all right." Lotti smiled.

"Aunt Lotti, I've missed you coming over and reading to me," Alina said. The girls had taken to calling Lotti and Lev their aunt and uncle.

"Yes, well, I haven't been getting out much this winter," Lotti said.

"Will you read to me now?"

"No, don't bother Aunt Lotti, Alina. We're going to the library. I'll read to you there. Or, better yet, you can practice reading."

"Aunt Lotti, I miss you reading to me. Will you? Please?" Alina asked.

Lotti's shoulders dropped. "Very well. Let's put on a pot of water for tea and I'll read you both a story."

And so it was that Alina, with the power that only an innocent child has access to, found a way to lift Lotti from the depths of depression. Instead of going to the library, Lotti spent the afternoon reading to Alina, while Glide sat on the floor in the kitchen arranging all of Lotti's pots and pans into neat piles.

Michal watched Lotti coming alive as Alina cuddled up to her, and she knew that this was a special day. What she didn't yet know was that from this day forward, Alina and Lotti would always have a bond between them that could not easily be broken.

"Are you sure you don't mind Gilde playing with all of your kitchen things?" Michal asked.

"I don't mind at all," Lotti said. "I'm glad to have all of you here."

Gilde sang softly to herself as she took apart the piles that were layered on each other and then found the tops that fit each pan and arranged them carefully on the floor.

After that visit, Lotti began to come back to her old self. Her eyes regained their sparkle. Twice a week, every week, Michal made it a point to take the girls to visit Lotti. And, after a few months, Lotti began to meet Alina after school, and with Michal's permission brought Alina back to her apartment, where they spent the rest of the afternoon baking or cooking. Lotti was an excellent seamstress, and she spent hours teaching Alina to embroider and sew. Alina learned to design and make her own clothes without a pattern. Lotti took her shopping for fabric. When she wasn't at school, Alina was at Lotti's house. Sometimes Michal was secretly a little jealous. She felt that the two had bonded and she'd somehow been left out. Still, she was glad that Lotti was no longer miserable. And, Alina could not have chosen a better friend.

CHAPTER 55

Berlin, 1931

Taavi was having breakfast and reading the morning paper. Although the state of the economy was getting worse in Germany, with Taavi's connections, he was still able to acquire small amounts of coffee and sugar. When he bought goods through the black market, he didn't use his rations, so sometimes Taavi gave their rations to an old widow who lived in their building. He would look at his family and his heart would swell with all of his blessings. Then something inside of him would compel him to share. After all, they weren't reliant on the rations. They had more than most. Although Taavi couldn't be sure, he thought the widow, Mrs. Marksmann, to be about seventy. She was a Christian woman, with a kind heart, who had always been good to his children. This month, he'd felt compelled to give her the last few lumps of sugar that they had. It would be a few weeks before he would be able to get more and now, drinking his bitter unsweetened coffee, he was mildly regretting his rash decision to be so generous. He smiled to himself, shaking his head, Taavi, he thought, you're such a soft old fool. At thirty-five, Taavi was hardly an old man; he was even more handsome than he'd been in his twenties. His hair was thick and sprinkled with just a touch of gray. His eyes were more deep, warm, and wise. From his physical work, his body had stayed muscular and strong.

Michal came into the kitchen and poured a little extra coffee in Taavi's cup. She glanced down at the newspaper.

"A new play is opening?" Michal read aloud, "The Three Penny Opera." She glanced up at Taavi. "I'd love to go and see it. I really like the theater and it's been years since the last time I saw a play. Let's ask Lev and Lotti to go with us, what do you think?"

"Who will babysit if Lev and Lotti are with us?"

"Maybe Mrs. Marksmann would be willing to watch the girls for a few hours," Michal said.

"I read the reviews on it and it's supposed to be an indecent play, not proper ... you understand, right?" Taavi said.

"Yes, of course I understand. I've been exposed to the Berlin art world long enough now to know what to expect."

"All right. I'll mention it to Lev," he said.

Taavi smiled at her. Then he went on reading the paper. He would talk to Lev about the theater. But that wasn't what was on his mind. Trouble was brewing. Taavi could feel it in his bones. There was an entire page devoted to Adolf Hitler's new bestseller, *Mein Kampf.* Unbeknownst to Michal, Taavi had read Hitler's book. He knew that Hitler was a complete anti-Semite and a dangerous one at that. Taavi'd read the book because he wanted to be forewarned and it bothered him greatly that the book had become a bestseller. To Taavi, that meant that many people were interested in what Hitler had to say. Taavi was keeping a close watch on the Nazi party, and he knew that they now had their own headquarters called the Brown house and that their popularity was growing every day. In fact, what had once been a small group of followers who had been viewed as crazy, was now the second largest political party in Germany.

None of his Jewish friends were particularly worried. They had discussed the situation and they were all sure that the Nazi threat would pass, but Taavi could not brush it off so lightly. Although he never mentioned anything to Michal, Taavi was uneasy like a wolf before a thunderstorm.

Lev and Lotti accompanied Michal and Taavi to the theater. This was the first play that either of them had ever been to and they enjoyed it immensely.

The play was outstanding, if a bit risqué. As Michal had hoped, Mrs. Marksmann was more than happy to watch the girls. After the play, they stopped at a café for a light dinner. Lotti looked like her old self. Her golden curls bobbed as she talked animatedly about the play. After the miscarriage, Lotti never returned to her former job at the factory. Lev didn't care. He'd lost his first wife to an accident at a manufacturing plant and it was nice not to have to worry about Lotti's safety every day. They had enough money to live comfortably. Lotti was back to her happy go lucky self, and Lev was glad that everything was going well.

"I have a surprise for all of you!" Lotti said. "I'm going back to work."

Lev cocked his head to one side and his eyes narrowed. "At the factory? I thought you hated it there?"

"Well, it's not exactly work. I mean, it's not paid work. And, no, it's not at the factory. I want to do volunteer work at an orphanage for Jewish children."

Although Lev was happy that Lotti wanted to get out and find things to do with her time, he was afraid that working with children would be a constant reminder to her that she was barren. "Are you sure you want to do this?"

"Yes, very sure. I was at the butcher shop the other day when I met a lady who told me that the Jewish Orphanage was badly in need of volunteers. You know how much I've always loved children."

"Yes, I know. But, how did the orphanage come up?" Lev asked. He thought that Lotti might be thinking about adopting a child and he had reservations of his own about the idea. Lev liked children, but he was not eager to raise one that wasn't his own. If he and Lotti had conceived, it would be a different story. But, as it was, he'd grown used to the ease of their way of life. Although he wouldn't admit it to Lotti, for Lev a child would be an intrusion.

"This woman and I were waiting in line for the butcher. You know how busy the kosher butcher is on Friday morning right before Sabbath? Well, it was Friday and I thought I would be there all day; the line was that long. So, anyway, she and I were waiting for our turn. And she had these two beautiful children with her, a boy and girl. I asked her how old they were. She told me they were twins and they were three years old. I said how fortunate she was to have children. Not just one, but two! Then she said that they were adopted. One thing led to another … and she mentioned the orphanage. Now, I know you, Lev; I know you would not want to adopt. You've sort of made that clear."

"Have I?" He wondered how she knew. Lev couldn't remember ever mentioning how he felt.

"Yes, you've let me know in several ways. But, I thought … well, if I can't take a child home, maybe there is something else I can do to be of use. So, the following morning I took the train out to the orphanage and asked if they needed any help. They said they could use volunteers, but were not able to pay employees. I hope it's all right with you, Lev. I said I would love to take the position." A smile spread over Lotti's face.

"You're sure this is what you want?" Lev took her hand and gazed into her eyes.

"Positive."

"If it's what you want, it's all right with me," he answered.

CHAPTER 56

In 1932, a famous and wealthy psychic named Erik Jan Hanussen made a prediction that Hitler would become a very important man. Hanussen was very popular and he performed in cabarets all over Berlin. News of the prediction reached Hitler, who, at the time, was at a political low in his career. Things were looking bleak for him as a future leader. Hitler decided to book private sessions with Hanussen. At one of these visits, Hanussen gave him a magic spell using a root called mandrake. The psychic promised Hitler that if he performed the spell he would take over as the leader of Germany.

Hitler followed Hanussen's directions and on the fateful day of January 30th 1933, Hitler was appointed chancellor of Germany.

Then slowly, very slowly so that no one would notice, things began to change in Germany. In mid-March, in a small village outside of Munich, Dachau, the first official concentration camp was opened.

Books written by Jewish authors were being burned in the streets, and then boycotts of Jewish businesses began. Next, Jews could no longer hold jobs at universities or in civil service.

Later that same year, Hitler discovered that his friend, Hanussen's real name was Herschmann-Chaim Steinschneider and that Hanussen was born a Jew.

In March, Hitler sent out a group of his thugs and had Hanussen arrested and murdered.

Then on April 26th, Herman Goering established an organization that would come to strike terror in the hearts of Jews and German citizens alike, the state police ... The Gestapo.

Children were encouraged by the Nazi party to watch their parents for any signs of disloyalty and to report them immediately. People who'd lived peacefully beside Jews for years now turned their backs on their neighbors out of fear for their own safety and the safety of their loved ones. The Gestapo had eyes around every corner; they were always watching.

Next, Hitler proclaimed himself Fuhrer and declared that the armed forces must now swear allegiance to him.

Then in 1935 the first set of Nuremburg laws were passed. They included over one hundred and twenty laws denying Jews their civil rights. Under "The Law for the Protection of German Blood and Honor," Jews were now considered a separate race. Judaism was no longer determined by religion or practice of religion. Now it was decided by ancestry and was determined by the government to be a race rather than a religion. Marriages and sexual relations between Aryans and Jews were now strictly forbidden by law.

CHAPTER 57

Lotti and Lev were walking a dangerous tightrope. Lotti's father came to see her and made another appeal to her to divorce Lev and return to her family before she found herself in serious trouble with the Nazi party. Lotti refused.

As Hitler's anti-Semitic views became more commonplace, they began to affect the Jewish children attending public schools. They were ridiculed not only by the other children but by the teachers who were no longer the adults that they could trust. Many children were afraid to go to school; they were singled out in their classes called names, accused of crimes they did not commit, and deemed a pariah on society. Walking home was even more dangerous; the boys in the Hitler youth waited outside to physically assault them. These young children knew that they could not turn to anyone for help; the principal and the teachers would not defend them.

Taavi was watching as the world was descending into Hell right before his eyes. Even before Adolf Hitler had been appointed chancellor and given himself complete power to make laws, Taavi had an uneasy nagging voice in the back of his mind warning him to beware. Michal told Taavi that she was beginning to feel threatened when she went out of the house. The boys of the Hitler Youth taunted her and she couldn't be sure that they wouldn't physically attack her. And she said she was very worried about the children at school. Perhaps they should leave Germany, Michal suggested. Maybe they should try to go to America. Taavi thought about what she said. But he'd worked hard and built his business and his life in Germany. In fact, he was known throughout the country for crafting the finest of furniture. Jews and Gentiles alike came to his store and placed custom orders. If he left Europe, he would have to start over again at thirty-nine. It would be a daunting task. Besides, it was hard to get into America, very hard. America was in a depression as well and her president, who was President Roosevelt, was limiting immigration because he wanted to create jobs and rebuild the American economy. If the country was flooded with refugees, they would need work. Roosevelt wanted to make sure his own people were employed before he opened the doors to others.

Taavi didn't know what to do. He didn't like to see Michal afraid, so he made light of the situation and told Michal not to worry. He said that he was sure that it would pass. Germany was too educated and civilized a country to accept this for very long. This was just a temporary problem. He told her, smiling and patting her shoulder reassuringly, that it would work itself out. But at night when Michal lay breathing softly and evenly beside him, Taavi's heart was growing heavier every day with fear.

CHAPTER 58

1936 Berlin

An Olympic stadium was erected to host the Olympics in Berlin. Hitler declared that no Jewish athletes would be allowed to compete. The U.S. threatened to boycott, but Hitler stood strong in his stance and only two athletes with some Jewish ancestry were allowed to participate.

The United States didn't keep their threat; they did not boycott. Instead, they sent an Olympic team. After Hitler bragged about the superiority and unbeatable athletic prowess of his Aryan race, to his chagrin, Jesse Owens, a black American track star, took most of the medals. Owens proved that there was no basis for Hitler's superior race ideology. And, of course, Adolf Hitler was furious.

Alina and Lotti remained close friends throughout the years. They spent as much time together as was possible. Lotti became very involved in her volunteer work at the Jewish Orphanage. Sometimes, with Michal's permission, Lotti took Alina to work with her, where Alina helped the other children learn to read and write. Alina emulated Lotti. She wore her hair the same as Lotti's, borrowed Lotti's lipstick, and spent endless hours at Lotti's apartment doing her homework.

Alina's sixteenth birthday was an event that Lotti and Michal were very excited to plan. They decided to have a surprise party at Lotti's apartment. Michal baked a cake. Lotti prepared all of

Alina's favorite foods, and they invited all of Alina's friends from school. Lotti called Alina and invited her out for lunch for her birthday.

"Come to my house and we can leave together from here. Dress up a little because I want to go to a nice restaurant. It's not every day that a girl turns sixteen."

"You don't have to take me out," Alina said.

"I know that; I want to take you out. Be here on Sunday afternoon at about noon. Would that be alright?"

"Yes, of course. Are you sure you want to do this?"

"Of course I am, silly."

Alina was completely overcome when all of her friends were waiting at Lotti's house. They yelled surprise and Alina's hand went to her throat. She felt tears run down her cheeks and, at the same time, she'd never felt so happy.

There were piles of gifts on the coffee table in the living room, but when Lotti gave Alina a tube of lipstick all her own, Alina hugged her tightly. Then Lotti and Lev gave Alina an envelope with money for her for college.

Michal and Taavi gave Alina a beautiful gold Star of David with a small sapphire in the center. It was beautiful. Michal kissed her daughter's cheek as she helped her to close the clasp.

"I'll never take it off. Never," Alina said. Taavi hugged his daughter.

Two days later, Alina asked Lotti to see if she would be eligible for a volunteer position at the orphanage. "I've always felt so needed here. I know why you do this," Alina said to Lotti.

Since there was always a shortage of volunteers, Alina was welcomed. Three days a week, after school, she took the train to the large brick building where the orphans were housed. Sometimes, Alina spent the Sabbath with the children instead of going home to her family. The little orphans were so alone in the world, so needy of her attention that many of them had borne their way deep into her heart.

Michal hated it, but she still felt jealous of the relationship between Lotti and Alina. For some reason, no matter how hard Michal tried, Alina always kept her at a distance. The bond between Gilde and Alina was undeniable. Gilde loved her mother. And Alina adored her little sister from the first moment that she'd seen her. She treated Gilde like she was her daughter. And for that, Michal was happy. But Alina was cold to Michal.

Gilde was the ray of sunshine in their home. She was equally close to her parents and her sister. She was always making jokes or singing songs. If one of the family members was having a hard day, Gilde would do whatever she could to cheer them up.

During the years that Michal and Taavi were separated, Michal thought that she and Alina had been very close. But, as the years passed, Alina became like a stranger to Michal. There was no doubt in Michal's mind that Alina loved her and that she loved her father too. In fact, Michal couldn't complain about Taavi; he had proved to be a wonderful father. But something along the way had been lost between Alina and her mother, and Michal had no idea how to retrieve it.

Occasionally, Alina took Gilde with her to work. At ten, Gilde already had a flare for the theater. She loved to play school and create puppet shows using old socks to make puppets with the other children at the orphanage. Michal had taught her how to make the puppets and she'd taught everyone

301

at the orphanage. Even though she was young, Gilde loved attention. In fact, she giggled when two of the twelve-year-old boys vied for her interest. The three of them had met the first time that Gilde came to the home for orphaned children with her sister. Elias was tall and slender, with deep dark eyes and short straight hair. He excelled at athletics and had no qualms about speaking up for himself. Elias was not intimidated by authority and it seemed he was always getting into trouble with the teachers and the volunteers. Lotti didn't like him very much; she tried to discourage the friendship that had begun to form between Elias and Glide. But the more she tried to warn Gilde to keep her distance, the better Gilde liked Elias. The other boy, Shaul, was a heavyset rather clumsy and awkward boy with black curly hair, thick glasses, and a sweet gentle disposition, who followed Elias around hoping that Elias would throw him a crumb of approval. Shaul was shy when he was with Gilde and that made her want to treat him like he was one of her dolls or her child. He never argued with Gilde. He did whatever she asked, while Elias just laughed when Gilde gave him an order, and did as he pleased.

One afternoon, Gilde came to the orphanage directly from school. She took the subway alone, without stopping at home first. "I need to see my sister," Gilde said to Elias. The skin around her left eye had begun to turn purple and yellow. The white of her eye was spotted with bright red blood and blood had crusted around a red cut on her top lip.

"What happened to you?" Elias asked. "You look like you fell down the stairs."

"No ... I got beat up on the playground during recess. I went in and told the teacher, but she refused to do anything to the kids that hit me. She said it was my fault. It wasn't my fault, Elias. I didn't do anything."

"Did you tell your parents?" Shaul asked.

"Shut up, Shaul. Tell me who did this to you. What are the kids' names? I'll find them and I'll beat the shit out of them," Elias said, his fists were clenched.

"A group of kids. Boys and girls. I don't know their names."

"What the hell started it? What the hell did they hit you for?" Elias frowned.

"For being a Jew. And, no, I didn't tell my parents. I came straight here. I didn't want to upset my mother. If she saw me like this she would be sick."

"I'm gonna sneak outta here and take a kitchen knife, then find them and stab 'em. You'll have to help me find them, Gilde; you're gonna have to point them out to me," Elias said, as he shook his head. He had a cigarette that he'd gotten through a friend who bought it on the black market. Leaning against the side of the building, away from the watchful eyes of the teachers, he lit it and began smoking.

"I can't, Elias. I don't want you to get into trouble. You're not supposed to leave here without permission, and if you go and do something like that, you'll end up in jail or worse. Forget it. I'm not going with you. I'm not pointing them out."

Elias crossed his arms over his body. "Then how the hell can I help you? If we let them get away with it, they'll keep doing shit like this."

Gilde just shook her head. "No, Elias. I can't help you do this."

"Does it hurt?" Shaul asked.

"Yes. A lot."

"I'm sorry that you got beat up. I wish I could do something to make you feel better." Shaul touched her arm.

"Yeah, well, I wish I could live here at the orphanage and go to the Jewish school here with you two. I'd be much safer."

"I wish you could too," Shaul said.

CHAPTER 59

Having spent a great deal of her free time at the orphanage, Alina decided that she wanted to become a teacher. She planned to finish school then go to university to study. At least, she hoped she would be permitted to go to school. More laws forbidding Jews their rights were being made every day. Things at her school had changed considerably. People who had been her friends for years were now avoiding her. Others were snubbing her, saying rude and offensive things. Evidence of the Nazi influence was everywhere. Boys she'd grown up with were now members of the Hitler Youth. Girls who she'd once giggled with at a lunch table when they were young children, now gathered to go to their meetings of the Bund Deutscher Madels. Alina didn't want to upset her family, so she never talked to her parents or even Lotti about the terrible changes she was encountering every day. She just found herself avoiding her non-Jewish classmates and spending her time at her volunteer job. Where Alina had once had friends of all religious backgrounds, now, except for Lotti, she had only Jewish friends.

The children were sitting at the long tables doing their homework, while Alina was helping with the regular chores that had to be done.

Alina was folding a basket of clean laundry a few feet away from the rest of the children. If they needed help, she was right there to assist. A pile of white towels lay on the end of the long table. Alina began folding a sheet, just as Shaul came in. He raced to Alina.

"Your sister is outside. Some kids beat her up real bad. She's looking for you."

"Where is she?" Alina dropped the sheet to the floor.

"Follow me."

Alina left all of the laundry on the table and rushed out behind Shaul.

When Alina saw Gilde and how badly she was hurt, Alina fell to her knees and hugged her baby sister. "What happened to you?"

"I got beat up. Some kids beat up on me for being a Jew."

"Does Mama know that you're here?"

"No."

"She'll be worried. I have to call her. Then I'm going to leave here and take you home myself. Did you ride the subway here all alone?"

"Yes."

"You know better, Gilde. It's dangerous for you to be doing that. You're too young." Alina shook her head, then she hugged her sister again. "Come on. Let's get you cleaned up."

Alina brought Gilde inside the building and sat her down on a small wooden chair. "Don't go anywhere. I want to wash all that blood off your face. But first, I'm going to call Mama so she knows where you are. She's probably going crazy with worry about you. I'll be right back."

Lotti came in and saw what had happened. She shook her head and tears came to the corners of her eyes when Gilde explained how she'd been hurt.

"Let me help. I'll clean you up," Lotti said. Then she went into the adjoining kitchen and got a rag and wet it with warm water. She came back and gently began to clean the blood off of Gilde's face.

Alina came back into the room. "Lotti, I just called my mother. She knows that Gilde is here and that I am going to bring her home. I'm sorry I have to leave."

"Of course. Is there anything I can do?"

"Nothing."

"Oh, Alina …I'm so sorry," Lotti said.

Alina took Gilde's small hand in her own and both girls walked out of the building. Lotti watched them and wiped a tear from her cheek.

CHAPTER 60

That night, the entire family gathered to discuss what had happened at school to Gilde.

Gilde told her parents everything. Then Alina added that she too had experienced a wave of anti-Semitism at school.

Taavi paced the room. He could not speak. Gilde was just a child. An innocent child. Michal watched her husband. She too was at a loss for words.

"She's afraid to go to school tomorrow," Michal finally said.

"I don't blame her. But she has to go. If she doesn't go, they'll never stop making her life miserable. If they see she is weak, they'll attack her all the time. She has to be stronger than they are. I'll go to the school with her. I'll talk to the teachers and tell them what happened. Maybe we can come up with a solution," Taavi said.

He picked up the phone and called Lev. "I'll be in to work late tomorrow. I have to take Gilde in to school and talk to the teachers about something. Can you just open the shop and wait for me?"

"Of course, Tav, don't worry about the business. I'll be there. You take care of your family."

CHAPTER 61

It was as Taavi had feared. He hoped he would be wrong, but he found that the teachers clearly didn't care about Gilde's safety. They were blatant anti-Semites, and had no problem telling Taavi what they thought of Jews. He did not leave Gilde at school that day. Instead, he took her back home and left her with Michal.

"Something else has to be arranged. She can't go to that school," Taavi whispered to Michal. He didn't want Gilde to hear him.

"What are we going to do?"

"I have some ideas. But, let me think about it and I'll talk to you when I get home from work tonight."

That night, it was decided that Gilde would go to school at the Jewish Orphanage. Taavi would drop Gilde at Lotti's home on his way to work in the morning. Then Lotti would take Gilde on the train with her to the orphanage, where she would go to school with the other Jewish children. Permission had to be granted from the authorities who ran the orphanage, but Lotti assured Michal and Taavi that she would be able to secure a place for Gilde.

And so the following week, Gilde began to attend school with the orphans. Since all of the students were Jewish, Gilde was safe from prejudice. And that was a relief for Michal and Taavi. Besides that, either Alina or Lotti were always available in case Gilde needed anything. When Gilde had attended public school, except for her love of music and theater, Gilde had always been a mediocre student. But since she'd changed schools, Gilde began to get better grades and even made the honor roll.

School became not only a place of learning, but a social outlet for Gilde. Every day, Gilde had lunch with her friends, Shaul and Elias. Then she returned to class, where no one mentioned that she was Jewish. After school, she waited in the main room and did her homework with the help of the other students and sometimes Alina, while she waited for Lotti to finish her work. And then Gilde took the train home with either Lotti or Alina or both.

CHAPTER 62

1938

Hitler decided that he must unite all German speaking people. He called this project *Lebensraum*, which means a natural development of a territory.

In March of 1938, Hitler took over Austria. The Austrian people welcomed the Nazis with open arms. It was a bloodless takeover that would come to be known as the Anschluss.

On April 6th, 1938, Elias turned fourteen. His voice had begun to change and was starting to notice how pretty Gilde was becoming. Although Gilde was only twelve, she was already beginning to develop the body of a young woman. She had begun to menstruate and Alina and Michal had both explained to her where babies came from and how important it was for a girl to respect her own body. With her father's golden hair and amber eyes, it was easy to see she was destined to be a beauty. Shaul, who had turned fourteen in February, noticed too. Gilde enjoyed all of the attention, but still had the heart of a child. She much preferred to climb a tree or shoot marbles with her friends, rather than trying to stop the boys from fighting. They'd started a ridiculous competition for her attention that sometimes caused them to hit or punch each other.

Meanwhile, Alina had begun dating the boy who brought cases of food each week to the orphanage. His name was Benny; he was a strong quiet boy who came from a religious family.

Every week, he and Alina saw each other when he made his delivery. At first, Alina had no romantic interest in Benny. But one day he jumped off the side of the delivery truck and walked over to her carrying an apple.

"I've been noticing you when I come here every week. Are you a teacher?"

"No, I'm a volunteer. I'm just finishing school."

"My name is Benny."

"I'm Alina."

"We just got this shipment of apples. They're very sweet. I thought you might like one."

She smiled and took the fruit. "Thank you."

"You're welcome. I hope you like it."

"I'm sure I will," Alina said, looking down at the apple in her hands. She'd never been alone talking with a boy close to her own age. She felt clumsy, awkward, and had no idea what to say. But she could see that Benny felt the same way.

"Well ... I'll see you next week?"

"Yes. Next week."

And so, each week they spoke a little more until finally Benny asked Alina if she would like to have dinner with him. She agreed and they went on their first date. Michal and Taavi were glad that Alina had finally shown an interest in a boy. She was eighteen and, before Benny, she had never paid much attention to the opposite sex.

After Alina said she had a nice time on her first date with Benny, Michal invited Benny for Shabbat dinner on Friday night. Afterwards, Benny and Alina went for a walk. It was late

June and the weather was beautiful. The sky spilled over with silver sparkling stars. They walked quietly for ten minutes, neither knowing what to say.

"It's a beautiful night," Benny said.

"It is."

Again, they walked in silence. "Look at all of the stars that are out tonight."

"They are beautiful," Alina said.

"So, what are you going to do now that you are done with school?"

"I'm going to the university next year. For now, I've applied for a paid position in the kitchen at the orphanage. I'll earn a little extra money over the summer."

"I'm attending school part time at the university now. I can't go to school full time because I have to work. My father's business hasn't been doing well. He had many Gentile customers who stopped coming to his store when the laws went into effect about Gentiles being forbidden to shop at Jewish stores. So, I went out and got a job with a steady paycheck to help the family."

"Do you have sisters or brothers?"

"Both, two younger sisters and a younger brother. I'm the oldest."

"It must be difficult for you."

"Yes, I suppose it is. I want to have my own life, but I can't just walk away from them and leave them to fend for themselves. We've always been a close family. They need me now, so I can't abandon them. At least not until my father's business improves."

Alina nodded. "What are you studying?"

"Accounting, my parents are convinced that, as an accountant, I can always earn a living."

"I suppose that's true. Although, with all of the laws discouraging people from doing business with Jews, it's hard to say what we can do to earn a living."

"Yes, it is hard to say. For now, all we can do is hope that things will get better for us soon. So, on a brighter note, what do you want to study?"

"I want to be a teacher. I love working with children."

"I can see that. The children at the orphanage love you."

"I love them. They give me a sense of purpose. Does that make sense?"

"Of course. You know that they have no parents, no families, so you are their family. It's a beautiful thing. You have a beautiful heart, Alina."

She shook her head and looked away, "You embarrass me."

He smiled.

"I was wondering if maybe you might have dinner with me again on Wednesday night?"

"Yes, I'd love to."

From that night on, Alina and Benny went out for dinner every Wednesday, and every Friday he came to Shabbat dinner at Alina's house.

Michal and Taavi discussed Alina's relationship and they both agreed that they liked Benny. He was a quiet, studious boy, who was always respectful. It was easy to see that he came from a good family who he was devoted to and he never came to dinner without bringing a basket of fruit or a box of candy.

CHAPTER 63

Because Lotti's father had forbidden it, Lotti had not seen her family since she married Lev. She missed her parents and her younger brother. However, the day Lotti married Lev, Lotti's father said that she was dead to her family and she was never to come near her parents or her brother again. He'd given her several chances to divorce Lev and come home, but when she refused, he'd completely disowned her and stopped trying to bring her home. She'd always feared her father. When he didn't get his way, he was known to have a violent temper. In fact, when she declared that she and Lev planned to marry, he slapped her across the face several times, sending her head flying. But Lotti didn't want to widen the gap between her husband and her family, so she never told Lev that her father hit her. Instead, she just told him that her parents did not approve of the marriage, but she said that she hoped they would change their minds. They never did. And Lev felt guilty that she'd lost her relationship with those she loved due to her love for him. But every time he mentioned it, she insisted that this was what she wanted.

One late afternoon at the orphanage, Alina and Lotti were helping the children with their homework. They sat on long wooden benches. Behind each of them, the children who needed assistance formed a line. One by one, they tried to give each child at least a few minutes of individual attention. Lotti was just finishing an explanation of an arithmetic problem to a seven-year-old girl, when a full grown man in his mid-twenties slid onto the bench beside her.

"JOHAN!!!!" she cried. "How are you? It's been so many years." Lotti hugged him tightly, smiling broadly. "Let me look at you. My God, you are handsome. The last time I saw you, you were just a teenager. Look at you now. Oh, Johan, I really have missed you."

"I've missed you too. Papa went crazy every time I said that I wanted to come and see you. And you know how mean he can be."

"I know."

"I thought about secretly disobeying him and coming anyway, but Mama has been so sick that I didn't want to upset her."

"Is she all right?"

"She's very sick. But, I actually came to tell you about Papa. Lotti, he had a sudden heart attack last week. He has passed away."

Her mouth fell open. "Papa is dead?"

"Yes, I'm sorry. Well, sort of sorry."

"Johan!"

"Yes, well his death has freed me. For years, he dominated all of us with fear."

"Oh, Johan. I know what you mean. He was a small-minded man full of hatred and anger. The threats of his beatings were a terrible part of our growing up. He hurt all of us, you, Mama, and me. Then when I met Lev, I think I fell so hard for him because he is the complete opposite of our dad. Now, I know

317

this sounds crazy, after all of the things he did to us, but I feel bad about his passing. I feel sad and maybe even a little guilty because I wasn't there when he died."

"He wouldn't let you come anywhere near him. It was his fault, not yours."

"I know that in my head, but my heart mourns. I guess it mourns for the man that I wished he had been."

"Lotti, you have always been such an optimist. And no matter what, you've always found a way to see the good in everyone. I always admired that about you."

She smiled.

"Does Mama want to see me?" Lotti asked.

Johan shook his head. "No, it's best that you don't come to see her. I'm afraid that she has lost her mind. Sometimes she doesn't even know who I am. There is very little that she remembers, and most of the time she is very angry. Sometimes she throws things or hurts me or herself."

"So you are caring for her alone?"

"I'm trying. But she is becoming impossible to handle. Last week, she started a fire on the stove. She was just sitting there in the living room and the whole kitchen was ablaze. It was a good thing that I got home in time or she would have burnt the entire building down with everyone inside. I'm ashamed to admit it, but I'm going to put her into an old age home. I have to work. I can't watch her constantly. At least when she's there, someone will always be around so she won't be able to hurt herself or anyone else. Can you forgive me?"

"Johan, of course. There's nothing to forgive. I understand. There's nothing else you can do. It's what's best for her too. She'll be safe there."

"I hope so," Johan said.

"Please, come to my house tonight. I want you to meet my husband. You and Lev have never met. He is a good kind man, and I am so happy to have you back in my life, my dear, dear brother." Lotti hugged Johan again, then she called across the room to Alina. "Alina, come over here; I want you to meet someone, someone very special." Lotti had tears of joy running down her cheeks as she pushed the hair out of Johan's eyes the same way she had done when they were growing up together.

Alina walked over.

"This is my brother, Johan. Johan, this is my very good friend, Alina."

A light flickered in Johan's eyes. He looked away. How could he be thinking about how beautiful this girl was when he had come to deliver an important message ... a somber message? He had come to tell his sister of the fate of their parents.

"Nice to meet you, Johan." Alina smiled and the flame that flickered in Johan's eyes lit a flame in Alina's eyes as well.

CHAPTER 64

Lev and Johan sat in the living room of the apartment, while Lotti prepared dinner. They drank dark bitter beer from heavy glass steins. At first, Lev didn't speak much. The conversation was stilted and uncomfortable. Johan wasn't sure how to relieve the tension, but he thought it might be caused by Lev believing that he had the same feelings towards Jews as his father had. Johan wanted to make sure that Lev knew that he was a different man than his father. Johan wanted to say that he had never disapproved of the marriage. But he was just a teen when his sister got married, and he didn't have the courage to stand up to his father. Even now, as a man, Johan was ashamed of his fear and weakness when it came to his father. He hated to admit it even to himself, but until the moment that his father had taken his last breath, Johan had been intimidated by him. It was strange because by the end of their lives together, Johan had grown taller and stronger than his father. Yet in the old man's presence, Johan still cowered, and when his father raised his voice, Johan was once again the child who had been beaten with belt buckles and hairbrushes. It was wrong to be joyous over someone's death. But his father's death had freed him and he felt light and hopeful for the future.

"I've missed my sister, and I just want to say that I am truly glad that you are happy together."

"We are. I feel like I have loved Lotti forever. In fact, I can't remember what my life was like before her."

"I just want you to know that I don't feel the same way about your people as my father did. I am not a Nazi … I am not involved with the Party." Johan took a gulp of beer.

"It's good to know that. You are my wife's brother and I want you to know that you are always welcome in our home."

"It's good to be here, to be reunited with my sister."

That night, Johan left with a promise to return for dinner on Sunday. As he rode the train back to his apartment, he thought about the serious, quiet, girl with charcoal-colored eyes. Alina. He whispered her name under his breath. She was Jewish. He was sure of it. The laws forbid relationships between Aryans and Jews. Lev and Lotti were walking a tightrope with the new laws. Was he as strong? Or was he a coward like his father always said he was? Johan took a deep breath. He hated himself for being weak and always afraid, but he knew it was best to forget the whole thing with the pretty Jewish girl. There were plenty of non-Jewish women that he could keep company with. Besides that, the Jewish girl was much younger than he and she would probably not be interested anyway. But she had such a mysterious way about her. She wasn't outgoing and free-spirited like his sister. She was dark, quiet, and brooding. *Alina*, he thought, *What goes on in that mind of yours*? He wondered what she thought of him. Did she find him attractive or was he nothing more to her than Lotti's brother? Perhaps she was married or had a serious boyfriend. Still, Johan could not forget her. In fact, he thought he saw a tiny spark of interest in her eyes when she looked at him. Had he imagined it? Maybe he was attracted to Alina because he was finally free of his father's heavy hand and his mother's needy illness? He didn't care about his father at all, but Johan was riddled with guilt over his decision to put his mother in a home, but he couldn't take it anymore, he had to be free of them. At twenty-six, he was handsome. There were millions of women all over Berlin. Finally, his life was his own. He was a fool to be thinking about becoming involved with a Jewish woman. Although he had no issues with prejudice, there was no reason to tempt the fates. It was his time to go to the beer halls and meet girls, to live, finally to live. Still ... those dark brooding eyes of Alina lit a fire in the back of his mind.

CHAPTER 65

1938

Michal and Taavi assumed that soon they were going to hold a wedding for Alina and Benny. Michal tried to talk to Alina about her future and her feelings. She tried to offer her daughter guidance, but Alina just brushed her mother off. It wasn't that she didn't want to be close to Michal, it was just that she had a hard time talking with anyone except Lotti. Lotti understood her. They had been friends since she was little, and when Michal and Taavi were first back together, Alina felt like a cement block had fallen between her and her mother. She loved Taavi, but before he came, even though Otto and Bridget were a big part of their lives, Alina and Michal were inseparable. Her father was kind and generous; she really had nothing to complain about. But, as she was growing up, sometimes she would lie in bed at night and wish that her parents would split up again. She adored her sister, but Gilde had added another cement block between Alina and Michal. Besides that, Gilde was so different from Alina. Gilde had no problem openly speaking of her emotions and asking for things she wanted. She complained loudly, declared her love loudly, laughed and cried loudly. Alina could never confide in Gilde; Gilde would never understand how twisted up she was inside. There was no doubt that Alina liked Benny, enjoyed his company, but her feelings for Benny were not strong enough to sustain a marriage, at least not with all the trials that she'd seen her parents face. She knew her mother wanted to know if she planned to marry Benny. But how could she explain what she really felt? What she wanted to say was, I don't want to have a marriage like the one you had with Dad. I don't know why you two broke up in the first place, especially when you were pregnant with me, but I don't want to be like you. I refuse to have a boyfriend while I'm still married. Then, after he dies go back and fix things with my husband. I don't believe it is acceptable to be unfaithful in the first place. Alina felt that Michal should have worked things out with Taavi before she left him, not after Otto's death. And then what about Bridget? She still remembered her friend. Her mother had stood by and watched as Alina became as close as a sister to Bridget. Then, when it was no longer convenient, Michal had sent Bridget away, leaving Alina heartbroken. Michal had promised that she would help Alina keep in touch with Bridget. But when they'd moved out of the apartment, Michal decided to leave no forwarding address and because of that, she'd lost contact with Bridget. Even as they were moving, she'd glared at her mother, angry and hurt. But Michal ignored Alina. When Alina was young and it was just Alina and Michal, it seemed as if Michal knew what her daughter needed and felt without Alina ever telling her. But once Michal and Taavi were together again, all of that deep understanding between Alina and her mother disappeared. Whenever she thought about her parents, especially Michal, Alina's intestines felt like they were in knots. If only she could say all of the things she felt, all of the things she'd left unsaid. If only she could scream and release all of the pent up anger inside of her that was eating away at her slowly.

CHAPTER 66

1938

Johan came to visit Lotti at the orphanage several times over the summer. Every time he came, Alina noticed his eyes following her when he thought she wasn't looking. There was no doubt that Johan was handsome, but she was still seeing Benny twice a week. And Alina had vowed to herself that, because of what happened with her mother and Otto, if she was involved with someone, she would be faithful. Predictable, reliable, Benny. He was kind and gracious, always considerate. If things between them continued on the course they were on, she and Benny would be expected to become engaged. So, why didn't she want to marry him? He hadn't proposed yet and she was glad that she didn't have to give him an answer. Because if he had proposed today, with the way she felt, she would have to say no, and then her parents would be upset. They would ask her a million questions ... questions that had no answers.

One late afternoon in early September, in the golden hours just before sunset, Lotti and Alina were taking the train home from work. As the train bumped and shifted along the rails, Lotti took Alina's hand.

"I need to talk to you about something. We have always been very close, so I want you to know that what I am about to say is for your own good."

Alina's eyes opened wide; she wasn't expecting a serious conversation.

"Of course, what is it?"

"It's none of my business, I know," Lotti said, speaking slowly, carefully. "But, I can see the way that you and Johan look at each other. And, believe me, I realize that my brother is a handsome man. But there is something that you don't understand about Johan. He is weak, Alina. You are Jewish and he is Aryan. If you two were to start seeing each other on a romantic basis, I'm afraid you would end up getting hurt. He could never be able to stand up to the Nazis the way that Lev and I are being forced to. Johan has never been a strong man. He would buckle under the pressure."

"What are you trying to say?" She hated to admit it, even to herself, but she was attracted to Johan. He was different, and that made him exciting.

"Quite frankly, I am trying to tell you not to fall in love with him. It won't work. Even as a boy, Johan was bullied at school because he never fought back. He was never one to stand up for himself. And right now with the climate of the country, an interfaith marriage would require more courage that Johan could muster. What I am telling you is to forget about him completely. It's what's best for both of you."

"Lotti? I never thought you'd say that to me."

"It isn't because I don't love you like a sister; I do. It's because I know that in the world we live in, you and Johan would do nothing but hurt each other. It could only end badly."

Alina didn't answer. She was at a loss for words.

From that day on, Alina found herself even more attracted to Johan and, at the same time, she was quite sure that she should be planning a wedding with Benny.

On October 15th, 1938, Adolf Hitler moved his troops into the Northwest area of Czechoslovakia, which is known as the Sudetenland, and took it over. He faced no resistance from any of the Western countries.

Then, on October 28th of the same year, seventeen-thousand Polish Jews that had been living in Germany were expelled. Poland refused to admit them, leaving them stranded.

Rosh Hashanah, the Jewish new year, arrived and lasted, as always, for two days. Then, eight days later, it was followed by the holiest day of the year, Yom Kippur. Jews believe that when the shofar is blown at the beginning of Rosh Hashanah to sundown on Yom Kippur, when the shofar is blown again, the book is open. This is the book where God reads over the deeds of the previous year and decides who will live to see another Rosh Hashanah. Sundown the night before Yom Kippur, the shofar is sounded and Jews over thirteen-years-old begin fasting as atonement for their sins. Then the following day, which is Yom Kippur, the Day of Atonement, the shofar is sounded again at sundown and the book is closed, sealing the destiny of all living creatures for the coming year.

Only the children over thirteen fasted, but the entire orphanage spent a good part of the day in the synagogue praying. At sundown after the sounding of the shofar, everyone went into the main dining room where food was served and those who'd been fasting ate for the first time since the previous night. Because of her age, Alina fasted, but Gilde was too young. They both ate something small as quickly as possible, then headed home. Michal had wanted them to be at home for the holiday. She'd wanted her family with her, but Alina wanted to go to the orphanage and Gilde followed her sister. Still, they had agreed to come home for dinner.

Even though she was not religious anymore, Michal still fasted. It was an old habit from her childhood and had become more of a custom than anything else. She didn't go to shul, but she prayed. Taavi, who had never been religious, fasted this year and thanked God for the good life he had.

When the girls got home, Michal had already set the table for the celebration. Taavi kissed his daughters on the top of their heads, then the family sat down together.

While they were dining, Taavi said to Alina, "You should have invited Benny and his family."

Alina smiled. "I didn't think about it."

Michal watched the expression on her daughter's face. Although Michal could not explain it, she had an uncanny way of feeling whatever Alina was feeling. And even though Alina would not open up to her, Michal's heart told her that something was troubling her daughter. She would not mention anything at the table. Instead, she would wait until later and then try to talk to Alina. It was doubtful that Alina would open up to her, but Michal would never stop trying.

Gilde was rambling excitedly about auditioning for a school play. Michal was glad that Gilde's animated conversation was filling what would otherwise have been a silent room.

As Gilde was reciting her audition piece, Michal watched Alina. Her daughter needed her; she would have to find a way to reach Alina … she had to. Whatever was bothering Alina, Michal wanted Alina to know that she was there and would always be there for her.

Later that night, after Gilde had taken her bath and brushed her long golden curls until they shined, Michal tucked her younger daughter into bed. Then she went back to find Taavi sitting under a lamp and reading in the living room. Michal sat down beside him and rubbed his arm.

"You fasted today?"

"Yes. I suppose I found God when I found you again. Today, I thought maybe I should fast for all of my sins." Taavi had recently acquired reading glasses. He removed them and looked at her.

"I asked God for forgiveness … for everything I've done."

"Oh, Taavi." She rubbed his arm harder.

"I'm afraid, Michal. Not for myself, for myself I don't care. But it is for you and the girls that I am worried. Things here in Berlin are getting worse for Jews. Look at what happened to Gilde at school. And then look at how the teachers reacted. It's becoming acceptable to torment Jews. Who knows how far this will go? A pogrom? I hate to say it, but it is possible." He sighed. "I don't know how you are going to feel about this, but I want to sell the business and take what we can get for it and then try to see if some of my black market friends can help us to get to America. I didn't want to do this. After all, we have built a good life here. Our best friends, Lev and Lotti, are here. Everyone we know is here. Alina and Gilde will have to leave everything behind, their friends, their school. And, in the beginning, until I can establish myself again, we won't have the nice things that we have now." He shook his head, "But, believe me, I have been doing a lot of thinking and I think it's for the best."

Michal took a deep breath; she let it out slowly. "Taavi," she said. "I will miss Lotti and Lev. I will miss the butcher shop and Mrs. Glick, the butcher's wife. I'll miss the rabbi and the neighborhood. And, I have to admit, I'll miss the comfortable life we have. I've been poor. I know how hard it is not to have what you need. And I can see where it will be difficult to start over, but I trust you and I trust your judgment."

"I love you so much, Michal. How foolish we were when we were young? Both of us so prideful."

"You're right; I think about it sometimes and wish I could have all those years back again. I love you with all my heart."

"We are lucky to have the love we have for each other, and we both love the children. No matter what kind of struggle is in store for us, we'll be alright, because we have each other. But, I think it's best that we don't say anything about this to Alina or Gilde until everything is set. I'll start to make arrangements to sell the business."

"What about Alina and Benny?" Michal said.

"I don't know. So far, there's no talk of marriage. We can't wait much longer for them to declare themselves. Then, if they are getting married, we have to see if they will want to come with us to America. Leaving Germany would mean Benny would have to leave his family behind."

"Yes, I agree. But, I couldn't bear to leave Alina here. They would have to go with us."

"Well, let's try to give them a little time. Let's see if they get engaged."

"I like him and I want her to be happy. But I won't leave her behind."

"All right. Let's not make any decisions today. I'll begin looking into selling the business, just to get some idea of how much it's worth. But I won't make any definite arrangements until we know what Alina and Benny are going to do."

Michal had planned to go and talk to Alina, but after her conversation with Taavi, she was spent, exhausted, and worried. Taavi would never be planning to leave Germany unless he had a serious sense of impending danger. His words were weighing on her. She washed her face with hot water, then changed into her nightgown and got into bed. But she couldn't sleep. She lay in bed looking out the window at the full moon.

When Taavi came to bed an hour later, Michal was still awake. She felt the mattress move as he got in beside her. The sound of his breathing soothed her and she rolled softly into his arms.

"You're still awake?" he asked.

"I couldn't sleep."

He gently caressed her back. "Michal, Michal. Please, don't be afraid. I will take care of you and the girls. It's my responsibility as your husband and the man of this house. I won't let anything happen to you. Do you trust me?"

"Yes, of course I trust you."

"We came here from Russia and started our lives over. We will do the same in America. It is not for you to worry about how we will get along. This is my job and I do it willingly because, for me, it's not a job, it's an honor to take care of my family. Put your faith in me, Michal. I won't disappoint you."

She kissed him. He turned her over and softly ran his hands over the sides of her face. Then he kissed her passionately, and for the next few hours, in the comfort of each other's arms, they forgot the challenges that lay ahead.

CHAPTER 67

1938

It was mid-October and the children at the orphanage were gathering leaves and branches to build a sukkah* outside the building in order to celebrate Sukkot (Feast of Tabernacles) The crisp fall air and brightly colored leaves added to the excitement of the event.

Lotti and Alina supervised the children, who sang as they worked. A blanket of leaves in crimson, deep orange, and burnt umber kicked up with the wind, which tossed Alina's hair about her head. She'd been wearing a silver clip to tame her locks, but the wind loosened the hair ornament and dropped it into a deep pile of leaves. Alina bent to search for her barrette. She heard the dead foliage crunch, and when she looked up she saw Johan.

"Johan?"

"Alina, how are you?"

"Fine."

"Are you looking for something?"

"Yes, my barrette fell out of my hair and I can't seem to find it."

"Let me help you." He bent down beside her and began sifting through the dried foliage. "What does it look like?"

He smelled like good cologne. Not a strong odor, just a hint of fragrance.

"It's silver with four small pearls," she said, sifting the leaves with her fingers.

Their hands brushed. Alina felt her face turn hot. She dared not look up, lest he see that she was attracted to him.

He touched the side of her face. She looked at him, stunned and embarrassed. "You look so pretty with your hair tussled."

She laughed, uncomfortable. "Thank you…" her voice was a whisper.

Johan moved just close enough for his lips to brush hers. Her heart began to race. He moved even closer, his lips soft, warm alive were now fully upon hers. Alina trembled and sighed as he kissed her. One of the children ran by, breaking the spell of the moment. Alina straightened up. The only man she'd ever kissed besides her father was Benny. And she'd never felt like this when Benny kissed her. This was magic. She was confused, frightened, excited, wanting more, and wanting less…then remembering what Lotti had told her. What was she doing?

"Oh, it's all right. It wasn't real anyway," Alina said, standing up quickly.

"I'm sorry? I mean, I don't understand? What wasn't real? It was real for me," Johan said.

"The hair clip. It wasn't real silver; it was plated, and the pearls were glass." Her knees felt weak and they were trembling.

"Oh … oh," he said.

"I have to go." She turned away from him and began to walk away quickly.

"Alina … Alina…" he called after her. "I hope I didn't offend you."

She dared not look back. Her entire body was shaking, but she'd never felt so alive.

CHAPTER 68

1938

After Alina and Johan kissed, Alina decided that it was best if she started to take her relationship with Benny more seriously. In the back of her mind, she heard Lotti's words repeated continuously. "Johan isn't strong enough for an interfaith marriage. He would not be able to stand up to the Nazis."

Alina thought about all of Benny's attributes. There was no doubt that Benny was a nice boy, a good boy. He was a hard worker and he came from a good stable family. But, most importantly, he was Jewish and she was Jewish. And that made all the difference in the world in Nazi Germany in 1938. Alina repeated these attributes to herself whenever her thoughts drifted to Johan.

So to move things along more quickly, Alina suggested marriage to Benny. It was unheard of for a girl to be so bold. At least Alina felt that it was a little outrageous. But the sooner she and Benny were engaged, the better. After all, she would be far too busy planning the wedding to think about that fateful kiss with Johan.

Benny was elated. He told Alina that he planned to ask her many times, but he was always afraid that she would refuse. He was glad she had asked.

"Let's get married in the spring," he said.

"I thought maybe June of next year would give us enough time to make plans."

"June would be perfect. I can't wait to tell my family. They'll be so excited. I want you to meet them, and we can tell them together. I'll tell my mother that I want to bring you to dinner on Wednesday. Instead of going out to the café, we can go to my house and announce our engagement."

"That sounds perfect." Alina smiled, but her heart was sad and empty. This is for the best, she thought.

"When should we tell your family?"

"Let's talk to yours first. Once we've told your family, we can make arrangements to tell mine."

CHAPTER 69

The days passed, and the closer Wednesday came, the more Alina was rethinking her plans to marry Benny. It was strange that trying not to think about Johan had brought him front and center in her mind. In fact, she'd begun to think about him most of the time. Her mind had begun to play tricks on her. She'd see small scenarios in her mind's eye where Johan came to her house and forbade her to marry anyone but him. Or she would imagine dancing in his arms, waltzing as the music played in a candlelit room.

Silly, she thought. (There can never be anything between Johan and me. Never)

On Monday, there was talk at the orphanage about something political. Everyone seemed upset, even Lotti. Alina didn't care at all. They were mumbling about a Jewish man who killed someone in France. The more everyone chatted about the event, the less she wanted to hear. How could the murder of a secretary of the German Embassy that took place in Paris, which felt like a million miles away, have anything to do with her? Right now, Alina had far more important things on her mind. She was about to make an announcement to marry Benny, which would change her life forever. Over lunch, Lotti was going on about the murder in Paris. Lotti told Alina that she was frantic because it had been committed by a Jewish man. Alina just nodded. She was bored with the subject already. And even if the killer was Jewish, what did that all have to do with her?

Benny arrived on time on Wednesday night, as he always did. He always made a nice appearance, but tonight he had dressed up even more than usual. Alina wore a simple three-quarter sleeve brown dress and low-heeled shoes. Tonight she was going to meet her future in-laws. And every step she was taking towards a future with Benny felt like a mistake. If she didn't back out now, in a few months she would be a married woman. Benny was smiling at her. She could see in his eyes how happy he was that they were going to be husband and wife. Perhaps she would learn to love him.

Her future in-laws welcomed her into their home. It seemed to Alina that they already knew what she and Benny had come to tell them. Surprisingly, Benny's mother was a smart dresser with her amber-colored hair in perfect finger waves. This was not at all how Alina had pictured her. Benny's father was a slender man, tall, and distinguished, with perfectly groomed silver white hair.

The house was decorated with fine furniture, but it was not overdone. Alina knew, because Benny had told her, that before Hitler had come into power, Benny's father had been a successful businessman. The quality of their home and its furnishings reflected the money he'd earned in the past. Benny's parents were gracious hosts. They asked Alina about her family and her work at the orphanage. Everything she said seemed to meet with their approval.

After everyone had finished eating, Benny's mother got up to clear the table. Alina began helping.

"No, please, you are our guest. Go and sit down in the living room. I'll clean up and when I'm done I'll bring some coffee and dessert."

"Are you sure I can't help you?"

"Absolutely positive. I'll just be a few minutes."

It wasn't long before Benny's mother appeared carrying a tray with a silver coffee pot, china cups, and a dish of cookies. She poured coffee for everyone. Then, as they sat sipping, Benny made the announcement.

"Mama, Papa, Alina and I have something to tell you."

"NU? So tell us already? Why the suspense?" Benny's father said, smiling.

"We have decided to get married."

"Mazel Tov!" his mother said and got up and hugged Alina. Then his father did the same. "Welcome to our family."

"I was thinking that once we are married Alina would move in here with us."

"Oy, such a blessing!" his father smiled.

Living with her in-laws? What had she expected? Of course they would have to move in with them. The family still needed Benny's salary to survive. They seemed nice enough, didn't they? Everything was moving so fast. Her future mother-in-law was hugging her.

"Yes, a blessing," her future father-in-law said.

Alina and Benny were betrothed.

It was that easy. She'd changed her life with just a few words. For the better? That remained to be seen. Benny put his arm around Alina as they walked towards her apartment.

"My folks like you; I can tell," he said, squeezing her shoulder. She pulled her coat closer around her body. A chilly wind moved a paper bag that someone had left on the sidewalk. Soon it would be winter and Alina could already feel the coming of the season. She'd always disliked winter. It was too still; it had always felt like a time of death to her, a time when nothing grew, nothing lived.

"They're very nice, Benny."

"So, you like them too? I'm so glad. I was worried that you might not like them." A big smile came over his face. "Now, we just have to tell your parents. Do you think they'll be happy about it?"

Alina opened her mouth to speak, but before she had a chance to say a word, their conversation was interrupted by a loud crash that sounded like a giant picture window had been shattered. It was followed by lots of noise and commotion. Somewhere in the direction in which they were walking, which was towards Alina's home and the Jewish sector of town, people were shouting angry curses, some were screaming, there were terrible cries of terror, and, above all of it, they heard the crashing of glass. The smell of something burning began to waft through the air. Alina's eyes burned; she rubbed them, then she saw black smoke pouring out of the top of the synagogue. "Our temple, the temple that we go to on the high holidays … it's on fire." Alina looked at Benny in disbelief.

"OH, MY GOD!" Benny said. "A fire must have started. That's what the noise is all about."

Alina and Benny rounded the corner and began to run towards the synagogue. They weren't sure if other buildings near the synagogue had caught fire and they wanted to help. The streets were filled with people running in all directions.

Some of them Alina recognized as her neighbors, but mostly they were teenage boys and young men in brown Nazi uniforms. The Nazis were shouting and singing a song with strange lyrics that Alina had never heard before. From the bits and pieces that Alina could decipher, they were singing something like, "If Jewish blood spurts from a knife, then all will go well." What was happening? Was this a pogrom like the ones her parents had talked about? She felt a pang of fear shoot through her. This had to be a nightmare; it couldn't be really happening.

"What the hell is going on here?" Benny said, not directly to Alina, but just voicing his inner feelings.

"Let's get to my apartment quickly. We should get inside and out of the street." Alina grabbed Benny's arm and started pulling him quickly towards her home.

The Nazis had clubs and bats, and they seemed to be having a good time bashing the windows of all the businesses. Even from several yards down the street, Alina could see that her father's shop had been vandalized. She had no idea how bad the damage was, but glass from the window was scattered all over the sidewalk and the wooden door lay crushed on the street. Alina pulled Benny harder and finally they got to the building where she lived. It looked as if the shop was entirely destroyed. Alina searched her purse for the keys to her apartment upstairs. But her hands were shaking so badly that she couldn't find them. Across the road, an old woman was crying and screaming in Yiddish. Two young boys in the uniforms of the brown shirts were beating her husband to death with a club.

Alina's fingers found the key. She put it into the door and it opened.

Benny turned to Alina. "Get in the house. I'll be upstairs in a few minutes."

She was afraid for him. "No, Benny, don't go over there. You don't even have a weapon. They'll hurt you!"

"Get inside." He pushed her.

"Benny!"

Alina was too late. Benny was already across the street. He'd taken the bat away from one of the boys and had begun to hit him with it. The other boy called out for his friends and, before Benny could turn around, he was surrounded by Nazis. Alina was screaming, but she didn't cross the street and go to Benny or go inside. She was frozen and unable to move. All that was unfolding before her was too horrible to be real. This had to be a bad dream.

Her father came rushing out of the building. Taavi and Michal heard Alina screaming; they heard the chaos and the breaking glass. "Get upstairs," Taavi said to Alina. "Now."

"I can't. Look, Papa. Those boys across the street … they're hurting Benny…."

"Go upstairs. Do as I say. I'll take care of it. Now, go."

"NO, Papa. Don't go over there…"

"Upstairs, now," Taavi said and he gave Alina a warning stare. She obeyed him. Then Taavi ran across the street.

From the window in their living room, Michal and her two girls could see across the street. Taavi was strong; he had beaten several of the boys down. Benny lay still in a pool of blood. Taavi hadn't had a chance to go to him; he was still fighting. But now the police had arrived and Taavi was being arrested. Michal bit her lip so hard that she could taste the blood. Two officers with guns forced Taavi into the back of a police car. Michal wanted to run out after Taavi, to beg the police to let him go, but she dared not. It was far too dangerous to leave the girls alone. She held her daughters in her arms and the three of them trembled and wept. And still, the violence on the street continued throughout the night.

Michal waited until morning for Taavi to return. But he didn't, and finally Michal couldn't bear the uncertainty any longer.

"I'm going to the police station. I have to find out what they've done with your father."

"I'll go with you, Mama," Alina said.

"No, please, you stay here and watch out for Gilde. Both of you stay inside. I'll be home as soon as I can. Your father is a good person. He was only trying to defend Benny and the old man across the street. The police probably don't know what happened. I'll tell them. I'll make the police understand. Wait for me here."

Alina sucked in her breath. Then she got up and hugged her mother. "Be careful, Mama," she said.

"I will. Watch your sister. Gilde, you listen to Alina; you do what she tells you and don't argue. Now, you two, take care of each other until I get back. Promise me you'll do as I say … both of you?"

"Yes, Mama," both girls said in unison.

Then Michal walked out of the apartment and down the stairs. Gilde and Alina were looking out the window. Both girls' hearts were pounding; they were afraid for Michal. Although it looked as if the perpetrators were gone, they couldn't be sure.

They stood there silently, watching their mother until she had walked so far away that they couldn't see her anymore.

Alina felt sick to her stomach. Benny's body was still there on the sidewalk. He hadn't moved and she was certain that he was dead. It was only right that she go to him, but she didn't have the courage. And her own weakness and fear disgusted her.

That fateful night in November of 1938 would be the beginning of a long descent into the darkest hour for the Jews, not only in Germany, but in all of Europe. It would be remembered forever as Kristallnacht, the night of the broken glass.

CHAPTER 70

Later that morning, Lotti telephoned.

"Alina? Are you alright? Is the family alright?"

"I'm fine. But Benny? I don't know what happened to Benny. He might be alive, but I don't think so. I think he's dead. I don't know. He's still lying in the street and there's blood everywhere. Everywhere, Lotti. So much blood. You see, last night the synagogue burned and there was a fight on the street … and then the boys were hitting an old man and then Benny was fighting with the boys. Papa came out and then he was fighting too. And then Papa got arrested and Mama went to find him." She was rambling, hyperventilating, she could hardly catch her breath.

"Slow down; I can't understand you. Are your parents there; can I speak to your mother?"

"No, I'm trying to tell you that Papa got arrested. Mama left this morning; she went to the police station to find out where he is. Gilde is here with me. We are alone. Mama insisted that we stay here and wait for her."

"I'm coming over right away with Lev. Don't leave the house."

"Are both of you all right?"

"Yes, we're fine. Shaken up, but fine. Stay put; don't open the door for anyone. Do you understand me, Alina? We'll be right over."

"Yes, Lotti. I understand."

As soon as Lotti walked in to the apartment, Alina rushed into her arms and broke down. "I'm so scared. It was the most terrible thing I've ever seen. Benny … a truck came and picked up his body a few minutes ago. He might be in a hospital. Or he might be dead. I just don't know. I think he's dead.…"

"Shh, it's all right."

Gilde walked over and lay her head against Lotti. "What are we going to do?"

"Well, for right now, we are going to wait until Lev comes upstairs. He's looking at your father's store to see how bad the damage is."

Lotti sat on the sofa and both girls curled around her. She put a hand on each of their shoulders.

There was a knock on the door a half hour later.

"Lev?" Lotti said.

"It's me," Lev answered.

Alina got up and opened the door. Lev came in; his face was the color of bleached sand. "Everything is destroyed. Everything we were working on, all of our inventory. Everything."

Lotti nodded. "That should be the worst of it. Let's just pray that Michal, Taavi, and Benny are all right."

When they had not heard from Michal or Taavi by nightfall, Lotti insisted that the girls leave a note for their parents and come to stay at her and Lev's apartment.

They packed small bags and left.

A week passed. Neither Michal nor Taavi returned. Alina stayed home from work with Gilde, who missed school. They barely ate. Neither of them had any appetite. By now, the streets were quiet. Only the damage that had been done was left. Blood still stained the sidewalk and broken glass shards littered the streets. The synagogue had burnt to the ground and the smell of fire and smoke still lingered in the air.

"What are we going to do?" Gilde asked.

"I don't know. Keep waiting here at Lotti's house for Mama to come back," Alina said, and it sounded ridiculous even as she heard her own voice. "Gilde, I don't know what else to do. I'm worried sick about our parents. I called Benny's house. His mother is distraught. They have no idea what happened to Benny. God only knows where he is and if he is even alive."

Another week passed. Lotti could see that the girls were becoming frantic. She, too, was frantic, but she couldn't let them know. If she broke down, they would have no one to lean on.

"I think it's best that you, Gilde, come back to school, and Alina, you come back to work with me. Our staying here at the apartment will not do anyone any good. The poor children at the orphanage will need us. Lev is here. He will be either here at the apartment or at your father's shop, trying to put it back into order. Either way, when your parents return, they will either come through the shop to your apartment and see him, or they will call here because of the note."

"I don't know if I can work," Alina said.

"I understand. But I believe it is what is best for you both right now."

The following day, Lotti and the two girls took the train to the orphanage. Gilde went to class and Alina went to work. No one questioned why they had been away for two weeks. Everyone knew what had happened.

Lotti was right; working helped. Alina was busy and, for a few hours, her mind was too occupied to think. After the children had finished lunch, Alina and Lotti sat down at the end of one of the wooden tables to have something to eat. Lotti spoke in a very low voice.

"There is something I have to discuss with you."

Alina nodded. "Have you heard something about my parents or Benny?"

"No, it's something else."

"All right, tell me."

"There is an organization, it's called, 'The Movement for the Care of Children from Germany'." The people in charge of this group are in the process of arranging for all of the children from the orphanage to go to England."

"England?"

"Yes, the plight of the Jewish children here was announced on the BBC and, from what I understand, five-hundred British families have offered to take them in."

"Really? That's remarkable. And very kind."

"Yes, Alina, it is. And … I think we should send Gilde with them."

"My sister? When my parents return she will be in England?"

"Alina, it's not safe here for Jews. Gilde is a child. She has an opportunity to get out safely. If she stays … well, who knows what's in store? Once this is all over, your parents can send for her and she will come back. But for now…."

"Gilde, all alone with strangers in England? Can I go with her? I can't just let her go all alone."

"I tried to arrange for you to go too. I wanted you to go. I lied to them; I told them you were sixteen. But because you work here, they know your real age is eighteen and you're too old to go."

"So Gilde will be all alone?"

"She has friends from the orphanage who will also be going. Gilde will stay with a British family until things settle down here in Germany. Then she'll come back."

"Lotti, I don't know. I wish my parents were here to make the decision."

"There isn't much time … only two weeks before the train leaves on December first. Before it's too late, I want to sign her up. I've twisted things around to make them work in our favor. I made up a few things so that she would qualify. It was a little contrived, but technically, she is an orphan. She can go. Let her go, Alina…"

Alina put her hand to her throat and shook her head. "I'm afraid."

"I know. So am I. But I believe in my heart that this is for the best."

"Will you help me talk to her about it? I know she won't want to go."

"Yes, we'll tell her together."

"OH … this is all too much for me. I've lost my entire family, and Benny too, all in a matter of one month." Alina's hands were shaking.

"I know, but you have me and you have Lev … and we'll take care of you until your family is all back together again. And it will be very soon, Alina. You'll see. This madness can't last long."

"Do you promise not to leave me?"

"Of course I promise. Can I go ahead and make the arrangements for Gilde? Do I have your permission?"

Alina nodded.

"Good … Thank God you agree. Gilde will be on the first children's transport out of Germany."

CHAPTER 71

If Alina had considered changing her mind about sending her sister to England, she was assured that she was making the right choice because of what happened that night when she, Lotti, and Gilde got back to the apartment.

Lev was waiting for them. It seemed he had aged twenty years in a few weeks. He sat at the kitchen table, staring out as if in a trance and wringing his hat in his hands.

"What is it?" Lotti ran to her husband and fell to her knees in front of him, so that she could look into his eyes.

"They took the business."

"Who took the business?

"The Nazis. Two men in uniform came and ordered that Taavi's store be turned over to the Nazis."

"Did they offer any money?"

"Nothing. In fact, if we want to survive, we must pay for all the damages that were done to the shop on Kristallnacht."

"What? That's crazy. They did the damage. I don't understand."

"From what I heard today, all Jewish students have been expelled from public schools and all Jewish businesses must be handed over to Aryans."

Alina and Gilde stood frozen to the floor listening.

"But, when Papa comes back he will find a way to get his business back. I know he will," Gilde shouted. "They can't do this to us. They can't," she said crying. Then Gilde ran into the room she was sharing with Alina, slammed the door, and threw herself on the bed.

"Your father had plans to sell the shop anyway," Lev said.

"I didn't know," Alina said. "He never said anything about that to us."

"He wanted your family, and Lotti and me, to go to America, but we would have needed the money from the sale of the shop in order for us to go. But, no one was offering to buy anyway," Lev said.

"Do you think we will ever see Mama and Papa again?"

"We can only hope that they're all right and they'll come back to us soon," Lev said.

"So? What will happen to you two and to my sister and me? How will we live? We won't have any money," Alina said.

"Well," Lotti cleared her throat. "As for Gilde, on the first of December, God willing, she'll board that train and she'll be on her way out of Germany to shelter in England. And, as for the rest of us, quite frankly, Alina … I have no idea. All we can do is hold on and pray that God will have mercy on us."

Coming soon: Book two in the "Michal's Destiny" series. "Watch Over My Child"

A Family Shattered

Book Two in the Michal's Destiny series.

In book two of the Michal's Destiny series, Tavvi and Michal have problems in the beginning of their relationship, but they build a life together. Each stone is laid carefully with love and mutual understanding. They now have a family with two beautiful daughters and a home full of happiness.

It is now 1938—Kristallnacht. Blood runs like a river on the streets, shattered glass covers the walkways of Jewish shop owners, and gangs of Nazi thugs charge though Berlin in a murderous rage. When Tavvi, the strong-willed Jewish carpenter, races outside, without thinking of his own welfare, to save his daughters fiancée, little does his wife Michal know that she might never hold him in her arms again. In an instant, all the stones they laid together come crashing down leaving them with nothing but the hope of finding each other again.

*Glossary of terms:

Chuppah: a canopy beneath which Jewish marriage ceremonies are performed

Shul: a synagogue

Mezuzah: a parchment inscribed with religious texts and attached in a case to the doorpost of a Jewish house as a sign of faith.

Yeshiva: an Orthodox Jewish school.

Nu: A general word that calls for a reply. It can mean, "So?" "Huh?" "Well?" "What's up?" or "Hello?"

Rebbe: a Yiddish word derived from the Hebrew word rabbi, which means "master, teacher, or mentor."

Goisha: a derogatory term that refers to something or someone who is not Jewish. Many people who grew up in very sheltered religious settlements feared non-Jews and non-Jewish ways of life.

Shidduch: a Jewish arranged marriage

Frum: devout or pious

Shamos: the candle used to light the other candles on a Hanukkah menorah

pe'ot: the Hebrew word for sidelocks or sidecurls

Minyan: the quorum of ten Jewish adults required for certain religious obligations.

Treif: the Yiddish word for any form of non-kosher food

Sukkah: a booth or hut roofed with branches, built against or near a house or synagogue and used during the Jewish festival of Sukkot as a temporary dining or living area.

Sukkot: a major Jewish festival held in the autumn (beginning on the 15th day of Tishri) to commemorate the sheltering of the Israelites in the wilderness.

AUTHORS NOTE

First and foremost, I want to thank you for reading my novel and for your continued interest in my work. From time to time, I receive emails from my readers that contest the accuracy of my events. When you pick up a novel, you are entering the author's world where we sometimes take artistic license and ask you to suspend your disbelief. I always try to keep as true to history as possible; however, sometimes there are discrepancies within my novels. This happens sometimes to keep the drama of the story. Thank you for indulging me.

I always enjoy hearing from my readers. Your feelings about my work are very important to me. If you enjoyed it, please consider telling your friends or posting a short review on Amazon. Word of mouth is an author's best friend.

If you enjoyed this book, please sign up for my mailing list, and you will receive Free short stories including an USA Today award-winning novella as my gift to you!!!!! To sign up, just go to...

www.RobertaKagan.com

Many blessings to you,

Roberta

Email: roberta@robertakagan.com

Come and like my Facebook page!

https://www.facebook.com/roberta.kagan.9

Join my book club

https://www.facebook.com/groups/1494285400798292/?ref=br_rs

Follow me on BookBub to receive automatic emails whenever I am offering a special price, a freebie, a giveaway, or a new release. Just click the link below, then click follow button to the right of my name. Thank you so much for your interest in my work.

https://www.bookbub.com/authors/roberta-kagan.

MORE BOOKS BY THE AUTHOR AVAILABLE ON AMAZON

Not In America

Book One in A Jewish Family Saga

"Jews drink the blood of Christian babies. They use it for their rituals. They are evil and they consort with the devil."

These words rang out in 1928 in a small town in upstate New York when little four-year-old Evelyn Wilson went missing. A horrible witch hunt ensued that was based on a terrible folk tale known as the blood libel.

Follow the Schatzman's as their son is accused of the most horrific crime imaginable. This accusation destroys their family and sends their mother and sister on a journey home to Berlin just as the Nazi's are about to come to power.

Not in America is based on true events. However, the author has taken license in her work, creating a what if tale that could easily have been true.

They Never Saw It Coming

Book Two in A Jewish Family Saga

Goldie Schatzman is nearing forty, but she is behaving like a reckless teenager, and every day she is descending deeper into a dark web. Since her return home to Berlin, she has reconnected with her childhood friend, Leni, a free spirit who has swept

Goldie into the Weimar lifestyle that is overflowing with artists and writers, but also with debauchery. Goldie had spent the last nineteen years living a dull life with a spiritless husband. And now she has been set free, completely abandoning any sense of morals she once had.

As Goldie's daughter, Alma, is coming of marriageable age, her grandparents are determined to find her a suitable match. But will Goldie's life of depravity hurt Alma's chances to find a Jewish husband from a good family?

And all the while the SA, a prelude to the Nazi SS, is gaining strength. Germany is a hotbed of political unrest. Leaving a nightclub one night, Goldie finds herself caught in the middle of a demonstration that has turned violent. She is rescued by Felix, a member of the SA, who is immediately charmed by her blonde hair and Aryan appearance. Goldie is living a lie, and her secrets are bound to catch up with her. A girl, who she'd scorned in the past, is now a proud member of the Nazi Party and still carries a deep-seated vendetta against Goldie.

On the other side of the Atlantic, Sam is thriving with the Jewish mob in Manhattan; however, he has made a terrible mistake. He has destroyed the trust of the woman he believes is his bashert. He knows he cannot live without her, and he is desperately trying to find a way to win her heart.

And Izzy, the man who Sam once called his best friend, is now his worst enemy. They are both in love with the same woman, and the competition between them could easily result in death.

Then Sam receives word that something has happened in Germany, and he must accompany his father on a journey across the ocean. He is afraid that if he leaves before his beloved accepts his proposal, he might lose her forever.

When The Dust Settled

Book Three in A Jewish Family Saga

Coming December 2020

As the world races like a runaway train toward World War 11, the Schatzman family remains divided.

In New York, prohibition has ended, and Sam's world is turned upside down. He has been earning a good living transporting illegal liquor for the Jewish mob. Now that alcohol is legal, America is celebrating. But as the liquor flows freely, the mob boss realizes he must expand his illegal interests if he is going to continue to live the lavish lifestyle he's come to know. Some of the jobs Sam is offered go against his moral character. Transporting alcohol was one thing, but threatening lives is another.

Meanwhile, across the ocean in Italy, Mussolini, a heartless dictator, runs the country with an iron fist. Those who speak out against him disappear and are never seen again.   For the first time since that horrible incident in Medina, Alma is finally happy and has fallen in love with a kind and generous Italian doctor who already has a job awaiting him in Rome; however, he is not Jewish. Alma must decide whether to marry him and risk disappointing her bubbie or let him go to find a suitable Jewish match.

In Berlin, the Nazis are quickly rising to power. Flags with swastikas are appearing everywhere. And Dr. Goebbels, the minister of propaganda is openly spewing hideous lies designed to turn the German people against the Jews. Adolf

Hitler had disposed of his enemies, and the SA has been replaced by the even more terrifying SS. After the horrors they witnessed during Kristallnacht, Goldie's mother, Esther, is ready to abandon all she knows to escape the country. She begs her husband to leave Germany. But Ted refuses to leave everything that he spent his entire life working for. At what point is it too late to leave? And besides, where would they go? What would they do?

The Nazis have taken the country by the throat, and the electrifying atmosphere of the Weimar a distant memory. The period of artistic tolerance and debauchery has been replaced by a strict and cruel regime that seeks to destroy all who do not fit its ideal. Goldie's path of depravity is catching up with her, and her secrets are threatened. Will her Nazi enemies finally strike?

Book Four in A Jewish Family Saga

Coming Early 2021....

The Smallest Crack

Book One in a Holocaust Story series.

1933 Berlin, Germany

The son of a rebbe, Eli Kaetzel, and his beautiful but timid wife, Rebecca, find themselves in danger as Hitler rises to power. Eli knows that their only chance for survival may lie in the hands of Gretchen, a spirited Aryan girl. However, the forbidden and dangerous friendship between Eli and Gretchen has been a secret until now. Because, for Eli, if it is discovered that he has been keeping company with a woman other than his wife it will bring shame to him and his family. For Gretchen her friendship with a Jew is forbidden by law and could cost her, her life.

The Darkest Canyon

Book Two in a Holocaust Story series.

Nazi Germany.

Gretchen Schmidt has a secret life. She is in love with a married Jewish man. She is hiding him while his wife is posing as an Aryan woman.

Her best friend, Hilde, who unbeknownst to Gretchen is a sociopath, is working as a guard at Ravensbruck concentration camp.

If Hilde discovers Gretchen's secret, will their friendship be strong enough to keep Gretchen safe? Or will Hilde fall under the spell of the Nazis and turn her best friend over to the Gestapo?

The *Darkest Canyon* is a terrifying ride along the edge of a canyon in the dark of night.

Millions Of Pebbles

Book Three in a Holocaust Story series.

Benjamin Rabinowitz's life is shattered as he watches his wife, Lila, and his son, Moishe, leave to escape the Lodz ghetto. He is conflicted because he knows this is their best chance of survival, but he asks himself, will he ever see them again?

Ilsa Guhr has a troubled childhood, but as she comes of age, she learns that her beauty and sexuality give her the power to get what she wants. But she craves an even greater power. As the Nazis take control of Germany, she sees an opportunity to gain everything she's ever desired.

Fate will weave a web that will bring these two unlikely people into each other's lives.

Sarah and Solomon

Book Four in a Holocaust Story series

"Give me your children" -Chaim Mordechaj Rumkowski. September 1942 The Lodz Ghetto.

When Hitler's Third Reich reined with an iron fist, the head Judenrat of the Lodz ghetto decides to comply with the Nazis. He agrees to send the Jewish children off on a transport to face death.

In order to save her two young children a mother must take the ultimate risk. The night before the children are to rounded up and sent to their deaths, she helps her nine year old son and her five year old daughter escape into a war torn Europe. However, she cannot fit through the barbed wire, and so the children must go alone.

Follow Sarah and Solomon as they navigate their way through a world filled with hatred, and treachery. However, even in the darkest hour there is always a flicker of light. And these two young innocent souls will be aided by people who's lights will always shine in our memories.

All My Love, Detrick

Book One in the All My Love, Detrick series.

Book One in the All My Love, Detrick Series

Can Forbidden Love Survive in Nazi Germany?

After Germany's defeat in the First World War, she lays in ruins, falling beneath the wheel of depression and famine. And so, with a promise of restoring Germany to her rightful place as a world power, Adolf Hitler begins to rise.

Detrick, a handsome seventeen-year-old Aryan boy is reluctant to join the Nazi party because of his friendship with Jacob, who is Jewish and has been like a father figure to him. However, he learns that in order to protect the woman he loves, Jacob's daughter, he must abandon all his principles and join the Nazis. He knows the only way to survive is to live a double life. Detrick is confronted with fear every day; if he is discovered, he and those he loves will come face to face with the ultimate cruelty of the Third Reich.

Follow two families, one Jewish and one German, as they are thrust into a world of danger on the eve of the Nazis rise to power.

You Are My Sunshine

Book Two in the All My Love, Detrick series.

A child's innocence is the purest of all.

In Nazi Germany, Helga Haswell is at a crossroads. She's pregnant by a married SS officer who has since abandoned her.

Left alone with the thought of raising a fatherless child, she has nowhere to turn -- until the Lebensborn steps in. They will take Helga's child when it's born and raise it as their own. Helga will now be free to live her life.

But when Helga has second thoughts, it's already too late. The papers are signed, and her claim to her child has been revoked. Her daughter belongs to Hitler now. And when Hitler's delusions of grandeur rapidly accelerate, Germany becomes involved in a two-front war against the heroic West and the fearless Russians.

Helga's child seems doomed to a life raised by the cruelest humans on Earth. But God's plan for her sends the young girl to the most unexpected people. In their warm embrace, she's given the chance for love in a world full of hate.

You Are My Sunshine is the heartfelt story of second chances. Helga Haswell may be tied to an unthinkable past, but her young daughter has the chance of a brighter future.

The Promised Land:

From Nazi Germany to Israel

Book Three in the All My Love, Detrick series.

Zofia Weiss, a Jewish woman with a painful past, stands at the dock, holding the hand of a little girl. She is about to board The SS Exodus, bound for Palestine with only her life, a dream, and a terrifying secret. As her eyes scan the crowds of people, she sees a familiar face. Her heart pounds and beads of sweat form on her forehead...

The Nazis have surrendered. Zofia survived the Holocaust, but she lives in constant fear. The one person who knows her dark secret is a sadistic SS officer with the power to destroy the life she's working so hard to rebuild. Will he ever find her and the innocent child she has sworn to protect?

To Be An Israeli

Book Four in the All My Love, Detrick series.

Elan understands what it means to be an Israeli. He's sacrificed the woman he loved, his marriage, and his life for Israel. When Israel went to war and Elan was summoned in the middle of the night, he did not hesitate to defend his country, even though he knew he might pay a terrible price. Elan is not a perfect man by any means. He can be cruel. He can be stubborn and self-righteous. But he is brave, and he loves more deeply than he will ever admit.

This is his story.

However, it is not only his story; it is also the story of the lives of the women who loved him: Katja, the girl whom he cherished but could never marry, who would haunt him forever. Janice, the spoiled American he wed to fill a void, who would keep a secret from him that would one day shatter his world. And…Nina, the beautiful Mossad agent whom Elan longed to protect but knew he never could.

To Be an Israeli spans from the beginning of the Six-Day War in 1967 through 1986 when a group of American tourists are on their way to visit their Jewish homeland.

Forever My Homeland

The Fifth and final book in the All My Love, Detrick series.

Bari Lynn has a secret. So she, a young Jewish-American girl, decides to tour Israel with her best friend and the members of their synagogue in search of answers.

Meanwhile, beneath the surface in Israel, trouble is stirring with a group of radical Islamists.

The case falls into the hands of Elan, a powerful passionate Mossad agent, trying to pick up the pieces of his shattered life. He believes nothing can break him, but in order to achieve their goals, the terrorists will go to any means to bring Elan to his knees.

Forever, My Homeland is the story of a country built on blood and determination. It is the tale of a strong and courageous people who don't have the luxury of backing down from any fight, because they live with the constant memory of the Holocaust. In the back of their minds, there is always a soft voice that whispers "Never again."

Michal's Destiny

Book One in the Michal's Destiny series.

It is 1919 in Siberia. Michal—a young, sheltered girl—has eyes for a man other than her betrothed. For a young girl growing up in a traditional Jewish settlement, an arranged marriage is a fact of life. However, destiny, it seems, has other plans for Michal. When a Cossack pogrom invades her small village, the protected life Michal has grown accustomed to and loves will crumble before her eyes. Everything she knows is gone and she is forced to leave her home and embark on a journey to Berlin with the man she thought she wanted. Michal faces love, loss, and heartache because she is harboring a secret that threatens to destroy her every attempt at happiness. But over the next fourteen tumultuous years, during the peak of the Weimar Republic, she learns she is willing to do anything to have the love she longs for and to protect her family.

However, it is now 1933. Life in Berlin is changing, especially for the Jews. Dark storm clouds are looming on the horizon. Adolf Hitler is about to become the chancellor of Germany, and that will change everything for Michal forever.

A Family Shattered

Book Two in the Michal's Destiny series.

In book two of the Michal's Destiny series, Tavvi and Michal have problems in the beginning of their relationship, but they build a life together. Each stone is laid carefully with love and mutual understanding. They now have a family with two beautiful daughters and a home full of happiness.

It is now 1938—Kristallnacht. Blood runs like a river on the streets, shattered glass covers the walkways of Jewish shop owners, and gangs of Nazi thugs charge though Berlin in a murderous rage. When Tavvi, the strong-willed Jewish carpenter, races outside, without thinking of his own welfare, to save his daughters fiancée, little does his wife Michal know that she might never hold him in her arms again. In an instant, all the stones they laid together come crashing down leaving them with nothing but the hope of finding each other again.

Watch Over My Child

Book Three in the Michal's Destiny series.

In book three of the Michal's Destiny series, after her parents are arrested by the Nazis on Kristallnacht, twelve-year-old Gilde Margolis is sent away from her home, her sister, and everyone she knows and loves.

Alone and afraid, Gilde boards a train through the Kinder-transport bound for London, where she will stay with strangers. Over the next seven years as Gilde is coming of age, she learns about love, friendship, heartache, and the pain of betrayal. As the Nazis grow in power, London is thrust into a brutal war against Hitler. Severe rationing is imposed upon the British, while air raids instill terror, and bombs all but destroy the city. Against all odds, and with no knowledge of what has happened to her family in Germany, Gilde keeps a tiny flicker of hope buried deep in her heart: someday, she will be reunited with her loved ones.

Another Breath, Another Sunrise

Book Four, the final book in the Michal's Destiny series.

Now that the Reich has fallen, in this—the final book of the Michal's Destiny series—the reader follows the survivors as they find themselves searching to reconnect with those they love. However, they are no longer the people they were before the war.

 While the Russian soldiers, who are angry with the German people and ready to pillage, beat, and rape, begin to invade what's left of Berlin, Lotti is alone and fears for her life.

Though Alina Margolis has broken every tradition to become a successful business woman in America, she fears what has happened to her family and loved ones across the Atlantic Ocean.

As the curtain pulls back on Gilde, a now successful actress in London, she realizes that all that glitters is not gold, and she longs to find the lost family the Nazi's had stolen from her many years ago.

This is a story of ordinary people whose lives were shattered by the terrifying ambitions of Adolf Hitler—a true madman.

<u>And . . . Who Is The Real Mother?</u>

Book One in the Eidel's Story series.

In the Bible, there is a story about King Solomon, who was said to be the wisest man of all time. The story goes like this:

Two women came to the king for advice. Both of them were claiming to be the mother of a child. The king took the child in his arms and said, "I see that both of you care for this child very much. So, rather than decide which of you is the real mother, I will cut the child in half and give each of you a half."

One of the women agreed to the king's decision, but the other cried out, "NO, give the child to that other woman. Don't hurt my baby."

"Ahh," said the king to the second woman who refused to cut the baby. "I will give the child to you, because the real mother would sacrifice anything for her child. She would even give her baby away to another woman if it meant sparing the baby from pain."

And so, King Solomon gave the child to his rightful mother.

The year is 1941. The place is the Warsaw Ghetto in Poland.

The ghetto is riddled with disease and starvation. Children are dying every day.

Zofia Weiss, a young mother, must find a way to save, Eidel her only child. She negotiates a deal with a man on the black market to smuggle Eidel out in the middle of the night and deliver her to Helen, a Polish woman who is a good friend of Zofia's. It is the ultimate sacrifice because there is a good chance that Zofia will die without ever seeing her precious child again.

Helen has a life of her own, a husband and a son. She takes Eidel to live with her family even though she and those she loves will face terrible danger every day. Helen will be forced to do unimaginable things to protect all that she holds dear. And as Eidel grows up in Helen's warm maternal embrace, Helen finds that she has come to love the little girl with all her heart.

So, when Zofia returns to claim her child, and King Solomon is not available to be consulted, it is the reader who must decide...

Who is the real mother?

Secrets Revealed

Book Two in the Eidel's Story series.

Hitler has surrendered. The Nazi flags, which once hung throughout the city striking terror in the hearts of Polish citizens, have been torn down. It seems that Warsaw should be rejoicing in its newly found freedom, but Warsaw is not free. Instead, it is occupied by the Soviet Union, held tight in Stalin's iron grip. Communist soldiers, in uniform, now control the city. Where once people feared the dreaded swastika, now they tremble at the sight of the hammer and sickle. It is a treacherous time. And in the midst of all this danger, Ela Dobinski, a girl with a secret that could change her life, is coming of age.

New Life, New Land

Book Three in the Eidel's Story series.

When Jewish Holocaust survivors Eidel and Dovid Levi arrive in the United States, they believe that their struggles are finally over. Both have suffered greatly under the Nazi reign and are ready to leave the past behind. They arrive in this new and different land filled with optimism for their future. However, acclimating into a new way of life can be challenging for immigrants. And, not only are they immigrants but they are Jewish. Although Jews are not being murdered in the United States, as they were under Hitler in Europe, the Levi's will learn that America is not without anti-Semitism. Still, they go forth, with unfathomable courage. In New Life, New Land, this young couple will face the trials and tribulations of becoming Americans and building a home for themselves and their children that will follow them.

Another Generation

Book Four in the Eidel's Story series.

In the final book in the Eidel's Story series the children of Holocaust survivors Eidel and Dovid Levi have grown to adulthood. They each face hard trials and tribulations of their own, many of which stem from growing up as children of Holocaust survivors. Haley is a peacemaker who yearns to please even at the expense of her own happiness. Abby is an angry rebel on the road to self-destruction. And, Mark, Dovid's only son, carries a heavy burden of guilt and secrets. He wants to please his father, but he cannot. Each of the Levi children must find a way to navigate their world while accepting that the lessons they have learned from the parents, both good and bad, have shaped them into the people they are destined to become.

The Wrath Of Eden

Deep in them Appalachian hills, far from the main roads where the citified people come and go, lies a harsh world where a man's character is all he can rightly claim as his own. This here is a land of deep, dark coal mines, where a miner ain't certain when he ventures into the belly of the mountain whether he will ever see daylight again. To this very day, they still tell tales of the Robin Hood-like outlaw Pretty Boy Floyd, even though there ain't no such thing as a thousand dollar bill no more From this beautiful yet dangerous country where folks is folks comes a story as old as time itself; a tale of good and evil, of right and wrong, and of a troubled man who walked a perilous path on his journey back to God.

The Wrath of Eden begins in 1917, in the fictitious town of Mudwater Creek, West Virginia. Mudwater lies deep in mining country in the Appalachian Mountains. Here, the eldest son of a snake-handling preacher, Cyrus Hunt, is emotionally broken by what he believes is his father's favoritism toward his brother, Aiden. Cyrus is so hurt by what he believes is his father's lack of love for him that he runs away from home to seek his fortune. Not only will he fight in the Great War, but he will return to America and then ramble around the United States for several years, right through the great depression. While on his journey, Cyrus will encounter a multitude of colorful characters and from each he will learn more about himself. This is a tale of good and evil, of brother against brother, of the intricate web of family, and of love lost and found again.

The Angels Song

The Wrath of Eden Book Two.

Cyrus Hunt returns home to the Appalachian Mountains after years of traveling. He has learned a great deal about himself from his journey, and he realizes that the time has come to make peace with his brother and his past. When he arrives in the small town where he grew up, he finds that he has a granddaughter that he never knew existed, and she is almost the same age as his daughter. The two girls grow up as close as sisters. But one is more beautiful than a star-filled night sky, while the other has a physical condition that keeps her from spreading her wings and discovering her own self-worth. As the girls grow into women, the love they have for each other is constantly tested by sibling rivalry, codependency, and betrayals. Are these two descendents of Cyrus Hunt destined to repeat their father's mistakes? Or will they rise above their human weakness and inadequacies and honor the bonds of blood and family that unite them?

One Last Hope

A Voyage to Escape Nazi Germany

Formerly *The Voyage*

Inspired by True Events

On May 13, 1939, five strangers boarded the MS St. Louis. Promised a future of safety away from Nazi Germany and Hitler's Third Reich, unbeknownst to them they were about to embark upon a voyage built on secrets, lies, and treachery. Sacrifice, love, life, and death hung in the balance as each fought against fate, but the voyage was just the beginning.

A Flicker Of Light

The year is 1943

The forests of Munich are crawling with danger during the rule of the Third Reich, but in order to save the life of her unborn child, Petra Jorgenson must escape from the Lebensborn Institute. She is alone, seven months pregnant, and penniless. Avoiding the watchful eyes of the armed guards in the overhead tower, she waits until the dead of night and then climbs under the flesh-shredding barbed wire surrounding the Institute. At the risk of being captured and murdered, she runs headlong into the terrifying, desolate woods. Even during one of the darkest periods in the history of mankind, when horrific acts of cruelty become commonplace and Germany seemed to have gone crazy under the direction of a madman, unexpected heroes come to light. And although there are those who would try to destroy true love, it will prevail. Here in this lost land ruled by human monsters, Petra will learn that even when one faces what appears to be the end of the world, if one looks hard enough, one will find that there is always A Flicker of Light.

<u>The Heart Of A Gypsy</u>

If you liked Inglorious Basterds, Pulp Fiction, and Django Unchained, you'll love The Heart of a Gypsy!

During the Nazi occupation, bands of freedom fighters roamed the forests of Eastern Europe. They hid while waging their own private war against Hitler's tyrannical and murderous reign. Among these Resistance fighters were several groups of Romany people (Gypsies).

The Heart of a Gypsy is a spellbinding love story. It is a tale of a man with remarkable courage and the woman who loved him more than life itself. This historical novel is filled with romance and spiced with the beauty of the Gypsy culture.

Within these pages lies a tale of a people who would rather die than surrender their freedom. Come, enter into a little-known world where only a few have traveled before . . . the world of the Romany.

If you enjoy romance, secret magical traditions, and riveting action you will love The Heart of a Gypsy.

Please be forewarned that this book contains explicit scenes of a sexual nature.

Made in the USA
Monee, IL
31 October 2023

45512107R00219